**B**EFORE LONG, DUSK WOULD BEGIN TO FALL OVER CASA ESPERANZA. The sweet aroma of night-blooming jasmine would scent the air and the rising moon would outline the stripes of surf as they slipped toward the shore. Bartenders would crate the unopened champagne, and caterers would haul away the platters and untouched food. Musicians would drag their scuffed leather cases to a waiting van, and everyone would call it just another day.

All that would be left of the Carristas' party would be souvenir pictures in the Palm Beach dailies and a full-page four-color photograph of Loretta and Chukker on the cover of the *Pictorial's* Easter issue.

Today Loretta had met them all. Every last one who was ambulatory had come to say hello. Yet now they knew even less than what they had thought they knew before they met her.

*Who was Loretta Worship?*

### SOMETIMES PARADISE
### by JUDITH GREEN

# SOMETIMES
# PARADISE

# JUDITH GREEN

BANTAM BOOKS
TORONTO · NEW YORK · LONDON · SYDNEY · AUCKLAND

*This edition contains the complete text of the original hard-cover edition.*
NOT ONE WORD HAS BEEN OMITTED.

SOMETIMES PARADISE

*A Bantam Book / published by arrangement with Alfred A. Knopf, Inc.*

*PRINTING HISTORY*
*Alfred A. Knopf edition published May 1987*
*Bantam edition / March 1988*

Bantam Books are published by Bantam Books, a division of Bantam Doubleday Dell Publishing Group, Inc. Its trademark, consisting of the words "Bantam Books" and the portrayal of a rooster, is Registered in U.S. Patent and Trademark Office and in other countries. Marca Registrada. Bantam Books, 666 Fifth Avenue, New York, New York 10103.

PRINTED IN THE UNITED STATES OF AMERICA

KR    0  9  8  7  6  5  4  3  2  1

FOR CHRISTINA AND NICHOLAS

NOTHING IS A FAIRY TALE
THAT YOU MAKE HAPPEN YOURSELF.

# PROLOGUE

The party had been called for noon on Easter Sunday.
Splendid even for Palm Beach, the Carristas' palazzo dazzled the mind. It sprawled beside the ocean like a sunning sea serpent; its turrets burst through the cloudless sky like sentries patrolling an endless grandeur. Many of the guests thronged the grand salon before making their way through the triple-tiered Etruscan arches to the marbled loggia. Others, drinks in hand, strolled the labyrinth of sculpture gardens that stretched to the soft, raked sands by the sea. This winter cottage was, if possible, more lavish now than it had been during the boomtime twenties, when Vanderbilt had commissioned Addison Mizner to build it.

Mixing centuries like cement, Casa Esperanza was unquestionably Mizner at his Spanish, Moorish, Saracen, bull-market best. In a town where the past is born quickly and play decrees the order of the day, only Mizner managed to create any lasting image. (How appropriate that he couldn't draft a floor plan and never became an architect!)

Within half an hour Via Pelicano, from Lake Worth to the Atlantic Ocean, was lined with Palm Beach gold, tarnished only occasionally by an American automobile. As the Dunbars approached Casa Esperanza, the long private road seemed more like a yellow-brick fantasy than a driveway. On each side and arched overhead a tropical Arcadia of colors blazed as if it had been there forever, while parrots and cockatoos screeched from root-twisted banyans and lushly vined perches. Some people thought it was out of Babylon, the Arabian Nights, the last days of the czars. Those in the know knew that it was out of sugar, out of rum, out of Cuba just in time.

Near the main entrance, row upon row of bunny-suited car parkers moved like jets in formation, channeling the continuous flow of gold. And just outside the massive Byzantine portico, a trio of tailcoated magicians whisked placecard-holding rabbits from hats shaped like giant Easter eggs. It was an opener that would surely have grabbed Daisy for Gatsby.

Loretta Worship Dunbar tightened her grip on her husband's hand. She couldn't believe that all this existed. Even in Europe, nothing she'd seen had approached such overabundance, such a total flooding of her senses.

But anyone whose eyes were trained on Loretta couldn't believe she was real, either. This was the first time anyone in Palm Beach had seen her. Even on second glance she looked younger than rumor would have her, perhaps because what one noticed first were her blue eyes, wide with wonder, her cheeks, red without rouge, and the Alice-in-Wonderland effect of the satin ribbon holding back her blond hair, all of which made her appear more a young girl than a woman in her twenties. Yes, in this unreal world Loretta looked especially unreal. Even her "right" dress was wrong. But then how was she to know that at parties in Palm Beach on Easter Sunday, you don't dress for church, even if that's where you've just been?

It wasn't long before word reached guests at the live-horse carousel and the Dom Pérignon fountain, where golden faucets spouted chilled champagne, and the claque of nannies by the kiddie pool: Loretta and Chukker had arrived. Suddenly, the excesses of the day were old news. *New* news was Loretta. Everybody wanted to see her, to know her, because everybody knew Chukker—"forever." Even if they didn't, they did. Just ask them.

Who was Loretta? What was she? Many swore she was a whore. Others knew, positively, she was a virgin—the worst kind, a holding-out virgin. What nobody here said was what she *really* was: nice. And smart; really smart.

"She's from a Dakota or out there somewhere."

"Nonsense. She hardly speaks English."

"She's eighteen."

"Ridiculous. She's nearly thirty. She only looks eighteen. It's peasant stock."

"The old goat met her recuperating."

"Wrong. He met her at X-ray when his wife was dying."

"She's had no education whatsoever."

"She grew up in a convent school."

"He gave her ten million dollars not to leave him and not to marry him."

"They were secretly wed in March."

"By a priest."

"By a judge."

"She has no interest in money."

"He bought her millions in jewels. She keeps them in Switzerland."

"She's a whore."

"That's what we said in the first place."

Chukker Dunbar, tall, lean, and angular, with abundant gray hair and deep-set blue eyes, had the look that everyone—

whoever wants class—wants. Although in a closet his blue blazer and knife-creased white pants might look like anybody else's, on Chukker they seemed custom cut. It didn't matter that his hair needed a trim, that he couldn't be bothered to wear socks, or that his ring was dented down the center of its Dunbar crest. What mattered most was that you couldn't buy what didn't matter.

Chukker knew all about days like today. His yesterdays included many just like them. Yet even he found it hard to recall an extravagance to match the Carristas'. It was a minor miracle that the laden buffets could support the massive weights of food. The lobsters tumbled over each other like waterfalls, and the oysters were piled into mounds resembling Alpine peaks. Giant birds and standing rib roasts had been carved and put back together with such skill that one almost dared not violate their perfection, while islands of orchids and cascades of white lilies festooned the entire feast.

Chukker knew that this day had to be, and that soon it would be over. And he knew that the people here would never dare tear the meat off Loretta's bones with words—not, at least, in her presence; not with him by her side. He knew the carnivores who couldn't wait, the beasts whose only burden was never having one—the ones whose families had made nothing into legends and who were now working even harder to turn those legends back into nothing. And he knew the hunger of the newcomers, impatient to sell themselves to these impoverished yet well-known names, and to whom no other names could smell as sweet.

Noreen Newirth also knew about days like this Easter Sunday. Too many times she'd smelled the flesh and watched the silently screaming victims attempting to escape.

After almost fifteen years in real estate, Noreen knew a

lot about the tribal rites of the coconut jungle. She'd been inside enough jungle closets to have seen four-figure price tags hanging from the lifeless sleeves of gowns that would never be worn and seen, too, the invisible price tags dangling from the homosexuals, the town tarts, the social swells. She'd seen souls swapped for cash and cash swapped for clubs and clubs swapped for lives. She'd watched the charityteers, the changed names, the scrambling pushers push for their photographs in her husband's weekly *Pictorial*.

Noreen had been twenty-eight when she married Bill Newirth. A little chubby, a little short, Bill hardly looked their society half next to his tall, willowy wife. Noreen had met Bill in New York while showing him the typical after-divorce apartment that no man really looks at, since all he's seeing is what he's giving to his wife. As long as Noreen and Bill lived in New York, their polyglot backgrounds fit their polyglot world. But when Bill inherited the *Pictorial*, the banquet Noreen expected turned into finger food.

In Palm Beach her dark good looks and bold features were immediately labeled "Semitic" by the very people who called such looks among their own "leonine." Had Noreen known then, fifteen years ago, the impossibility of not getting hurt on a daily basis when one lives on a perpetual dateline where the rich and idle meet the sun and surf, she never would have stayed. Like Loretta, she hadn't been to Palm Beach before she married.

As she watched Loretta being heaped with hugs, Noreen again felt marrow drain from her bones. Because she had inherited Judaism instead of alcoholism, Noreen had too often encountered stinging nettles disguised in nosegays and barbed wishes buried beneath smiles. She knew Loretta must be sensing something similar—not the same pain, but pain nonetheless. Instinctively, Noreen wanted to help—not to warn her to run away but to whisper how to stay, how to cope a little and then a little more. Noreen made a promise to herself that she would call Loretta, and soon.

"So, this is Loretta!" Mary Dodd kissed the air beside Loretta's cheeks.

Before Dodd, the name had been Algernon; before Algernon, Trumbull. According to Mary Dodd, there had been nothing before Trumbull. But before Trumbull the name had been Manchetti. And before Manchetti, Wolf. Carlo Manchetti was Mary's first husband. She had been with him the day he was shot, just before he was to turn state's evidence.

Mary Dodd looked Loretta up and down in much the same way that a madam might inspect a new girl. Mary was never a person to be accused of thinking with her brain. One of the few facts she had ever read and retained—and, after all, memory does follow interest—was that it takes the average man two point eight minutes to achieve orgasm and the average woman thirteen.

Although Mary Dodd was sufficiently past sixty, the goods in her window were still for sale. That was evident in everything about her, from her too-short skirt to her bulging blouse to the thin, overbleached hair framing the powdered white skin and garish red cheeks. Even the designer clothes could not camouflage the ample body.

Maria Manchetti had arrived in Palm Beach early on— not quite with the Seminoles, as she was fond of saying, but right after that Chicago shoot-out in the early thirties . . . which was right after Maria had buried her Bronx beginnings. When she'd met Frazier Trumbull, she was not quite the "recreation director" of the new Boca Raton Club, as she fancied herself then; she was the head hatcheck girl and unofficial director of after-hours recreation. It was well known that until Frazier Trumbull found Mary, he'd suffered from what was politely known as "the Duke of Windsor disease."

It was also well known that the duke was a great chum of Frazier's, and that Wallis had become his duchess by adopting many of Mary's boudoir techniques. The duchess had shown her gratitude for this priceless tutelage by placing the Trumbulls on a lifetime retainer that allowed them to pay for much of the Windsors' style. It was this *oblige* from the *noblesse* that gave Maria Manchetti her leg up and out of the big Italian boot.

"Yes—it's Loretta," Chukker said, staring at Mary Dodd.

"Chukker! I must be the first to have a little luncheon for Loretta."

Since Mary's husbands had left her little in the way of money, Mary needed these luncheons to introduce anyone new to the butchers, the bankers, the boutique owners . . . all the willing players of Palm Beach's most popular and most expensive sport: kickback.

"Thank you, Mary," Chukker said dismissively.

Lennox Knox—"Fort" to his friends—leaned over and whispered to his teenage daughter, "I'd have known her without him."

"That's mean," Christina Knox replied intuitively.

"You're thinking what I am or you wouldn't think it's mean," Lennox Knox said.

Christina moved from her father's arm. "I think she's pretty. I like the way she looks. She's like Alice in Wonderland."

"She's in Wonderland, all right," Fort said. He flicked his filter tip into the meticulous hedge, walked up to Chukker and slapped him on the back. " *Fab*-u-lous, Chukker— *fab*-u-lous! A-ONE-er. You sly bastard, you! She's the best look—"

A liveried waiter carrying a huge bowl of caviar threaded his way toward them, followed by another servant bearing a giant silver tray laden with Easter egg trimmings. A third brought up the rear, pouring Polish vodka from iced crystal decanters.

"Caviar, my dear Loretta? Would you like some caviar?" Mary Dodd asked in an affected voice as she hovered conspicuously near Loretta. Under the influence of Polish vodka, or any spirits for that matter, Mary would slip in and out of accents—the product, she apologized, of her English nanny and her French governess and her "childhood abroad."

"No, thank you," Loretta replied. Not that it didn't appeal to her; she simply wasn't hungry.

Mary Dodd shook her head knowingly, glancing around to make sure that she had an audience. "Of course, my dear Loretta," she said, heaping the glistening, buckshot-size eggs onto her plate. "It's an acquired taste."

As Loretta blushed, Noreen Newirth wondered why Chukker had decided to unveil his bride today. There must have been a hundred more appropriate occasions; Chukker was invited everywhere.

Suddenly, from the corner of her eye, Noreen saw, stampeding toward Chukker and Loretta, those Palm Beach gents, those resort regulars Noreen secretly referred to as "Crayolas." For as long as she could remember, she'd never seen them wearing anything but lemons and reds and greens and pinks. They were ageless and faceless, with suntans that defied the seasons, and with everything about them interchangeable, even their wives and albino children.

As the Crayolas clustered around Chukker, Letitia Barton seized the opportunity to welcome Loretta. A porcine woman with wooden red hair, Letitia had a face that no one ever said was once beautiful.

"Welcome to Palm Beach, Loretta. I can say 'welcome' because I've been here so long I've begun to believe I really did float in with the coconuts." Letitia threw an insincere laugh to the group while resting her layers of chins on her layers of pearls, pearls the size of antiaircraft missiles, given her years before by an extremely grateful "lady" turned du Pont. It seems Letitia had discovered that Her Ladyship's "aristocratic" threads were more synthetic than nylon.

As she gazed at Loretta's hand, it wasn't the large, cushion-cut sapphire that caught Letitia's eye. It was the bracelet. A charm bracelet? As if whirling a Rolodex, she flipped by Big Ben, the Eiffel Tower, an ancient coin, a gondola, past them all.

"It's a souvenir from every place we went. The gondola's my fav—"

"I love them," Letitia said, fixing the smile on her face. "You're certainly a fresh breath in this stale air."

Loretta wanted to pull away, yet something stronger made her stay. She had no way of knowing that Letitia was the acid-tongued society columnist aptly bylined as "Mouth."

"Charming, just charming," Letitia continued. Her voice was soft, her enunciation precise; yet her words made Loretta shiver.

Suddenly, velvet slippers, madras pants, and an oversized pink blazer with gold fox-head buttons boomed toward Chukker. Except for slits for eyes and a nose that almost didn't exist, the face was all shiny red cheeks.

"Looks great, doesn't he?" Murphy chortled to the others, waving his hand toward Chukker, as if he were on exhibit. "We sure did it, didn't we?" Much too familiarly, he thrust his arm around Chukker's shoulder. There was never an unostentatious hello from Dr. John Murphy. His greeting was always an assault.

John Murphy had been on the staff of Good Samaritan Hospital since he'd arrived in town five years earlier. Doc-

tors of his sort were becoming common in Palm Beach.
They'd come to make it big and make it fast. Their bedside
manner was more monied than medical, their research more
into backgrounds and bank accounts, and their experiments
usually conducted in motels. That old Hippocratic oath
seemed to have been rented along with the caps and gowns,
and somewhere between the second martini and the eighteenth green, it was forgotten.

Certainly the very married Dr. John Murphy forgot it
when he met Angela Seagrist.

Throwing her arms around Chukker, then stepping back
to shake hands with Loretta, Angela Flagler Seagrist looked
every long, cool, blond inch the stereotypical image of Palm
Beach. Always recently divorced, she was a paradigm of
devotion to herself—but it worked. She looked fantastic for
forty, meaning people believed "I'll be thirty April second."
On that same date back in 1894, Angela's great-grandfather's
railroad had connected Palm Beach to the rest of the world.
Singlehandedly, Henry Morrison Flagler put an end to fron-
tier life in Palm Beach by introducing what Henry James
would later call "the hotel world." After that first train ride,
Palm Beach would never again be joined to the real world
except by its three bridges.

On Angela Seagrist's mother's side, somewhere between
the balance sheets and the percales, lay one of Isaac Singer-
sewing-machine's eighteen illegitimate children. This particular bastard went on to create the Addison Mizner masterpiece
among country clubs: the stucco and red barrel-tiled Ever-
glades Club, which Paris Singer not only owned but ruled
like a warlord in order to keep all the other bastards out.

The house where John Murphy first met Angela Seagrist
was where Angela had gone after leaving yet another husband. It was "Mummy's house," but Mummy was never
there. Its scale and extravagance, with its miles of swagged

and tasseled damask, room-length sofas, and countless photographs in faded velvet frames, recalled the days of ocean-going schooners, vases in motor cars, and gentlemen in plus fours—the days when house painters such as John Singer Sargent and Giovanni Boldini would move right in and not move out until everyone in the house was hung. As if she were still on Gaga's lap, Angela remembered every word of her grandmother telling how "poor Alfie Vanderbilt" went down on the *Lusitania* with his wife's priceless pearls in his pocket and how "that drunken old fool," Evelyn Walsh McLean, had forgotten she'd hidden five million dollars of her jewelry in the back of a radio she'd given her chum Addison Mizner.

Angela's involvement with John Murphy had begun in that house the night she made an emergency telephone call to Good Samaritan Hospital.

"It doesn't matter what doctor, just get one here fast." The call was for Nanny. For the past twenty-five years, Nanny had been living out her last days on Wild Turkey. This time she'd fallen down a whole flight of stairs. There was blood. She wasn't moving. Dr. John Murphy got her moving. He even got her off the booze. And onto afghans—within six months, every bed in the house was covered with crocheted squares. Long after Nanny was able to visit the doctor's office, John Murphy still came to visit her. But his visits now lasted no more than a few minutes, after which Angela would hurry him through the portrait-hung corridors, past the Florentine hunting scenes and the other ransacked European treasures, up the massive mahogany stairs, past door after door, until they came once again to the bright, smallish room whose balloon wallpaper and matching curtains had been hanging since Angela was born.

Dr. Murphy's relationship with Angela Seagrist was a Palm Beach dream that even his first upwardly mobile marriage couldn't match. Naturally he wanted to marry Angela and have her proclaim her love for him to the world. It was Angela who had given him the gold fox-head buttons, the Cartier cufflinks, the Patek Philippe, and the swizzle stick he had no idea how to work. Angela would pick him up at the hospital after hours, before hours, during hours—whenever he could get away. He would run down the corridor, shedding his white coat in the process, not wanting to miss a moment. She would slide across the rich leather and he would get behind the wheel. The champagne would be iced. They'd drink from the same glass, then throw it to the sea. Under her grandmother's frescoed ceilings, atop mounds of down, they'd make love: he with the courtliness of the social climber, she with the lust of the overbred.

Sometimes they would make love in his office. Driving there, Angela could think of nothing else. Her muscles squeezed tightly together, she would cut in and out of the geriatric traffic along South County Road; speeding over the middle bridge into West Palm Beach, she would race down Flagler Drive, brushing past traffic lights as they turned red. Once in John Murphy's office, Angela would remove only the panties beneath her tennis skirt.

Now Angela watched as Murphy made a fool of himself in front of Loretta and Chukker, tapping his toe to draw attention to his shoes, shooting his cuff to show off his watch. Murphy never understood that old money was worn so it didn't show. Angela sighed. Murphy was becoming insufferable; it wouldn't be long before he went the way of her former lovers.

Julietta Carrista was fortunate that nobody stepped on her during her dash toward the Dunbars. "My little Julietta of the spirits," Jorge Carrista called his tiny wife, who had not only told Castro where to keep his Coronas but had talked enough family out of Havana to start her own village, and gotten enough money out to keep them all rich. Down to the smallest turquoise-earringed grandchild, Julietta Carrista ruled her new Cuba like an old conquistador.

There were no small steps amid the great strides she had made for her family. Long ago her father had told her, "Don't stay a minute after you've stayed a minute too long." That's when Julietta's clan had found its way to Palm Beach. Although she believed that luck never carried one on its shoulders forever, she also understood how immense wealth could be used as a shield, and so she and her troops had hardly expected to hear the word "spic" directed at them so often. Yet Julietta had proved herself so successful a fighter that the old guard now boasted when one of their children married a Carrista.

And today she had the Dunbars. It was indeed *fantástico!* Julietta's deep red lips caught the side of Loretta's neck— that was as high as she could reach. Chukker smiled, noting that the bejeweled cross dangling from Julietta's neck was the sole reminder of this special Sunday.

"*Lindísima*," Julietta Carrista said to Chukker, putting her arms through his and Loretta's and marching them to where Jorge was filling a gold Easter egg with a thousand-dollar bill for the end of the children's hunt.

"They may not know poor, but they know loyalty and gratitude," Chukker had told Loretta in the car. He admired the Carristas. If the big Carrista money was occasionally misplaced, the big Carrista heart never was.

Before Julietta reached her husband, she stopped abruptly to throw her arms around two attractive, well-dressed young men. One of them could only be called beautiful, Loretta thought—beautiful like Rudolph Valentino.

"These are my boys, my decorators, my Michael and David," Julietta said. "David, Michael, this is Loretta. Chukker you know.

"When I say they are responsible for my house, I mean it. But when I say they are more responsible for what you don't see, I mean it more. Always I want to do and fix and buy more and more and more. They stop me. A very, very rarity," Julietta said, tiptoeing to pinch the beautiful one's cheek.

"She's the rare one," Michael said.

"I adore them both," Julietta said, once again turning to the Dunbars and threading her arms through theirs.

Jorge Carrista's eyes gleamed with pride and his teasing smile spoke welcome. In his nubby linen suit and shiny black-and-white patent shoes, Jorge looked every inch the successful Cuban planter. "You need a Latin," he said to Loretta, his wink followed by a laugh.

Just as there was never any economy in the Carrista hospitality, so there was none in their gestures. Fingers and arms moved extravagantly as Jorge and Julietta kept talking through each other's sentences. But what impressed Loretta most was their laughter. She had known so little of that when she was growing up.

"Look! Loretta! Chukker!" Jorge Carrista called out, pushing them both as he waved in the direction of the long reflecting pool. Loretta was transfixed as she watched spirals of spray rise from the mouths of bronzed dolphins to the rhythms of "Easter Parade" and delicate streams splashed onto the thousands of yellow Inca lilies floating in a pool of giant goldfish.

Some of Loretta's earliest memories were of flowers. Often she had helped make crosses from the dandelions and day lilies she'd gathered from the field behind the church. When life had seemed almost unbearable, only the flowers made her feel free. Sometimes she stayed in the fields for hours, long after she'd gathered enough, waiting for the flowers she'd picked to flop over their stems so she would have to pick some more. She never really wanted to get back.

Loretta felt somebody leaning against her. Not pressing hard, merely brushing.

"Quite a sight, huh?" Sam Bayberry slurred. "You know, it wouldn't surprise me if Ponce de León jumped right out of the frigging fountain." He looked heavenward and made the sign of the cross. "How many fun-filled years ago is 1513? Maybe he could hand us a little drink and make us all three again." Sam smiled. He liked thát. "By the way, I'm Sam Bayberry."

Loretta, shaking his hand, felt she was steadying as well as greeting him, "Hi, Sam. I'm Lor—"

"Let me guess. What could it possibly be?" Sam laughed. He also had a laugh Loretta liked.

Although Sam Bayberry had not yet seen his fortieth birthday, he could easily pass for fifty with his dark eyes sunk deep in their sockets, and the flesh around them sallow and loose. His slouching shoulders and years of paunch made even the uniform of blue blazer and white trousers look wrong, almost as if they'd been tailored for someone else.

"Best part of the caviar," Sam said, throwing his head back, downing what was left of his vodka.

"How are you, Sam?" Chukker asked, giving his friend an affectionate pat on the back.

"You don't really want to know. Anyway, you don't have to ask *me*. Anybody'd be only too glad to fill you in. You know why Bradley once named a horse Bad News? Because it travels fast." Sam took a long breath. "Anyway, how about you? Not that I have to ask." Sam clutched Chukker's arm and glanced toward Loretta with tears in his eyes. "You know something, Loretta? This is a prince. A real prince.

My father's oldest friend. No. That's a lie. If my old man had a friend like Chukker he wouldn't be my old man. Oldest acquaintance? Yeah . . . maybe." Sam Bayberry raised his glass. "Should old acquaintance be—" He stopped suddenly. "You know what they say—'Fill the glass that's empty and empty the glass that's full.' Or is it just me who says that?" As he stepped away, Loretta noticed Sam's limp. She wasn't sure quite why, but her eyes misted.

Nobody knew better than Chukker the portions of childhood Sam had never been fed. Sam was a product of all the luxuries and none of the necessities of life. Sam's father and Chukker had played polo together in their undergraduate days at Virginia. Neither one had ever had to do anything else, and Sam's father never did.

Before Sam Bayberry could walk, his father would hold him in front of him on the saddle and gallop endless lengths on his private polo field. Before Sam learned to ride, his father made him midget-size mallets and spent uncountable hours teaching him how to swing, to aim, to lift those shots between the posts.

When Sam was hardly eight, Porfirio Rubirosa, Philip Iglehart, and the Aly Khan were amazed by the boy's grace, his form, his promise. Then, soon after his twelfth birthday on the carpet-grass haunts of the rich, exclusive North Shore, *it* happened.

The boy wonder was playing with his father alongside the likes of Pete Bostwick, Winston Guest, Jock Whitney— the best the valleys of Long Island and the harbors of Maine had to offer. It was yet another rematch in a longstanding rivalry, and this time even the horses seemed braced for blood. The ball was smashed down young Sam's side of the field. It was his shot. Sam's father raced to get it. Mallet high, eyes low, he charged toward the target. But as he leaned from his mount, he misjudged his mark; his mallet

caught the forelegs of his son's horse. Young Sam fell hard
to the ground, his pony on top of him. After eleven opera-
tions, and years of rehabilitation, the multiple fractures in
Sam's left leg still refused to heal. His father never forgave
him.

The photographers from Jack Newirth's lacquered *Pictorial*
were making their way toward Loretta and Chukker. Even
through the piercing shards of sunlight, their cameras flashed.
Flashes were a must in Palm Beach. Flashes rubbed away
years. And rubbing years away was what much of Palm
Beach was about—especially for the acres of "girls" who
still saw themselves as they were before they traded the
name Ziegfeld for that of a famous car, a well-known tobacco, or a New York telephone exchange.

For Loretta, there seemed no end to the stream of people
coming to greet her. She never let go of Chukker's arm as
she watched them all watching her, standing in their tight
clusters, nodding their heads, their hands half-shielding
their mouths. She was uneasy yet exhilarated.

Nothing in what she knew so far of Chukker's world had
prepared Loretta for this. Nothing could have. Although it
looked like Eden on earth, Loretta would soon feel the
tension that rolled through this paradise, the undercurrent of
schemes and sloth and jealousy, with people continuously
climbing over each other en route to that better address.
People were kind for the wrong reasons, as you might be
kind to a kidnapper because he hasn't bothered to kill you.

Before long, dusk would begin to fall over Casa Esperanza.
The sweet aroma of night-blooming jasmine would scent the
air and the rising moon would outline the stripes of surf as
they slipped toward the shore. Bartenders would crate the
unopened champagne, and caterers would haul away the
platters of untouched food. Musicians would drag their scuffed

leather cases to a waiting van, and everyone would call it just another day.

All that would be left of the Carristas' party would be souvenir pictures in the Palm Beach dailies and a full-page four-color photograph of Loretta and Chukker on the cover of the *Pictorial's* Easter issue.

Today Loretta had met them all. Every last one who was ambulatory had come to say hello. Yet now they knew even less than what they had thought they knew before they met her.

*Who* was Loretta?

# PART I

*1*

Loretta's name was Jean when she was dropped at the front door of the orphanage on the outskirts of Tallahassee. The sisters knew it because "Jean" and "2 1/2" were printed on a card pinned to her sweater. It was obvious that whoever had left her still loved her. In fact, even after they were sure she was safely inside, the man and the woman stayed in a hidden part of the roadway wiping away tears, before churning up dust and driving away forever.

Loretta could still remember that little blue sweater with its clusters of tiny red roses blooming down the front and across the bottom—and not because of the photograph the sisters took the day they found her, the photograph they gave to the Worships, the one Luke Worship shook whenever he told Loretta how lucky she was.

Before a year was up, the Worships came and adopted Loretta from Hilltop House. Luke and Lillian Worship had gone through so many shy, sad faces that when Loretta's picture popped from between the protective pieces of cardboard, Mama couldn't believe her eyes, or Luke his luck. In the return mail, he wrote Sister Maria Josefa: "That little girl's smile has already dug deep into our hearts." Only

Luke knew how well that smile would dig into God knows how many pockets.

Luke Werner's career began after answering an ad.

*Baptist Preacher Wanted*
Young. Experienced. Married.
First Baptist Church, Trainerville, Florida.
250 miles Southwest of St. Petersburg.

As an able-bodied former seaman suddenly turned not only Baptist but self-appointed minister, with a name just as suddenly akin to God as his profession, Luke Worship wrote his reply. Although he wondered if Second or Third Baptist churches existed, there was never a doubt in his mind that he was on his way to being anointed by an altogether unsuspecting parish.

The year was 1951 when the First Baptist Church of Trainerville, Florida, reopened for business as the Sunshine Parish, with Luke Worship as the new pastor. How lucky the parish was to have a "chaplain" who was not only a three-time winner of the Purple Heart but the youngest bearer of the coveted Navy Cross. Aware that to his flock such tangible symbols seemed links to heaven, Luke was never seen without them. And when he realized that miracle preachers were more in demand than the nonhealing clergy, he began practicing this special brand of medicine. He learned about advance men, poster plastering, tent raising, fund raising, and money; about badges, pamphlets, slogans, marathons, telethons, and money. On cue, he could turn worship into vaudeville and theology into theatrics.

He studied the sermons of John Wesley, the father of evangelism, and learned how a stone thrown at a preacher draws not only blood from the stone but the mob to the preacher's defense. Luke's twist was to crush a capsule of red dye to his face, and as the mob grew wild, he'd continue "bloody but unbowed."

He learned from Marjoe Gortner and Elmer Gantry, Reverend Ike and Father Coughlin. He became a student of the teachings of Hitler, Nietzsche, Lenin, Gandhi, and Jesus. He realized that the "freedom" craved by the masses could be attained only when the chains of choice and responsibility are removed, that what people really crave are the confines of order, structure, and command. He recognized that people rise against weakness, not against wickedness.

And no matter his whereabouts, Luke always sported that eternal tan associated with show biz. If Ed Sullivan and Lawrence Welk were thought of as cheek-to-jowl with God, why not Luke Worship? While Oral Roberts's audience laid hands on their radios for contact with God, Luke Worship's congregation would one day touch their TVs for their private sessions with the Lord. If selling Jesus like cornflakes was what it was all about, then, by God, Big Luke would sure make that bandwagon. That's when he "indulged" his wife's whim and decided to adopt Baby Loretta. Their six-year-old son, Paul, was certainly not Luke's idea of big bucks. He needed a girl for his act.

Although it wasn't yet nine a.m. when they set out for the orphanage, already that morning Luke had stirred the souls of his Sunshine parishioners, urging them to tell every God-fearing, God-loving congressman to use any statute he could find to outlaw the desegregation evil preached by the

Supreme Court. Until he was hoarse, Luke Worship warned that "we must start today, before he grows even more dangerous, to defrock that rubbish-ranting black devil—blackened by the ashes of hell—who dares to call himself Martin Luther; with the crowning blasphemy of 'King.' "

At about the same time that Luke's congregation was heading home, Sister Maria Josefa and Sister Martina Angelica were trying to calm a squirming, sobbing little girl about her beautiful new life with her nice new family. After all, her new father was a man of the cloth, sent by God Himself.

The May morning was unusually hot. Lillian Worship sat in the front seat, fanning herself and babbling. "Just like Mama named me Lillian for Lillian Gish, I'm naming her Loretta for Loretta Young. Tell me, Luke Werner—I mean Worship—just tell me if you can, if you've ever seen anybody prettier in your whole life than Loretta Young? Can you? Of course not. Nobody can."

Luke wasn't even listening, and, anyway, Lillian's monologues never required participation.

"Do you know," she asked, turning to Paul in the backseat, "what an Oscar is?" He, too, knew when no response was required. "Just tell me about her coming through that door! Is that sunshine or is that sunshine?"

Luke drove past the pier and beside the last stretch of beach, heading north onto Route 19. He smiled as he came to the Weeki-Wachee Springs billboard.

100,000 GALLONS A MINUTE FLOW
THE WORLD'S GREATEST UNDERWATER SPECTACULAR
STARRING A REAL LIVE MERMAID

He thought of the day he did that special sea duty after showtime with that real "live" mermaid. He remembered how she wriggled out of that fake shimmery thing. As he passed the arrows to the Silver Springs Dollhouse, he grew indignant at the idea of taking some kid to see dolls. No way he'd ever do it. Never.

Luke's anger waned as he noticed the signs on the opposite side of the highway. "Hey, all of you, look— look out my side." He backed up and then drove slowly forward.

SHE KISSED

THE HAIRBRUSH

BY A FLUKE

AND THOUGHT IT WAS

HER HUSBAND LUKE

BURMA SHAVE

Luke backed up again. They all got out so that Paul could take Luke's picture with Mama pointing to his name. "You be sure to get the 'Luke' in. You sure, boy? You better be."

Back in the car, Lillian Worship rearranged the skirt of the dress she'd bought specially for the sisters: black and white polka dots, with prismed jet buttons and a black patent belt that cut her roundly in two. Her shiny white plastic bag matched the shiny sandals, except for the colored flowers around the toes. Lillian loved flowers almost as much as she loved movie stars.

Her hair was dyed red to match Rita Hayworth's, her eyes mascaraed to mimic Elizabeth Taylor's, and her lipstick faithfully carved like Joan Crawford's—the unfortunate results of a careful study of photographs torn out of movie magazines and pasted on the walls of her kitchen. Although she was only thirty-one, a year younger than her husband, any trace of girlishness was gone.

While weight added years to Lillian Worship's looks, Luke's pudginess subtracted years from his. Whatever "style" he'd pulled together came from his careful study of split-level America. The white short-sleeved shirt, the initialed belt buckle, the polyester checked jacket, even the Kiwanis ring (the only one that fit at the pawnshop)—all presented a nonthreatening image to his audience. Only Luke's eyes, dark as thunder clouds, betrayed him. Even the thick butterscotch hair and toothy smile couldn't conceal their permanently engraved meanness. But Luke Worship knew enough about performing not to let his faithful come too close.

Paul reached over the front seat and turned the radio up full blast. "Hound Dog" exploded through the car.

"You gone nuts?" Luke Worship yelled, spinning around. "That jungle rot's for niggers and crazy men." His temper was hotter than the screaming rubber that swerved to miss their car.

Neither Lillian nor Paul said a word; neither wanted to breathe. Only by freezing could they survive the fury.

Lillian reached like a blind person for her lipstick. She didn't want to move more than her arm, or even turn her eyes. Balancing her purse on one foot, she made sure the bag slipped silently to the floor until another crisis had passed.

The dome of the state capitol loomed high above the buildings as Luke searched for the intersection of Adams and College avenues. Sister Maria Josefa had sent a hand-drawn map, noting that after the university the orphanage was a sharp left before the stadium.

Suddenly they saw the sign: Hilltop House. Once the home of Florida's first cattle king, the rambling old colonial with its huge shade trees and sloping lawns looked anything but institutional.

"Let's not make it all day," Big Luke said, rolling his wrist without glancing at his watch. "Gotta make it back, too, you know."

Lillian Worship got out of the car and tried to smooth the creases in her dress, but they were too deep to flatten. Noticing that Luke and Paul had walked ahead, she ran to catch up.

In a show of respect for "Chaplain" Worship's naval record, the sisters had dressed three-year-old Jean in a white middy, red tie, and blue skirt. But as soon as the outfit was on, Jean had wanted it off. She wanted her pink smock, like the ones all the other girls wore. The sisters even tried bribing her with her favorite playmate, a no-eyes teddy, but Jean had thrown it on the floor and kept crying. She didn't want to leave. She wasn't "a lucky little girl." She hated her beautiful new name. She didn't even know how to say it, and she didn't want to try.

It was a red-eyed Loretta, looking more like a toy than a toddler, who stood between the enveloping sisters to meet her new family. Lillian rushed from her husband and pulled the tiny body to her. Of course she hugged too hard. Of course Loretta cried even more and ran away.

"She's shy."

"So loving."

"And so smart. So fast to learn."

"We love her."

"We're all she's really ever known, so she doesn't know how lucky she is."

"She's still only a baby."

When the sisters brought Loretta back, they gave the Worships the glossy snapshot of Jean in her rosebud sweater, taken the day she had arrived at Hilltop House. They gave Loretta a small, red patent-leather suitcase with white stitching on the outside. Inside they put some clothes and, as a surprise, the no-eyes teddy.

"No. There's no time. Not now," Big Luke said to his wife, who desperately wanted to take pictures.

"Just one? Just one of us all?"

"We'll do it at home." Luke kept on walking.

"It'll be dark then, Luke." Lillian didn't move.

"That's what I'm saying. It's late. It's a far piece back and I don't want to be driving in the dark." When Luke got into the car and turned the key in the ignition, the old wagon leaped forward, then jerked back, stalling. His having left the clutch in gear was a good excuse to explode.

"Get in! Now! God damn it! Get in," he shouted, gunning the motor and blasting the horn.

After Baby Loretta came into Luke's life, the Reverend Worship decided to move his Sunshine Parish from St. Petersburg to the outskirts of Tampa. "St. Pete's got too many old and not enough rich." It was entirely St. Pete's fault he wasn't rich, Luke decided, after hearing about the big bucks Oral Roberts, Robert Schuller, Rex Humbard, and especially "Fuller Brush Billy" were bringing in. Luke was positive the new arena and, in due time, the one-two punch of Luke and Loretta on the same bill would be enough to flatten the most heavyweight wallet.

But so obsessed was Luke with himself, it was impossible for him to push the product, to sell Christ instead of Big Luke. He would have to be reborn a thousand times to be able to learn what being a Fuller Brush salesman had taught Billy Graham about marketing; to be able to say of himself, like "Fuller Brush Billy," that he was "a sinner who'd been saved." After all, Big Luke was the savior.

What Luke Worship never believed was that you had to believe. Yes, you could be part charlatan, part liar, and part thief, but still you had to believe you were doing it for God. Luke thought he could make it in spite of God. And for a while, by changing locations, he did. But Big Luke merely stunned his prey, never knocked them out. As good as he was at getting, Luke was a poor keeper. It was never long before the disillusioned took their souls to another savior.

# 2

The massive lucite tub was being lowered to the middle of the reinforced platform in preparation for another Big Luke Miracle Mass. Workmen nailed a sparkling white carpet to the corners of the plywood while the local fire department waited for its cue. Just before the service began, the firemen would be given the Lord's blessing to supply the thousands of gallons needed to fill God's own seaquarium-in-the-round. Were it done any sooner, the dust from the drought would blur the purity of the pulpit and its pastor who swore God had promised rain.

The previous afternoon, posters had been slapped all over and speaker trucks driven everywhere ballyhooing the one-time-in-a-lifetime Miracle Mass. Throughout the night the huge tent-topping cross flashed its neon lightning, igniting the souls who sought salvation.

"A miracle—a true miracle!" Luke Worship shouted into the mike, his voice reverberating through mammoth speakers scattered around the big top, each time more loudly, each time with more bravado.

So strong was the heat under Big Luke's fire from God that when he raised his arms to the Lord, the perspiration ran through his white satin suit. Luke always wore all-white for his one-time-only Miracle Masses, right down to his mother-of-pearl buttonhole rose.

"A miracle! For the first time in her twelve years on God's earth, our baby, our Loretta, has heard His call."

While the piped-in hymns lent a welcome familiarity, they also created the right rhythm for the good reverend. Luke never missed a beat, even when the time came for the huge circular screen to be lowered. At that moment life-size pictures of Baby Loretta, from newborn to now, would flash rapidly in succession. Loretta's favorite was the one that showed her in the sweater with the tiny rosebuds. Luke's favorite was the just-born shot he had taken of "Loretta" —the day he sneaked into Tampa General's nursery and "that ugly old bitch in maternity finally held up a kid that didn't look like a raisin." One of the few occasions Lillian heard Luke really laugh was when he told her the newborn he'd snapped was a boy.

Whenever Loretta's days weren't completely taken with her enforced tutoring in the tricks of Big Luke's parish, she was dragged to other performances. Big Luke's favorite had always been Marjoe Gortner. But what truly tortured Loretta was that Luke forbade her to go to school. Even after Mama taught her to read, if Luke caught her with a book that Paul had sneaked to her—or worse, something that she'd bought with "money stolen from God"—he would become crazed. And that's when he'd beat the living bejesus out of her.

Like the day after his return to Tampa. Luke had left the house "to minister," he claimed, "last rites to the new owner of Morgan's Mortuary." The absurdity of the lie delighted Luke. In fact he'd met up with another devil's disciple and gone to a nearby bar to leer at what he referred to as "pink high-school things." The kind of feral lust Big Luke felt at such moments could be cooled only by dousing it in a grateful Lillian or in one of the broads he picked up in Tampa bars.

When Luke got home, he was still wearing the cowboy hat he put on whenever he left the church. Even in summer he'd wear the finest fur-felt Stetson God's money could buy, crease it just so, snap the brim just right, and beat a dent down the middle to rival Roy Rogers.

As Big Luke pulled the refrigerator open for a beer, he spotted Paul in Loretta's room.

Even with the paint peeling from its walls, Loretta loved her little room off the kitchen because from the window she could see Mama's little garden, and this meant that Mama was always nearby. If Mama wasn't tending her roses, she was sure to be in the kitchen with her pasted-up pictures of movie stars.

The kitchen always smelled of garlic and onions and, in season, Mama's garden prize, the deep-red Imperial Rose. From the moment its fat floppy petals opened, it looked like some blowsy madam ready for work. But Lillian Worship saw it only as God's most beautiful bloom, and with the utmost care she would arrange as many as would fit into the heavily sculptured milk-white vase that Big Luke had stolen from a grave.

How Mama loved sitting around the kitchen table, with the roses in the vase, reading her poetry book to Loretta. From all kinds of magazines Mama had clipped all kinds of poems, and collected them all in her black-and-white composition book. Emily Dickinson, Wordsworth, and Hallmark shared equal space. Mama didn't know who the poets were; she just liked what they said.

Still standing at the refrigerator door, Big Luke glared at Paul as he watched him hand Loretta a slender book. Paul was almost sixteen, but he looked like a child, with his bright, button eyes, shy smile, and curly hair the same butterscotch color as his father's.

"You're going to like *The Little Prince*," Paul said. "He even looks like you, Loretta. See? His eyes are even your blue."

Gently, Loretta caressed the book's cover, her fingers tracing the small boy's face and the myriad stars circling his golden head. Paul had introduced Loretta to Huck Finn, the Hardy Boys, even Lad, a Dog. He wanted to share everything he liked with her. It was their unspoken bond that they knew their life wasn't what it should be, but it was okay for now because someday things would change.

"You know how we love to watch sunsets?" Paul asked. "The Little Prince says nobody should ever be too busy to watch them." He showed her the line.

Paul had the power to make Loretta happy. What would she do without him? As she threw her arms around Paul's neck, Big Luke stumbled through the door.

"Whore! Cock-teasing whore!" Grabbing the book, he ripped through its cover as if it were tissue. "Make me crazy, will you?" Spittle slid down his chin. "I'll show trash like you—and you, too!"

Loretta's eyes glazed with terror as Paul stepped between them, pushing her back and kicking hard at his father.

Big Luke felt nothing. His eyes narrowed as he twisted Loretta's wrist. "Trash! Gutter trash! That's where you came from and that's—"

Loretta bent her head over the arm that held her. With the savagery of a wounded beast she bit into the hot, hairy flesh, gagging on the blood, but not letting go until Luke released his grip. She thought she heard him cry out, but she wasn't sure, because as she let go she slammed the door so hard behind her that everything fell from the shelves.

Running wildly out of Luke's reach, she collided with Mama, who was racing toward the hurricane's eye. Only when Loretta felt Mama's arms tight around her and saw Mama's tears did she begin to cry.

Luke's drunken scenes never stopped hurting. But the ache was deep down where nobody could see, and the tears wouldn't go. To ease the pain Loretta would sometimes pray silently, in the way that only He Who mattered heard.

Now, as Loretta stood dwarfed in the middle of the gigantic big top, heads were beginning to spin as spectators put what they saw together with what they heard. A real live *miracle*—it could happen to them. Miracles *do* happen!

"It was just one week ago this very morning," Luke said slowly, pressing his finger to his nose, pretending to remember. "It was just about the time the sun was washing the very last star from the heavens when my little girl first came to me and said: 'Daddy. I'm ready. Jesus called to me, Daddy. Like you said He would. Daddy, take me to Jesus. I'm read—' "

Big Luke stopped, put the onion-drenched handkerchief to his eyes, and wept uncontrollably. His heaving sobs were amplified through the big top. Bravely, he resumed.

"Our baby, our miracle from God, said to me, 'Daddy. I'm read—' " Clearly, Daddy still wasn't. He stopped for more tears. Luke Worship's eyes did not merely water; they blossomed into a sympathy-swollen fuchsia. Peering through his lids, he judged that the crowd was nearly ready. " 'Daddy,' she said to me," he continued, " 'I'm ready to be . . .' " Pause . . . another ripple to heaven . . . one more pass of the handkerchief. " '. . . REBORN!' "

Loretta had lost count of how many times she'd been totally immersed for her eternal salvation, how many times she'd stepped down one ladder, her skirt billowing high over her tiny pink panties, then stepped up the other side, the thin cotton of her dress clinging to her erect nipples.

Luke stepped solemnly back, leaving Loretta to stand alone before the mesmerized mob. Slowly, she turned, smiled, and blew kisses, shouting: "Reborn! Reborn! Reborn!"

Little Loretta was a slice of heaven in Big Luke's world. Long, lean, fair-skinned, and flaxen-haired, with deep blue eyes, she bore little resemblance to the rest of her family, as much a standout among the Worships as Oliver Twist was at the orphanage. But Loretta never thought much about being adopted, except on the occasions when Big Luke reminded her of her incredible good fortune.

On cue, a choir from one of the local churches, dressed in the flowing white robes that Big Luke always provided, appeared inside the tent. Luke had once seen, and unfortunately never had forgotten, the Easter pageant at Radio City Music Hall. In a thunderclap of a cappella harmony, the choir now intoned the pious verse that Luke himself had penned to the tune of "76 Trombones"—

> Baby Loretta heard like the Christ child heard
> But Baby Loretta heard from Him . . .

—over and over until everybody clapped and sang, sang and clapped. Soon the audience, moved by the spirit, would march right on down.

> Baby Loretta heard like the Christ child heard
> But Baby Loretta heard . . .

Yet no matter how Luke manipulated the strings of his miracle marionette, there was always an awkwardness to Loretta's performance. Loretta enjoyed being loved, but she didn't like what she had to do to be loved. She knew that love from strangers was not like the love of Mama and Paul. She believed in God—the God she and Mama talked about, not the one Daddy did for a living. She didn't like having people touch her. They scared her, yelling and praying, grabbing for her. And she didn't want to have to touch them.

" 'The blind receive their sight, and the lame walk, the lepers are cleansed and the deaf hear.' Matthew eleven," Luke Worship screamed at the feverish worshipers, his sweating palm planted firmly atop Loretta's head. "And that same miraculous healing of Jesus has been lent here to our own little miracle."

Loretta didn't want these people to come to her, to believe in her, simply because they'd seen her heal the shills Luke had planted in the audience, whose pains miraculously left with her touch. She didn't want them thrusting sick babies into her arms because they'd watched her take crutches from the arms of "crippled" children.

Loretta stood shivering onstage trying to shut out the cries from the audience as well as from Big Luke. None of it had meaning. All that had meaning for Loretta was the faces of the frightened, the vulnerable. They were there for *her*, and she knew she couldn't help them. She trembled, and the audience thought it was part of her miracle rebirth. They kept staring, waiting for a sign.

As Baby Loretta grew older, the number of sons, husbands, fathers, and brothers who sought salvation had also grown. Now when they watched this shapely missionary rise from her spiritual baptism, they could feel the devil taking possession of their bodies. The deeper this "evil" struck their flesh, the more these men felt they were in desperate need of being saved. "*And the child shall lead us!*" One by one they stepped forward to receive salvation in the supreme unction of hypocrisy.

In the nearly nine years since Loretta's first "rebirth"

before an audience, hordes of hopefuls had followed her down the shady aisles of Luke's Sunshine Church.

If ever she became ill and couldn't go on, Luke would scream, "Don't you call me Daddy! Don't make me your blood! You could be half nigger for what I know about you!" And when he finished with Loretta, he'd turn on Lillian. "Coddling and cuddling that white trash like you do is sick. Do you hear? Sick! So whatever sickness she's got, she's got from you. You understand what I'm saying?" He would rub his brow, worried about how he could perform the Miracle Mass without Loretta. "The whole lot of you's sick!"

As time went on, Loretta noticed it seemed less and less convenient for Luke Worship to tell the truth. Now, even Christmas came wrapped in Luke's lies as he traced Loretta's ancestry back to Bethlehem. Amen!

# 3

Luke Worship's new Celebration Mass was to be held in the First Baptist Church of Tallahassee, only about a mile from the orphanage where the Worships had first met Loretta. Mama couldn't wait for the sisters to see Loretta again. She wanted to show off how pretty she was now, at sixteen, and what good manners she had; how much Loretta knew about books and about nice things such as flowers and poetry.

"You know, Loretta sweetheart," Mama said, taking her hand off the wheel to pat Loretta's hand, "I'm so proud. I never have been prouder. It's like dreaming when you're awake."

"I love you so much, Mama." Loretta leaned over to kiss her.

"Now don't get all mushed up and start spoiling your dress." Mama groped through her pocketbook for the handkerchief she always carried. She bought only ones with roses on them. "Here," she said, shaking the handkerchief open. "Use it. Keep it. The pink in the middle there matches your dress."

Loretta's dress would have looked more appropriate on a

child than on a teenager, but Mama wanted her to look like a little girl. It was all part of Mama's way of looking at a hateful world with loving eyes.

"Why won't you tell where we're going?" Loretta asked.

"Just for a drive."

"No, Mama. We wouldn't have gotten dressed up like this just for a drive."

"We're going to visit some nuns."

"Nuns?" That didn't seem likely to Loretta. Not that Mama wasn't religious, but she had enough of it every day with Luke.

"Did you ever think," Mama asked, "it's funny that Loretta Young's a Catholic when she was born in Salt Lake City? Isn't it funny she's not a Mormon?" She shook her head.

Loretta looked out the window at the houses leaning into the hillside and thought how Mama should be the one wearing this dress with all the roses. It was she who was still the little girl.

Lillian switched on the radio and the car filled with "The Sound of Music."

"Loretta, honey, do you think if Julie Andrews had played the lead in *My Fair Lady*, which she should have, she'd still have won the Oscar for *Mary Poppins*? I mean it would have meant she'd won two in two years." Again, Mama shook her head at her own question. Mama's movie questions were always answered by Mama.

"You know, you look like Julie Andrews," Mama said, looking Loretta full in the face as they stopped at a traffic light.

"Maybe my hair when I'm out in the sun, but that's all, Mama."

"You're tall like her."

They both laughed. How Loretta loved her mama. It

made her joyful just to see Mama so happy. She knew the only way Mama could bear the daily boredom of her life and Luke's drunkenness was to imagine those things to be the celluloid, and the movies to be her real world.

"You know, Loretta, when I was a girl, gangsters were like movie stars. Gangsters were heroes. Every magazine, every newsreel followed them. Everybody knew everything about them: their girlfriends, their families, their funerals. Everybody was so poor, and they were the only people who weren't afraid. You know? They weren't afraid of anything and everybody else was afraid of everything."

Loretta kissed her mama's hand. She sensed that Mama had been afraid all her life. One day Loretta would do something wonderful for her, something so wonderful that Mama wouldn't believe it.

When finally they arrived at the orphanage, heavy rusted chains held the gates together. "No Trespassing" was posted on the sign that once had read "Hilltop House," and high weeds overran the lawn. Only the long, dusty driveway remained the same. Lillian bit her lip to keep from bursting into tears. Where had they all gone? Mama took Loretta's hand in hers, they smiled at each other, and once more Mama thanked God for Loretta.

Big Luke's just-completed tour of Georgia and Alabama had been a godawful disaster since Loretta's rebirth was no longer on the bill. While all across Dixie, other representatives of the Lord's video vicarage were buying into prime time TV, Luke could hardly afford local spots. His act had been seen too often for the scam that it was, and Luke now desperately needed his vilely conceived Celebration Mass as his new gimmick.

Also, times were changing and it was harder than ever for Big Luke to deliver his firebrand segregationist sermons to the land of cotton. People were keeping pretty much to themselves and it took something special to flush out the rednecks from behind their hooded sheets and .44 Magnums.

Yet Luke felt confident about his upcoming Florida tour. From Tallahassee to the tip of the Keys, Luke's Celebration Mass would canvas farm and factory, milking old and new sacrificial lambs. The once-in-a-lifetime occasion Luke was celebrating was that his blessed son, his special gift from God, had enlisted in America, having heard his call from Jesus to fight for freedom. At exactly the same time that Vietnam was making parents throughout the United States pool their last dimes to send even illiterates to college, Luke Worship plucked Paul out of his senior year and forced him to sign up.

"On no roll call anywhere, especially on the one that counts, will *my only boy* be called a traitor," Big Luke shouted, lifting his head toward the Lord's ledger. "With communism the murderer of Jesus, what would you call a draft dodger? A killer of God! And what better way to hammer down a blood-hungry Christ killer than to impale him on his own sickle of death?"

Paul only gave in to this pious prostitution because he knew of the Sunshine pulpit's desperate need for dollars, and he hoped that some might filter through to Mama and Loretta. So as Chaplain Luke Worship reclaimed his full naval regalia from its mothballs and toured the Florida landscape, Paul donned khakis and passed the months prior to his induction waving and saluting from the altar with Loretta at his side as Miss Liberty.

Big Luke's new vitality turned every Celebration Mass into a fiery rally as he raised his uniformed arm along with Paul's to grab hold of Loretta's torch while bellowing like a madman. "Just as the Lord sent His only Son to help the world, so I . . ."

Each sermon would end with an impassioned plea for funds. "How can we help Our Lord meet the enemy and make him His? Help Him rid the world of this Goliath against God—how? By buying a share in freedom. And Jesus turns deaf ears to the jingle of coins," Luke shouted, as people reached into their pockets. "He knows too well the death rattle from pieces of silver. Dig deep. Let's hear paper!"

Then Luke's legion of ministers, hired for the day, would parade down the aisles, baskets in hand, stepping in time to the deafening sounds of Luke's favorite military marches. At the end, he would administer a benediction for "our boys everywhere," while Loretta struggled to shut out the noise and prayed silently for her brother.

The hurricane season had passed with the summer, and it was at last time for Paul to leave. Luke's free freedom ride was over. Tomorrow his son would be gone, the train pulling out before most of Key West would awaken.

Luke's final Celebration Mass managed a fair-sized catch of local "conches," and Big Luke managed some better-than-fair-sized tears—not for his son's departure, but for losing his gimmick.

The late-September evening was light and fresh, and a small breeze floated in from the Atlantic. Loretta and Paul sat without talking. They had too much to say. Although they were happiest watching sunsets, tonight they felt lonely and apart, and the greedy sea seemed to gulp the fiery ball faster than ever. Why did it have to set today? Why couldn't it stay half on this side of the world and half on the other—just so it didn't all go?

"Loretta, don't let him bully you," Paul said finally.

That's like saying, "Don't let the sun go down," Loretta thought, as the last of it slipped away and the afterglow blazoned the sky.

"No matter where I am, I can help. And I'll write. Please, Loretta. Promise me you won't let him. Say it. Say, 'I promise.' "

"You're too good to go," Loretta said quietly, looking straight ahead at the horizon. "We won't even see the sun on the same day. You'll have seen it already. But when you're there and I'm here, you know what I'll think? I'll think it's you who sent it to me. And you can pretend I'm sending it back. And that way, every day we'll be together."

Paul smiled and reached into his pocket, pulling out a tiny gold Saint Christopher medal on a thin gold chain. "Loretta, promise me—you must swear—you must swear on this." He pressed the medal into her hand. "Swear."

"And Paul, you must swear to come back." She didn't look at him, because now was not the time to cry.

His hand pressing hers, they said it together. "Swear."

Even Loretta's delicate fingers had difficulty opening the minuscule clasp. Tiny as the medal was, it shone like the first star against her tanned chest. "I'll never take it off," she said as she kissed her brother's cheek.

Embarrassed, Paul rubbed the side of his face. Looking down at the jetty, he picked up a mollusk covered with barnacles. He turned it over and over as if in a trance, then tossed it out to sea. "Loretta, when you get back to Tampa, put my shells together with yours. Even the ones in the glass lamp."

Captiva . . . Boca Grande . . . Sanibel Island . . . their best moments together, when they'd followed the tides to find the best tellins, molluscas, olives. Once they'd even found the rare golden olive. They'd stoop and dig until their necks were stiff and their backs felt permanently bent. Then they'd rush back, rinse away the sand, and sort through their treasures with a delirium greater than that of doubloon-crazed pirates.

"Asia's near Australia and Australia's where the Barrier Reef is, where the Chambered Nautilus is—remember?" Loretta was making an inept effort to be lighthearted. "When you get out of the Army, before you get home, I'll meet you there." Hearing her own words, she knew she could never make Paul believe them.

"I hope it won't be long," he said, his voice drifting.

"Paul? Don't be afraid." She took her brother's hand. "Please, Paul. Are you afraid?" Loretta looked at his eyes and saw that they were empty. Tentacles of fear stabbed the cool she had promised to keep, as she felt herself growing hotter.

"No," he lied. Then he grabbed her shoulders. "Loretta, I'm so afraid. I'm so afraid to die," he sobbed.

Loretta had a sudden vision of a khaki-clad misfit in the thick of combat, crawling through mud, his bottom half trapped under low-hanging barbed wire. His buddy tries to free him but can't. A hail of shrapnel. Grenades explode. Troops break loose. Paul can't move. Thrashing like a child learning to swim, he flails in the slime. Unable to shake this terrible image, Loretta shivered in the warm sea breeze.

"I don't want to fight, Loretta. I don't know who or what I'm protecting. I only want to protect you. You know how Daddy says, 'It's all shit up there?' What if Daddy's right? What if all there is, is here? What if this is the one time Daddy's right, and I don't come back?"

Loretta had no answer. Silently she and Paul walked in the surf, shoes dangling from their fingertips, until the moon changed places with the sun.

# 4

The very day Paul left for boot camp, two imposing, oversize portraits of Private Worship assumed their place on either side of the altar. The huge fabric-covered frames were quilted in Betsy Ross stripes, and from the ceiling hung blue-spangled stars, each with "Christ wins" written in silver at its center. The *t* in "Christ" was a crucifix. There were exactly seven hundred and eighty-seven starbursts that Loretta, still fettered as Liberty, had counted and recounted during each Sunday's weekly force feeding of Jesus. Loretta was clearly not the only one bored, but Luke Worship seemed blind to the shrinking size of his congregation.

In the time since Paul had gone away, heavy clouds had gathered over the Sunshine Parish. Once the reverend himself had even been booked for driving with a considerable bit more than the communion cup; but Luke presented a self-defense invoking his poor soldier son that Mama rated with Barrymore. After his release, Luke celebrated his innocence with the sequined hostess at the Tampa Tampico. Several months later he found himself slapped with a paternity suit. With the same self-righteous pleading Reverend

Worship once again shook his head toward heaven: "Ladies of easy virtue always see easily, but never accurately, in the dark." His testimony was corroborated by other "ministers" and by a horrified Mama. In fact, it was Mama who made the judge believe Luke was innocent. Mama simply *knew* such a thing couldn't have happened, since in all their years of marriage Luke had rarely showed much interest in the bedroom. "Certainly now," Lillian Worship cried to the judge, "with our son off to fight and our flock dwindling, Luke's got enough to worry about without some crazy lady throwing threats like those people in *Peyton Place*."

If ever Mama allowed herself to admit the truth about Luke, then all of Mama's life would be a lie. It was impossible even to think about.

Loretta couldn't abide any picture of Paul in uniform at her bedside. Instead, she framed the one from his yearbook with the pink-mottled sky, the padded shoulders, and the equally unreal smile. It was, at least, a less damnable fraud than the larger-than-life hero straddling the altar.

Paul's last leave before being shipped to Vietnam was so sad Loretta thought her throat would never heal from her swallowed sobs. Everything about Paul and Vietnam didn't make sense. The only positive thing was how good he looked. Having slimmed down and shaped up, he seemed inches taller, and with his soldier's ruddiness he finally looked more man than boy. The tailored jacket, close-fitting pants, and mirror-shine shoes reinforced the impression of physical strength. Perhaps Paul would be okay after all. Maybe he would come back to her. Maybe the fat boy trapped beneath the barbed wire would succeed in wrangling loose.

"Won't be long now, son," Big Luke mumbled through one of the mouthfuls of food he forever seemed to be chewing. "I'll never stop getting cranked up when I think of those slanty-eyed bastards I killed. Shoulda killed more. Shoulda killed every one of those yellow midgets." Finishing his plate with his fingers, he pushed it at Mama, who, conditioned by years, got up and loaded it with seconds.

"You're welcome," Loretta said loudly, unable to stand the ugliness of Luke's overstuffed body and overflowing plate. She felt as if there were no oxygen left, as if Big Luke had sucked it all out, just as he'd drained so much else from everyone in his life.

"You bet I'm welcome, you rotten little orphan," Luke said, picking at a back tooth. "You're goddam right I am!"

Mama clutched at her neck as if she, too, were in need of air, and cast one of her "don't answer" looks at Loretta.

Big Luke narrowed his eyes on Paul. "She's gotten pretty sassed up since you've been away," he smirked, waving his arm at Loretta. "Found her mouth, you might say. But she'll find a fat lip if she keeps it up. Hear me? In case *she* can't, I'm warning all of you to clue her in."

"You lay one hand . . ." Paul stood up, shaking with rage.

"Sit down, kid," Luke said. "I wanted to see something and I saw it. A fighter. I like a man who fights. For chrissake, General, sit down. This is no war. It's a party. Get in the spirit. Drink some of it." Luke dumped another shot of whiskey into his coffee.

"Know the only good thing any preacher ever did?" Luke went on. "And do you know, too, why I'm asking a bunch of idiots like you? 'Cause you're here! . . . The only good thing any goddam preacher ever did was invent bourbon, that's what. And that includes all those brown-robed, fat-bellied faggots who thought brandy was the come-all!—get it? Cumall? Let's hear it for the great Reverend Elijah Craig of Bourbon County, Kentucky. Seventeen hundred eighty-nine.

Ring dem bells. Ding-dong. How's everybody's ding-dong doing? My ding-dong's doing just fine," Luke said, leering at Loretta. "You know something, honey? You don't ever give me credit for being educated. Didn't you just now learn something from me? Date and place and everything? What about that? Don't that deserve a little preacher's punch?"

Big Luke lifted his cup and winked obscenely at Loretta.

"I hate him. Period," Paul said to Loretta as they sat alone on a red leather banquette watching a wedge of moonlight divide Tampa Bay. "He's nuts, Loretta. I never saw it so much before. You've got to get out."

The candlelight that outlined Loretta's delicate features made her look soft and defenseless, and made the tiny, glistening medal seem little protection. "Loretta, please. You've got to get away. He's no good. Mama doesn't see it. She can't. What else is there for her? But for you there's something better."

His surprising forcefulness made Loretta believe more fervently than ever that he would survive. "I'll go when you come back. You can't be gone more than a year. It's the law." She smiled and clasped his hand between hers. "I can't leave Mama. For me as much as for her. Anyway, I've got this," she said, squeezing the Saint Christopher.

Paul understood. In a way, he didn't really want her to go. How could she? Where would she go?

"You know, Paul, I'll have my mail-order diploma in two months."

"What do you want to do when you get away?" Paul asked.

"Just that. Get away. Learn more, so I can work. And I want to help sick people. Really help them."

"Do you believe in God, Loretta? Not Luke's God— though I never thought much about the real one until my buddy Joe took me to his church. Now I think about Him a lot. I can't believe I believe, but I do. First thing when I get out, Loretta, I'll come to take you away." Again, Paul sounded strong. Just let it stay with him, Loretta prayed.

Since Paul had left for Vietnam, Loretta received letter after letter that unskillfully tried to hide the fear, the boredom, the waiting for whatever.

Mama took more and more to gardening, to planting new seeds she kept getting free at the bank, few of which bore anything close to a decent return.

Apart from the constant dread about Paul, these last months had been almost easy for Loretta. Since Luke was drinking more, there were fewer trips and fewer masses, more time with Mama, with reading in the kitchen, with movies.

One of the best times Mama and Loretta had was when "The Forsyte Saga" was on TV. Mama didn't even care that Luke stumbled home drunk night after night. Only once did he notice that the TV was on.

"Even those nigger Supremes are better than that shit. You two think that phony accent's gonna make you any better? Fuckin' sick. Both of you."

"He's so tired," Mama said, turning the volume back up once she'd heard Luke crash on the bed. "A poor parish takes a lot out of a man's soul."

"Only if the man has one, Mama."

Mama merely squeezed Loretta's hand.

Unlike tropical Florida, Tampa has a northern spring with crocuses and robins. And as the buds burst forth and the trees became a fuzzy green, Loretta wondered why, if God is so faithful to His flowers, He made peace so unreachable for us.

Standing on the porch, waiting for Mama to come back from the market, Loretta heard a car door slam. It took her a moment to realize that it wasn't Mama.

At first, all she saw was a sparkle of buttons and bars. As he came closer, the sun caught the small gold cross in his left lapel. Holding his cap in his hand, he asked, "Is this the home of Private Paul Worship?"

Everything inside her froze. Her eyes became glass, her fingers stone. She stopped breathing until her pulse broke through her flesh. "No!" she cried hysterically, turning and racing through the house. Yanking the shell lamp from her dresser, she hurled it through the window. Jagged spikes of glass flew everywhere, some ricocheting toward her neck. She wiped her fingers in the blood, rubbed them on the walls, on the kitchen walls, the living room walls. Crazed, she ran to the church squeezing her gashes for as much blood as would spurt out, then smeared it across the ob-scenely huge, draped portraits of Paul. Kneeling at the altar, she picked up a crucifix, over which her scarlet fingers curled as she collapsed in sobs of grief.

Chaplain Bender accompanied the Worships when they met the metal casket and stayed with the family through the funeral. He was also a Baptist. Yes, that's what the Army did now—wasn't it considerate? They kept a file on the religious preferences of their corpses.

After Paul, what sunsets would ever again give Loretta pleasure? She knew only that she wasn't yet ready to leave Mama.

Luke, consumed with the failure of his "soon-to-be-discovered genius," was hardly ever off the bottle. And only on rare Sundays did he make any effort to preach, and then only to be able to afford more of the Supreme Being's libation.

It was after just such a service, when the collection plate would buy him barely a bottle, that Luke Worship's sinning became its most grotesque.

Slobbering and staggering, he lunged for Loretta as she was tidying the altar. Catching her by surprise, he ripped away at her dress, shoved her to the floor, and tore off her underclothes.

"You move while I'm doin' this, you try to move away from me, and I'll beat you to a pulp," he said breathlessly, using his weight to keep her from moving. "I'll kill you. You understand, you little whore? Now, tell me you want me. Tell me you want me to be the first. Say it, or I'll rape you in front of your precious Mama. Then I'll tie up Mama and rape her in front of her precious you."

In a desperate gasp for survival, Loretta tried to say what Luke wanted to hear.

Suddenly, a scream, a wail, an animal's howl sounded next to them. Luke jumped off, and more claws sprang toward Loretta. More hysterical screams. Who dared seduce her man, God's man, in God's own house? Blindly, Lillian Worship slapped the harlot . . . then opened her eyes to the shocked and contorted features of her beloved Loretta.

# 5

Even the children seemed old and listless in the seedy waiting room of Tampa's main bus station. Loretta stared at the happy family in the poster.

GREYHOUND GOES EVERYWHERE *You* WANT TO GO.

She supposed she was the "*you*," because she was the one going. But there was no place in particular she wanted to go. She just wanted out.

She kept looking at her watch. Impossible it wasn't yet noon. Was it only a few hours ago, when the day was still wrapped in silence but already hot, that Loretta had stolen into Mama's room, reached quietly under her bed, and pulled out her cherished Loretta Young issue of *Photoplay*, shaking it until nine one-hundred-dollar bills fell from between the pages? Whenever Mama had squirreled away enough fives, tens, and twenties, she'd rush to the bank to exchange them for a crisp hundred. Big bills were more fun to look at. More important, they were easier to hide, easier to sneak into her wallet when she hurried off to buy whatever clothes her favorite stars were wearing or whatever makeup they professed made them beautiful. Loretta took only four of the bills. But she allowed herself the entire contents of Big Luke's pockets as he lay sprawled in a snoring stupor. The total came to about seven hundred dollars. Not much for fifteen years of forced labor.

Loretta didn't put the money into her purse, which she thought was too easy to lose. Instead she buried it in her raincoat pocket. Over and over she felt to make sure it was still there. She was sorry to be stealing Mama's money; she was sorrier that there wasn't more she could take from Luke. Despite her love for Mama, there was no way for her to go on living in that house. Someday, Loretta vowed to herself, she'd come back and take Mama away from here too.

SEE AMERICA FIRST—GO GREYHOUND

HISTORY, BEAUTY, INSPIRATION—ALL COME ALIVE IN
WASHINGTON, D.C.

Maybe she would too. A wall-length Kodacolor poster depicted the Capitol dome, the Washington Monument, and the lit-up, sculpted memorials. Perhaps this was some kind of sign, an omen that Loretta should go to Washington. All she knew as she approached the ticket window was that she wanted to go north.

"Round trip?"

Was he crazy? Loretta almost laughed. Back to here? Didn't he know that the only good thing about here was that it made *there* look that much better?

The excitement and the fear of knowing 'hat she controlled her own life suddenly terrified Loretta. Mama's poem about "master of my fate" was never the real world.

"Round trip or one way?" the man snapped without looking up, wiping perspiration from his forehead. "What's the matter? Can't you hear? You don't understand?" For the first time he looked through the bars at Loretta, and in spite of himself he smiled. He didn't expect anyone white or young or so pretty. Even in the sweltering Tampa summer Loretta looked cool. With her shiny hair tied back and her face unadorned by makeup, she appeared not only very young but very innocent—except to somebody who stopped long enough to notice the ancient eyes on that young face.

"You no speak no English?" he asked slowly. Like most people, he seemed to think that broken English was somehow easier for foreigners to understand.

Loretta gave him a wry, sad smile. "I speak English. I'm sorry. Just one way, please." Please God, just one way. Loretta was lonely and scared enough to want to prove to this man that she wasn't crazy or an imbecile. She wanted to prove it to him so that she could be sure of it herself.

The man was still smiling as he counted her more than fifty dollars' change. His hand lingered on Loretta's as he handed her the ticket—a comforting, fatherly linger. "The bus leaves at eleven-thirty. You'll be getting to Jacksonville around four, and you'll change there for an express. You should make Washington by about ten tomorrow morning. It'll be hot there too," he said, dragging his arm across his forehead once more. "Real hot."

It was kind of him to tell her all that. He hadn't said anything to the lady in front of her. For a moment Loretta wondered if he said so much to her because he thought she was crazy.

"You have a good trip now. You should be able to sleep good, too. The seats go pretty far back."

"Thanks. Thanks a lot." Loretta smiled again, reassured by his mention of sleeping. He simply thought she was tired.

\* \* \*

The first of forty-three possible passengers to board the big sixteen-wheeler, Loretta felt that once she was aboard she was already on her way. The gears in her head had shifted; her life from now on was not only going to go somewhere; it was going to be *worth* something.

The blue of the driver's uniform matched the blue of the stripes on the bus and the blue of the plastic seats. Loretta placed her cherished red suitcase on top of the blanket in the overhead compartment. She stowed the travel brochures in the elasticized pouch in front of her and unfolded the map to trace the journey.

She looked at her watch again. The bus was already late, but people were still boarding. Nobody, as yet, had sat next to her. Most people came in pairs. The day was getting hotter, and she wished they'd get underway so the air-conditioning would go on. It was beginning to smell: babies, food, people, sweat.

"Anybody sittin' here, child?"

"No," Loretta said, moving closer to the window as if to make room on her own seat.

The woman was enormous, and she looked especially so sitting next to Loretta. After much arranging and settling in, she heaved a sigh, folded her hands, and waited for the bus to take off. She gave Loretta a quick once-over and smiled.

The woman fetched a hanky from between her large breasts and dabbed the dark brow beneath her brittle gray hair. "Whew. That climate control's outa control. Lost its cool's more accurate." "Acc-ur-ate" was how she pronounced it. She replaced the damp hanky carefully, making sure that a corner of lace still showed. Loretta wondered whether this was for decoration or ease of access.

"I hope, child, I'm not takin' too much room, 'cause there's nothing less I can take," she said in a kindly way, flashing a big white smile at Loretta. "I'm just plain fat—

and I'm also Zinnia. Zinnia Tyler." She patted Loretta's thigh with a hand that was smooth and childlike, though large. Her short, rounded nails were buffed to a fine gloss.

"I'm Loretta."

"That's pretty. Real pretty. Lo-retta." Zinnia sat back and nodded. When she nodded, her whole body nodded, as if she were in a rocking chair on a wide veranda. "Nothin' after Loretta?"

"Worship. Oh, I'm sorry. Loretta Worship. Sorry." She paused. "Zinnia's pretty, too." Immediately, Loretta heard how stupid that sounded. She didn't even like the name Zinnia. It was pretty only as a flower, like Rose.

Zinnia was too large to turn full around, but years of rearranging had taught her that a certain body angle and a soft voice could create the same intimacy as direct eye contact. "I'm the last of Thomas Jefferson's side of flower children, child," she said with a laugh. "Every girl from the Jefferson tree—and I had girl cousins on every branch—was named right from the garden. Except for Q. Since there's no Q flowers and Mama didn't want to break the alphabet, thinkin' it might split the family, she gave my brother Q. Called him Quince for the fruit. Lord, we'd kid him about that. Don't doubt that's why he joined the Army, old as he was." Zinnia's voice lowered.

"He died D-Day. Never even made the beach." Her voice trailed away as she felt again for the lace edge of the handkerchief.

But wasn't that the war when everybody came back, the war Loretta watched over and over in the movies she saw with Mama? "Off we go into the wild blue yonder . . ."—and then they came home? Those were the good old days. . . .

In a rare torrent, Loretta told Zinnia about Paul and Vietnam, about Mama, about the flowers and the poetry. That was as much as she could tell. She could never talk about Big Luke, who attacked her. Or how her mother had attacked her, too.

Yet it was clear that she had said enough, because Zinnia was reaching alternately for her hanky and for the cross that hung around her neck.

"No use lookin' back, child. 'Better fish in the sea than ever was caught.' That's what Grandmother Jefferson'd say. Lookin' back means you got no creativity in your soul." She drawled out "cre-a-tiv-i-ty." "Tomorrow should be busyin' you. Backwards is for backwards people. Where you headed?"

"Washington. Washington, D.C.," Loretta said.

"You don't sound so sure, child. You sure you want to go there?" Zinnia cocked her large head like a tiny bird.

"I'm sure," Loretta nodded, and Zinnia let it lie.

"Washington's not a whole lot past where I'm goin'." With that she threw her head back and closed her eyes, shutting everything out so she could concentrate on what to do next.

Zinnia Tyler must have spent hours whiting those sturdy shoes of hers, Loretta thought. Even the tops of the laces were wondrously white. Zinnia's dress, with its oversized floral print, was garden fresh and probably contained each of her Jefferson cousins. Her large, horn-handled navy pocketbook was too old-fashioned to be new, but it was obviously "good." If Mama saw that pocketbook she would say, "They don't make them like that anymore."

The big Greyhound rolled north. To Loretta it seemed that there was little difference between the scenic route of Highway 4 and Interstate 95. Every now and then patches of grass grew where there were no dingy little houses, but mostly Loretta saw Bar-B-Q's, big golden arches, and the Colonel.

She watched the blurs of red-and-white Florida license plates become fewer and those of the Peach Tree State more numerous. Loretta consulted her map. Savannah next. Then Florence, South Carolina; Fayetteville, North Carolina; then—what? Virginia came after the Carolinas. But Loretta didn't want to be past them, because after that would come Washington, and what would she do then?

Loretta looked at Zinnia and wondered if her family had been slaves. President Jefferson had a lot of slaves; so did President Tyler. Did he give Zinnia's family its name? "Slavery's kin to Godliness," Luke always said. "Bring it back and blacks can have a use instead of just gettin' welfare." The voice in her head made Loretta shudder.

Zinnia Tyler reached into her purse for a paper fan. One side read "Jesus brings us life"; the other advertised "Your Home Before Heaven—Harte's Funeral Parlor." She fanned herself in short, dignified strokes so as not to bother Loretta.

"I don't know what you was taught about the Civil War, child," Zinnia started up again, this time pulling each word from some important place. "People in Richmond got hurt more than any other people, North or South. One thing they know about's hurt. Sure and simple, Richmond was then and still is today the last nice city in the South and the last nice city in the North. It never knew why it was fightin'. It was snarled midway. There was never gonna be no winnin' for them." Her words were paced, deliberate. Talking this way was hard for her.

"I'm with my daughter now, in Tampa. She's teachin' school and I'm teachin' her children before they're old enough for school." She closed her eyes tightly, not wanting to lose her concentration. "I'm goin' to Richmond for a hip operation. All Dr. and Mrs. Crestbourne had to hear was 'my hip' and here I am goin' to Dr. Crestbourne's hospital and stayin' at Foxrest. Foxrest's among the finest homes in Richmond." She wasn't showing off. She was proud. "To me I'm me and that's all. To them I'm one of them and that's all. They don't hear nothin' else." Again she paused.

"I was workin' at Foxrest almost no time when Mrs. Crestbourne said, 'Zinnia, Foxrest is your home.' That was more than thirty years ago." She shook her head. "Over thirty years. First time I've been back since I left. It's three years gardenia time. And that's now. They're always askin' me, but my daughter's husb . . ." Her voice trailed away, then started strongly again. ". . . Raised all four Crestbourne boys. Raised Mrs. Crestbourne right along with them." Zinnia laughed. "I used to call her the worst of the lot. She knew how I meant it. I loved the devil outa her because of the devil *in* her." Zinnia's smile stretched extra wide. "Child, if ever you get to Richmond, you call on the Crestbournes. Just knowin' we're friends, their hospitality'd be spread from breakfast through Christmas. Christmas, that's the time. . . ." Zinnia talked and laughed and waved her fan to and fro.

"Marie, my daughter, called Dr. Crestbourne 'bout my hip. He near jumped through the phone thinkin' I was goin' elsewhere. Mrs. Crestbourne got arguin' at me that there was no other way and that Henderson would pick me up. Nothin' like that hospital in all the world. And there's a college there, too. Jonathan, my boy, graduated from the pharmacy school. I wanted Julie to go through nursin' school, but she . . ." Zinnia's voice faded again, but only briefly. She had a job to do, and it wasn't done yet.

"Virginia's sent four governors to the White House," she went on proudly, as if she were largely responsible. "Good people in Virginia. Fine people. And Richmond's a fine family city. You don't find people leavin' there.

"Lordy, I rocked each one of them Crestbourne babies to 'Carry Me Back to Ol' Virginny,' and I swear even though they're grown men they still try to jump in my lap, embarrassin' me to tears since I don't blush." Her tone became serious. "You look like you could use some rockin' yourself, child."

As the bus rolled through the fertile green acres bordering the thick timber stands of the Shenandoah, Zinnia laid her arm around Loretta's shoulder. Suddenly a torrent of tears, not unlike the earlier outpouring of words, rushed from Loretta. Her body shook with sobs. Every emotion seemed to surge and resurge through her tears—despair, fury, ambition. But mostly hope. Perhaps it was because the heaviness of Zinnia's arm took some of the weight from Loretta's shoulders.

"Welcome home," Henderson said, greeting Zinnia with a smile as wide as the world. "Mrs. Crestbourne's real upset she can't be meetin' you herself, but she's got another meetin' over at the hospital. She said she'd be home soon as she could. She said to give you these and tell you it's gonna be a fine year, 'cause Zinnia's home to see the gardenias blossom."

Zinnia began to cry as she smelled her favorite flowers, then held them for Loretta to inhale.

"Bless her heart," Zinnia said quietly. "Henderson, this is my friend Loretta Worship. Remember, child, I told you about Henderson, the newcomer to the old place. Henderson's been only twenty-five years at Foxrest." Zinnia and Henderson chuckled at their private joke.

"A pleasure, Miss Loretta," Henderson said.

"We'll be taking Miss Loretta to the Madison Residence on our way home."

Henderson nodded. "I'll get the wagon and bring it up close. See she doesn't move, Miss Loretta," he cautioned as he picked up her suitcases.

The lobby of the Dolley Madison Residence was small and spartan. There were no sofas on which to linger, just several straight-backed chairs along the dark walls. The light, such as it was, came from a too-high chandelier with insufficient wattage. If it hadn't been for the portrait of a bonneted Dolley above the fireplace, Loretta would have gone back out and rechecked the plaque on the door.

"Seven dollars a day. Forty-five a week. One hundred seventy a month. No drinking. No entertaining men. No cooking in the room. Dinner is three dollars and fifty cents and is served promptly at seven." Miss Hollins was small and sharp, but not nearly as unsympathetic as she sounded. After years of checking girls in, she had learned to register much more than mere names. She noticed such things as Loretta's near-empty duffel and her doll-sized red suitcase.

"We have a lovely service here," Miss Hollins said, after Loretta ventured that she might be staying awhile. "It's called our like-new closet. It's actually a small room filled with like-new clothes that our girls have for sale. How many times have we all bought mistakes or gotten a little thinner or a little fatter?" Miss Hollins stopped as the pain became apparent in Loretta's smile.

"Here's two weeks' rent in advance," Loretta said quietly, reaching deep for one of Mama's hundred-dollar bills.

As she picked up her suitcases, Loretta noticed an easel with buckling plastic letters on the counter beside the check-in desk.

GREYHOUND TOURS OF RICHMOND—$1.00

Loretta laughed to herself. She knew she had to be crazy to get off one bus and onto another the same day. But then, why not? It was a perfect early-summer day, and with luck, she wouldn't have too many more of those free. She'd find out for herself whether Zinnia had been exaggerating about Richmond.

Superstitiously, Loretta chose the same seat for the tour

that she'd taken for the trip up from Florida, once again huddling close to the window. The conductor's voice was all syrup and drawl. Funny, Loretta thought, in Florida, so much farther south, there wasn't even an accent.

"On the left is our grrr-ate state capitol dee-zined bah its first occupant, the grrr-ate Thomas Jefferson. As we pass the grrr-ate rotunda . . ."

Loretta squeezed her eyes shut and leaned against the window, thinking about her mama, worrying, wondering if Mama would ever miss her, especially after she discovered the stolen money. One day she would bring Mama to live with her in a beautiful house with beautiful flowers. They'd go to Hollywood together and visit the stars. Loretta could see it all. She just couldn't see tomorrow.

". . . on the left, on the right, all around is not only the medical college, but the hospital. Virginia's pride and joy, MCVH . . . established in eighteen hundred and . . ."

Was this where Zinnia would have her operation? Where Mrs. Crestbourne attended meetings and Dr. Crestbourne practiced?

"Broad Street, Richmond's grrr-atest thoroughfare, got its name from its grrr-ate size. When Richmond was gonna be the new capital of the new U-nited . . ."

The glory of the huge magnolias, the nobility of the monuments, the grandeur of the rich brick mansions along the river all seemed to echo a beauty and a permanence that Loretta had never known, never dreamed of.

# PART II

# 6

As Loretta perfected the crease on the bedsheet and folded it under the mattress, she wondered how many corners she'd turned since she'd arrived at the hospital. Sometimes, when she felt dismal and lonely, she'd look to the window and imagine folding the sheets into birds or planes and floating away on their wings. And then there were those other times when she'd imagine her patients floating away on the sheets, waving happily and laughing, unable to believe that they'd been cured.

"You have a healin' way about you, child," Zinnia had told her. "And that's gonna help heal up what's inside you, too."

Although Loretta's days contained few idle hours after nursing school, the hospital, and her job at the museum, what time was left Loretta spent with Zinnia. And Zinnia was right about her. Nursing had begun to heal the pain of Loretta's childhood. In time her state of mind came to reflect the bright candy-cane colors of her uniform. She loved nursing and had taken an overload of courses so she could graduate as soon as possible.

The Crestbournes, whom she had met through Zinnia,

seemed to mean what they said when they told Loretta, "Our home is your home." And Zinnia concurred: "The Crestbournes are your kind of people—the kind of people you should be seein', child." Still, Loretta couldn't take their offer seriously. She couldn't credit that those high iron gates opening onto Foxrest's sumptuous sweep of lawn had anything to do with her.

When Zinnia was finally well enough to leave Richmond, Loretta felt lost. She tried to shrug off her loneliness with more work, pretending that was all she needed. She hadn't realized how much she had come to rely on Zinnia. The Dolley Madison remained for her little more than a bed and a radio, where nameless faces came and went. Although she'd made a few friends at the hospital, most of her free time, when not with Zinnia, was devoted to solitary, educational pursuits. She discovered that she had a passion for art, and through art, a passion for history too. Yet only in the hospital did Loretta feel that she could redeem her guilt for her part in the hundreds of sham miracles that she had helped Big Luke perform.

It was a day in mid-August that Mrs. Crestbourne called Loretta to ask whether she might be willing to work as a hostess at a Washington benefit for the Virginia Museum, which was planning to display its Fabergé treasures at the Phillips Collection. The relatively unknown Phillips Collection had become Loretta's favorite museum; it seemed to own all the same paintings that Mama owned, although Mama's were on cookie tins and spiral calendars. But as much as Loretta would have liked to help out, she felt that she had no place among the museums' society circuit.

"Hostess? I don't—"

"You don't what?" Mrs. Crestbourne countered. "Know how to say hello? Now what else is worrying you? Something

to wear? That might be the best investment the museum ever
made. Loretta, you now more 'bout those eggs than all the
Fabergés put together. Times I see you staring so hard, I
swear one's going to hatch before your eyes. Loretta, someone smart and pretty as you will have people doubling their
donations. Doubling, hell—*tripling!*"

The hundred-dollar ticketholders, who seemed not to
mind being crushed and having drinks spilled on them,
fascinated Loretta almost as much as their disinterest in the
exhibit. The brilliantly lit cases of Fabergé that lined the
walls beneath the fabulous paintings drew little attention
from this Capitol Hill crowd, and the few people Loretta
approached who seemed at least to be looking at the displays soon drifted off, often in the midst of her description
and usually without so much as a thank-you. Mrs. Crestbourne
had done her best to tell everyone to listen to Loretta, but
people weren't even listening to Mrs. Crestbourne.

Half-filled glasses were set down, discarded, and replaced with new ones, as platter after platter of hors d'oeuvres
was picked over with a vicious whimsy by people who
wanted only to see what was in them.

While Loretta was watching the crowd, Randy Byrd was
watching her. Something special about her, he thought—not
the usual matron with a hostess badge. As he ran a hand
through his pretty-boy brown hair, Randy Byrd made his
way toward Loretta, assumed his well-rehearsed smiling-
politician's stance, and launched yet another campaign.

"Hello, Loretta. I'm Randy Byrd. Lovely dress . . .
maybe the prettiest here."

Loretta blushed, although not uncomfortably. She was
flattered. Here was someone who at least was paying some
attention—to her dress rather than her words, but still . . .
He had even bothered to read her name tag.

"Thank you. I bought it for this. I mean, I bought it for tonight but I'll wear it again." Where? Loretta wondered, as she laughed nervously, embarrassed.

When America was still but a baker's dozen colonies, the Randolphs and the Byrds *were* Virginia, especially to the Randolphs and the Byrds. Not only did a branch of Byrd territory become Richmond, but the Randolph family tree stretched so far along the James River that any other plantations existed only in its shadow.

Like most old-line Virginians, Randy Byrd's blood was two hundred and fifty years of glory unjustly soiled by an ignominious defeat in The War. And in Virginia, where names were still akin to land grants, receiving three illustrious ones at birth had assured Randolph Macon Byrd of a seat anyplace he chose to sit. At the age of thirty he had chosen Congress. Now, at thirty-six, he was entering his fourth term.

Tall and wide-shouldered, Randy Byrd had green eyes and a strange, unruly smile that made him look almost rugged in spite of his wavy hair. His most interesting feature was the crescent-shaped scar that ran lengthwise across his chin; it suggested sabres from Heidelberg rather than the unseen limb of a copper beech that had knocked him from a horse when still a boy.

Randy Byrd's fixed gaze on Loretta roved from her legs to her hair to her slim fingers before he realized she was pointing to the Fabergé.

"The miniature pictures inside the egg revolve. That one's the Winter Palace. The egg was a gift from Nicholas to Alexandra in 1896. It's because of Fabergé that people believe the days of the czars were filled with elegance and opulence, but really . . ."

Randy Byrd tried to place her accent, but it was unfamiliar, just as her manner seemed to have no origin that he could define. When finally she paused before moving on to another egg, he asked, "Where are you from?"

"Florida."

"Where in Florida?"

"We traveled a lot. I live in Virginia now." Her sad expression and carefully measured tone seemed somehow to connect Loretta with experiences she appeared too young to know.

"The museum's Lillian Thomas Pratt Collection is the finest Fabergé outside of the Hermitage or Mrs. Merriweather . . ." Then, too, there was her vigorous mind, with its fortress of facts he had no desire to hear.

"Where did you learn all this?" Even as her display of erudition wearied him, it also impressed him, made him more curious about her.

"I work at the museum."

"Where?"

"The Virginia Museum. That's what this is all about, this benefit," Loretta said wistfully.

Oddly for Randy Byrd, he felt uneasy with Loretta. The more she spoke, the more he was struck by her singularity, and the more she fascinated him.

"Hey, Congressman," a deep drawling voice bellowed as a fat hand slapped Randy's back. "Make sure she's not from the district." The man's laugh was as salacious as his leer. Luckily, Loretta heard nothing after "Congressman."

"Congressman? I've never met a congressman," she said. Suddenly she felt shy again, excited and frightened at once.

"Shucks, ma'am," Randy Byrd said, shuffling, seizing the moment to kiss Loretta's cheek. "Every southern family has a crop failure, and I guess I was elected from mine." He bowed with a sweep of his arm. "I just didn't know how to go out and make honest money." Congressman Byrd's kickbacks from tobacco companies in the face of the surgeon general's report made this last statement probably the first honest words he'd uttered since his election.

"Congressman . . ." Loretta shook her head while turning the word slowly, then stopped for fear she sounded like an idiot, and abruptly changed the subject. "Why are you wearing a white suit? I mean, it's autumn and all. Is it something everyone knows about?" Immediately she felt even more idiotic. It upset her to know that he must be thinking what a moron she was.

"Mark Twain said, 'Pin stripes are for Yankees.' Said it while watching Babe Ruth bat. At least that was his excuse. Mine is so they'll see me coming and going and remember the nut in the white suit. Sometimes I even travel with my own ice cream cart."

He had a wonderful laugh, Loretta thought. A real sense of humor. All this and a congressman, too. Never once did Loretta connect Big Luke's white suit with this fine southern gentleman.

What Randy Byrd thought as he stood next to Loretta was how it might feel to lie naked next to her. He imagined doing things he suspected she'd never done before—things he didn't think she'd mind doing, though—and the notion made him feel even wilder inside.

As she stood next to Congressman Byrd, Loretta considered that no matter how stupid she sounded, there was no denying the fact that he was still there. The vague discomfort she felt must have something to do with his being a congressman. Surely it hadn't anything to do with the way his body kept touching hers as he moved to let waiters pass by who weren't even close. And when he grasped the tag on her chest, squinting to read her whole name, Loretta had to step away so that he would not hear or feel the rapid pumping of her heart.

Randy Byrd was a complete contrast to the young medical students Loretta knew. How different and worldly he seemed! And what was particularly strange was that Loretta felt a kind of kinship with him.

Randy Byrd had explained that of course he wanted to stay, but after all she had her job to do, and he might as well take advantage of the time to do some catching up on his. He had written the name of the restaurant where they would meet after the benefit, as well as his office number, on a cocktail napkin that he pressed into her hand. Not until he was gone did Loretta notice that he'd folded in money. "Taxi money," he had written. But, my God, so much! Naturally, she'd give him the change.

But in the excitement of seeing him at the restaurant that night, she forgot. Congressman Byrd didn't.

The tufted plush of the banquette was soft and comfortable. Strains of Joan Baez and Crosby, Stills, and Nash emerged from strategically placed speakers and filtered through the bar. The people here were young, mostly couples, sitting close and talking quietly.

". . . So that's why I say," Randy Byrd said, "a slogan is just a substitute for facts. People don't want slogans. People want facts. The *how*. How's that chicken getting into every pot? How?"

"By taking it from the refrigerator and putting it there," Loretta said, giggling.

Randy Byrd threw back his head, laughed his best politician's laugh, and inched closer to show appreciation for her wit. Without bothering to signal for a waiter, he pulled the champagne from its bucket.

Loretta was having such a good time. She couldn't wait until Congress made the special appropriation for the museum. And she promised, of course, not to breathe a word about it to anybody until it came through. She felt that she was beginning to understand the workings of government.

"Now tell me about Loretta," Randy Byrd said, his eyes focusing on hers. "What does she like to do? Where does she like to go? Who is she?" His voice sounded exaggeratedly southern as it became soft and confidential.

If he only knew, Loretta thought. The brightness in her eyes dissolved into melancholy, and again Randy Byrd felt her strange connection with something deep, something beyond here and now.

"I'm just me, Loretta. A nurse. Almost a nurse." Her eyes avoided his.

"All right, Almost-Nurse Loretta, I have three wishes to grant you. Anything you want. What would you wish for? Tell me?"

Loretta took a deep breath. Three wishes, Mr. Congressman? That's so easy it's sad. You might pity me if you knew the truth, but if that were the case you wouldn't be here. Not a gentleman like you, Mr. Congressman. Three wishes? How about bringing Paul back, for one? How about bringing Mama back from hell, for two? And for three, how about bringing me, Loretta, back from the damned?

Loretta forced her face into smiling, her thoughts into words. "I wish I could travel all over the world. I wish I could be a really great nurse. I wish I could hear Leonard Bernstein at the Kennedy Center. I listen to all the . . ."

Randy Byrd's mind wandered. He thought back to an evening a few weeks ago, to an outrageous charade he'd performed when he'd told his wife that he had no other choice but to finish the final draft of the fishery protection bill he was sponsoring . . . how it would take all night and he would have to sleep in his office again. Again—with that young girl he'd moved up from the steno pool. And once more, Donna-Jo Byrd had asked her sister to escort her to the Kennedy Center.

Only when Loretta stopped talking was Randy Byrd aware that he'd stopped paying attention. The last thing he'd heard was something about a nurse. In a flash, Randy Byrd saw himself lying on a bed. Nurse Loretta was peeling back the sheets. Softly, gently, she raised his hospital gown. Warm water . . . a sponge . . . smooth, silky soap.

". . . Well, what do you think? There they are. Are they dumb?" Loretta asked timidly.

"What about money? You do want money, don't you?" he asked. He had listened just closely enough to know that she hadn't said the word "money." Randolph Macon Byrd was very, very rich.

"I guess so. No, I don't guess. Of course. It could pay Mama back and pay my tuition. It could help with the travel, too," she half-laughed, self-consciously.

Again Randy Byrd nuzzled close and reached into the bucket, pouring more champagne as he wondered what she must think about the money, about how much he'd want in return for the amount he'd already paid her. He certainly knew what he wanted. But at the same time he felt an unaccustomed desire to unravel the contradictions in Loretta's life, to fill the blanks between her whippet good looks and her ignorance of what to do with them, between her soulful, knowing eyes and the naiveté in her manner.

Loretta was already tipsy. She could feel the waiter's stare, and then she realized, blushing, that she was still wearing her name tag. She giggled and fumbled with the pin.

Randy Byrd was happy to help. His hands flew toward the blue crepe bodice.

"I never wore a badge like this before," she said. Her fingers mingled with his. What air there was between them grew hot.

Loretta extricated her hand and covered her glass with her palm. "No, no more, thank you," she said to the waiter.

"Come on, just a little. A little more for Mama," Randy Byrd whispered.

"Who?" Loretta blinked.

"Your mama. The one we're gonna pay back. It was one of your wishes, remember?" Imperceptibly, Randy signaled the waiter.

Loretta nodded slowly. "Yes, I remember. Pay Mama back."

Again, Randy saw the eerie look in her eyes.

"Yes. To Mama." Loretta held her glass high.

"Tell me about her."

In all her life no one had ever asked Loretta to describe Mama. What would Mama want her to say? She took a big gulp of champagne. "Mama is very, very beautiful. As beautiful as a movie star."

Randolph Byrd wasn't surprised.

Mama, Loretta thought, I'm telling a real congressman what you are like. And he believes me, Mama. And you know why? Because it's true.

"And she reads beautiful things. She reads poems, and the ones she loves best she pastes in a book. And Mama loves flowers. She loves roses the best. She's special with roses. She talks to them and they do whatever she says, because they want to make her happy." As Loretta spoke, she toyed with the pin on the back of her badge.

"Mama cuts only the roses that are too full and then only because it's good for the ones that haven't budded yet. 'I will be the gladdest thing under the sun/ I will touch a hundred flowers and not pick one.' Mama had that hanging on the refrigerator. Know who said it? I mean, Mama used to say it, but you know who *wrote* it? A poet whose name sounds almost like a poem—Edna St. Vincent Millay." Loretta's voice glided through the smoky noise of the restaurant.

Was this girl putting him on? She'd kept the money. She was here, showing no resistance. She claimed she didn't want champagne, but she was drinking it.

"Tell me about your father," he said.

"Papa's dead." If Loretta's tone when she spoke about Mama held all the affection of an adoring daughter, her tone for her father carried the warmth of an unmarked grave.

"Doesn't it ever scare you, being so important?" she asked, again changing the subject. "Your being able to make things that matter happen?"

The only thing Randolph Byrd wanted to have happen was Loretta. And if playing her game would get him there, then so be it. "What would you want me to make happen? More wishes?" He moved closer, picked up her hand, and patted it like a child's. "Tell me."

"I'm serious," Loretta said. "Like the Pentagon Papers helped Vietnam. Like busing is going to help. You can help."

Randy Byrd shuddered. What the hell kind of thing was she into? "Repeatedly I've let my constituency know how the President's been fumbling Vietnam, but I'll be hard-pressed finding any sweet sap flowing out of southern pines for any niggers." His tone was fierce.

All at once Loretta saw the image of Big Luke.

"Now don't take me wrong, Loretta," Randy Byrd hastened to say as he felt Loretta stiffen. "I'm talking about nigg—blacks like those killer Panthers, who, for chrissake, teethe on white meat like you and me. And let me tell you just how much they're helping the cause of those nice, quiet, God-fearing blacks who God, and me too, certainly know are in the majority. They're pushing them right back into the trees. Why I even believe so much in good blacks I've given more of them jobs than anyone anywhere in any state." As the lies flowed from Randolph Byrd's lips, he felt Loretta begin to soften again. "Damn right, busing's a start. Does me proud seeing those little things all braided and starched stepping onto those buses."

How Randy Byrd wished he had a crony here. No matter how much he allowed himself to laugh inside, it wasn't half as good as sharing the thigh slapping.

"You know," Loretta said, as the flame of the candle on their table dilated before her eyes. "You and me, we can help stop prejudice now."

"You're right, Loretta. We both better do a little hustling from what we want to call tradition into what we know is tomorrow. And now. You're right. Right now." Congressman Byrd feared that if such exuberant virtuousness continued, he might be in danger of losing his seat.

"Right." Loretta clinked her glass against his. "Ban the bigots!" If she made even a small impression, she thought, on someone as important as Randolph Byrd, it could mean a lot.

"It's my new slogan," he said, as he ever so lightly kissed her cheek.

Loretta thought Congressman Byrd's office was awfully nice, even though the brass-and-glass tables and drawerless glass desk looked more like sculpture than furniture. Loretta felt overwhelmed being alone with someone who had been photographed with Presidents. Someone who knew Presidents so well that they autographed the pictures "For Randy." As she picked one up, she couldn't help grinning back at the congressman's constant smile, the perfect hair, the pristine white suit. While Loretta admired the photograph, Randy Byrd managed to shove under the sofa a picture of himself embracing George Wallace.

And the view—my God, it was the most beautiful she'd ever seen, especially with the Washington Monument lit up like on the poster. Standing awestruck by the window, Loretta unconsciously accepted the glass of champagne Randolph Byrd handed her.

With the arm that wasn't around Loretta's waist, he gestured toward the panorama of the city as if all of Washington were his. "No doubt about it," he said, shaking his finger at the brilliant white obelisk piercing the night sky, "that's got to be the prettiest piece of marble in all God's world. I guess I've taken more people up those eight hundred ninety-eight steps more times than I care to count." He nodded with pride as he spoke. "Unless they were crippled or dying, I'd make them walk. Their groans were music to my ears, kind of a prelude to the sweet 'ahh's I knew I'd hear at the top."

The only time Randy Byrd had ever walked up the Washington Monument was on a dare, and then only because he'd been horribly hung over. And the only way he had made it to the top was by taking breaks at each of the fifty landings. Having once told the story as a joke, however, he found his audience so eager to believe that he entered it right alongside apple pie, the flag, and Mark Twain in his repertoire.

"For me, this little District of Columbia *is* America the

Beautiful. . . . Almost, Loretta, as beautiful as you." He brushed her lips softly with his.

Loretta realized she didn't mind, and this realization made her uneasy. She pulled away from his arm and turned to a picture she'd noticed earlier. "Are these your children?"

"I take full responsibility," Randy Byrd replied. "Maudie-Lee is seven and Chip—look at him!—isn't he one off the old block?—he'll be ten next month. He's popping his buttons thinking about those double digits, having another one up on his sister." He laughed again, buying time to sound more natural, more convincing for what was coming next. "I'm separated from their mother." And indeed he was—for tonight. Mrs. Byrd was at their home in Virginia with Maudie-Lee and Chip as he basked in the light of his favorite monument, the proud testament to the man who never told a lie.

Loretta smiled uncertainly, thinking she sensed something a little too slick; but then, wanting to believe him, just as his constituents did, she dismissed it. Anyway, who was she to be skeptical of someone so high and mighty?

"I've been thinking," Randolph Byrd said, as he'd said so often with the same chin-scratching gesture. "Before Congress'll get to act on the museum, maybe I could persuade our good state of Virginia to appropriate some of *their* money. Money earned by my hard work. They owe me a couple—more than a couple, I'd say." He watched her as he pretended to be lost in his own thoughts. "Maybe even before that I could wrestle something up from the foundation." Turning directly toward Loretta, he narrowed his eyes as if he were still thinking out loud but letting her in on it. "Foundation's a family thing. And as far back as I can think, I can't recall anything they've done for the museum. Be a fine idea. Be a fine idea to help Mama, too. You know, Loretta, helping always makes me feel good. Makes all good people feel good." His smile was now bigger than ever. "I don't doubt that's how come you're a nurse. Right?"

He'd certainly read that part of her right, Loretta thought. She wondered if her whole life might be this transparent to him.

Randy Byrd tried once again to ply Loretta with champagne. This time, however, she moved while he poured, and the champagne spilled onto the beige zigzag of the carpet. What the hell was he doing, he wondered, chasing her around like some slapstick waiter! He set his glass down on a table and moved closer to her. "Loretta," he said, as he put his arms around her, ". . . Loretta, you're the one who's beautiful." Instinct warned him to move very slowly, very gently. He caressed her back with one hand as the other traced an imaginary line on her cheek. Then he kissed her tenderly, again and again.

He's treating me like a lady, Loretta thought as his kisses deepened. He has no idea who I really am or how I feel about myself, yet he really wants me. And for some reason, I want him to do what he wants to do to me.

When Loretta's arms tightened around him, Randy Byrd fought the urge to throw her on the carpet and take her right there—his usual method of lovemaking with willing partners. Instead, he dimmed the lights and carefully led her into the room where he slept on those frequent nights when he and his wife were separated. So intent was he on putting Loretta at ease that he failed to notice her strangely sober, defiant walk, almost as if she were marching before a tribunal that would one day reverse its judgment.

He spread Loretta across the pale, shiny sheets and eased a silky pillow beneath her back. His breath soon quickened, and somehow Loretta realized what she should do, how she should pretend to respond. As her fingernails

raked across his back, she felt a surge of relief that Big
Luke was no longer the last man to have touched her.

The seemingly ordinary act of driving Loretta back to
her hotel was in fact an altogether extraordinary act for
Randolph Byrd. And all the while it frustrated him that she
leaned so close to the door that she nearly fell out of the car.

"I'll call you at the hospital. Is that the easiest place to
get you? Is that the best, Loretta?" Usually it was someone
else who was asking Congressman Byrd those questions.

"No. No, not the hospital."

"The museum? Is that better?"

"No. No, not really."

"But you say you're not home much. Where is it you
are?"

Randy's nervous laughter made Loretta feel a twinge of
anger. But she supposed it wasn't his fault—that all men
acted the way he did. Clutching her purse, she was comforted by holding the key that would soon lock her into
herself.

"Tell me where."

"Where I live, at the Dolley Madison. That's the best."
She tried being kind. "Early or late are the best times to
reach me."

And while Randy Byrd contemplated the calls he'd make
to her, Loretta thought about how she would fend them off.

Back in her room at last, Loretta leaned like a grateful
prisoner against the locked door. Although she had seen
Randy Byrd push something into her purse, she hadn't
wanted to look while they were in the car. Now she dumped
the contents on the bed, careful to avoid the clean sheets.

Good God! Not only was the change from the taxi still
there, but there was something folded in a card. As if she

were afraid someone else might see, Loretta palmed the card, opening it close to her face. "For Mama," it said in letters as small as Randolph Byrd's crossed-out name. Inside were two more hundred-dollar bills.

Loretta ran to the desk and pulled the hotel stationery from the drawer. The faster she sent the money away, the better she'd feel. "I love you, Mama," she scribbled, and then drew smiling faces in the *O*s.

The night clerk was surprised to see her again so soon and even more surprised that she waited until he stamped the envelope and slipped it into the brass-plated slot.

# 7

A racing scene by A.J. Munnings and a pair of chestnut stallions by Sartorius replaced the posters of Degas dancers and a still life by Renoir. A tray table with reading lamp, dictionary, the latest *Chronicle of the Horse*, paper tablets, and a canister of felt-tipped pens was put next to a leather chair. Amidst all the confusion, especially her own, Loretta wondered about those felt-tipped pens. Was he able to write already? She walked across the room to his chart to see exactly when he had been admitted, when exactly the CVA—the cerebrovascular accident, the stroke— had occurred. But the chart wasn't hanging where it should have been, at the bottom of the bed. Odd? Not really. Once Loretta realized that *everything* was abnormal, the absence of the chart seemed only fitting.

All Loretta knew was that this room had been redecorated overnight for a male stroke patient: a highly important patient whose aggression and anger had suddenly turned into deep depression.

"He could've made it home much easier a week ago," said one of the young men in white.

"But when you're H.W. Dunbar, every Blue Ridge

mountain comes to you," another orderly said, rolling a blood-pressure machine into the closet.

"If they don't tell him what they're doing and they wait to surprise him, he could have a stroke." Both young men laughed.

In a matter of minutes, more personal belongings were carried in to replace nearly all the items on the hospital checklist.

Loretta was to be the new "stroke team" for this special patient. Occupational therapy, physiotherapy, speech therapy —she'd done them all. She'd learned about the physiology of recuperation, the rebuilding of muscle tone, the reteaching of tiny tasks to giant brains and of speech to nonstop talkers. But something else Loretta had learned from the masses of data she had studied was that masses of data don't necessarily result in survival.

"The most important factor for survival is to bring the stroke patient back to his usual environment. Only then will he have the incentive to work, to make his rehabilitation effective." She'd underlined the words as she'd read them. And now, unexpectedly, she was to participate in testing that theory. Yet nobody knew better than Loretta that therapy is the one game you can't help losing when you're up against a player who doesn't want to win.

Kim, one of the trainees, flitted about like a butterfly as she checked the room. "Who's coming in here?" Loretta asked.

"His name is Harrison W. Dunbar, Jr., and they say his initials are like IBM," Kim replied in an awed tone. "They say that when he first came in he was nice, then he got terrible. After that he didn't care. That's how he is now. Did you ever see a room so beautiful?"

No IBM or HWD or anything, thought Loretta, could buy protection from the mortal hell of a CVA.

Since she'd completed nursing school and her special-ized training, Loretta had seen a lot. But one thing she'd never seen was the complete relandscaping of a hospital room.

Suddenly, a group of hospital department heads marched onto the scene of transformation. Although stroke patients are customarily treated by more than one specialist, it seemed that every top "ologist" within a hundred miles was on call for H.W. Dunbar.

"Sure wish my house looked like this," the neurologist said.

"This is going to make all the difference for Dunbar," the urologist said.

"These things are his favorites," Benton Hartman, the cardiologist, said, hoping to impress his colleagues with his personal knowledge of Dunbar's home. Only then did he notice Loretta. "Yes?"

"I'm Worship." She smiled and held out her hand. "Loretta Worship. I'm the—"

"Where've you been?" Benton Hartman demanded. "We've been looking for you." He introduced her to the group and began giving her a quick rundown on Dunbar's condition.

But with the mere mention of Dunbar's name, the ologists were at it again. Each of them was convinced that Dunbar's survival was attributable to his own particular life-leasing actions, although in truth the procedures performed on Dun-bar's case had all been fairly standard.

"Cerebral infarction, CVA. Diagnosed upon admission. Dunbar was lucky when he arrived, because I . . ."

"In just two weeks he was doin' great, because I . . ."

"Even in intensive care his spirits were good. Got out in five days because I . . ."

"Clot in the left-middle cerebral artery. Good thing he's

a southpaw. Boy, that right side was completely paralyzed until I . . ."

"Chukker Dunbar's one of the finest gentlemen I ever met," Benton Hartman was telling Loretta. Dunbar had arrived in the emergency room not knowing if he was going to live or die. "Dynamite man. Looked a lot younger than sixty-two until this happened. I can't figure why after doing so well, he's gone back to being more dead than alive."

"The will just won't," one of the ologists offered. "He doesn't care about moving, eating, talking—anything."

Suddenly a new voice spoke up. It was a very proper-looking woman of some indeterminable age past forty, obviously not part of the hospital staff, who efficiently and unobtrusively had been placing all Dunbar's belongings about the room. The doctors all fell silent, studying the floor as if in mourning.

"Nonsense," she said, turning to Loretta. "He has his business to run. You have no idea about all the lawyers, the accountants, the papers, the meetings. Dunbar Enterprises is enormous, global. And it's all H.W. It's not anyone else. Everything that's worth anything is inside H.W.'s head." A mammoth hairpin fell from her stiff upsweep as she shook with emotion.

"The first Monday of every month, H.W. has meetings," the Efficient One kept explaining, directly to Loretta. "After that they know what to do. The Three Musketeers, I call them: Carstairs, the attorney; Anthony Scotto, the accountant; and Peter Nicholas, the president. They take notes. They listen. I watch them. What you don't under—" When the Efficient One finally turned to Hartman, he was no longer there. In fact, as soon as she had started talking he had walked away, obviously preferring the sound of his own insincerity.

"What about his family?" Loretta asked.

"There's one son, Wilson," the Efficient One continued. "He's H.W.'s whole family. He's a journalist. He doesn't like business." Loretta realized that the woman was fighting back tears. "H.W. made us all swear we wouldn't call him. Looks as if we may have to now." Her voice broke.

Loretta picked up one of the leather frames. "Is this Wilson?" she asked, pointing to a tall, angular, yet boyish-looking man standing with his arm around a young woman in front of the Taj Mahal.

"Yes. He was on his way to Ceylon. It was still called Ceylon then." Again she sniffed back tears. "That's ten years ago. He'd just turned twenty-one. He'd no sooner gone than his mother died. We held up the funeral until we could find him. H.W. thinks worlds of that boy. He's all he's got."

The Efficient One, whose name was Florence Collier, was one of those women about whom people often remarked that if only they'd wear makeup or loosen their hair they'd be attractive. In fact, she had tried both and neither worked, so now she concentrated on dressing corrrectly and stylishly: color-coordinated outfits in muted hues, bags and shoes that matched. Her prized possession was a sapphire circle pin that had belonged to H.W.'s wife. He'd given it to Florence one Christmas.

Loretta watched the way the Efficient One kept readying the room, fluffing and refluffing, picking up and setting down. It was evident that this woman loved H.W.

Loretta was slowly beginning to form a picture of H. W. Dunbar—from what the nurses said, from the room that the Efficient One was installing, from the doctors' stories. Gradually, she was making order of the chaos that had marked the six weeks since Harrison Wilson Dunbar had been admitted to Medical College Virginia Hospital for treatment.

He'd arrived in Virginia the week before that, flying

directly to Rosefields, his estate in Middleburg, from his home in Florida.

Three days before his attack, H.W. had suffered a "nothing" episode. The butler recalled that Mr. Dunbar had dropped his coffee cup and that as he bent to pick it up, he'd almost fallen. He'd said something about being dizzy, a little light-headed, but the butler could barely understand his slurred words. Whatever it was obviously disappeared quickly, because Dunbar went out to dinner that same night. In fact, he didn't give the episode another thought until the "nothingness" returned in an acute form almost seventy-two hours later.

In only a few short moments a horrible dizziness, muddled vision, and paralysis of his right side set in. He tried to shout for help, but his voice failed him. His eyes veered to the left, and he was unable to move them in any other direction. His mouth fell open, limp.

At sixty-two, H.W. Dunbar had not entered the hospital on the sunny side of statistics. The critical hours after a stroke are the first twenty-four. Nearly a quarter of all stroke victims never make it, and the death rate doubles with each decade of the patient's age. Not until two agonizing days after the seizure had H.W.'s chances of survival begun to improve.

Skull series, brain scans, EKGs—every possible test had been performed and reperformed during Dunbar's five days in intensive care. Loretta had read the results and knew that the infarction, edema clot—whatever medical term for stroke they used that day—had been nearly absorbed after the first four days. The critical stage was over, and Dunbar was going to live. That's what the ologists had written. And because it was written, it was so.

Remarkable how well he responded, they all said, how fine his spirits seemed, how fast the imminent danger disappeared. The brain maps could now plot a complete recovery with no damage. Loretta read the prognoses and charted how all of them had the patient bound for home before the fear was gone, before he realized what grit he would need for the months ahead. What their scans failed to tell the ologists was that a man like H.W. Dunbar couldn't tolerate any sort of reduced competence.

After the machines stopped, Dunbar's treatment would have been a rapid barrage of therapy for everything from speaking to walking, from occupational to recreational recovery. Most of the therapists who now worked with Dunbar had been with him since he'd left intensive care. But during the past three weeks, the primary therapist, Loretta's predecessors, seemed to change more often than his bedsheets.

Loretta noticed that in the most recent reports on Dunbar's condition the word "uncaring" appeared with increasing frequency. Only Dr. Briggs didn't write it. He had noted "sad," "quietly desperate," but not "uncaring." Nobody, thought Loretta, who responded to the beautiful things in this room could be uncaring. "Mean," "nasty," "cantankerous" —those might be words to describe the man in the silver frames the Efficient One had arranged around the room: playing polo, receiving an honorary degree, in a rose garden with his dogs—but never uncaring.

"He's coming," Kim announced as she fluttered into the room. Without hesitation, everyone lined up in two rows on either side of the door, like soldiers awaiting inspection.

A moment later, a wheelchair with padded arms was rolled into room 1247. The patient was then transferred to his bed, but through the phalanx of bent backs and craning necks it was impossible for Loretta to see. When Dunbar was propped into place, the ologists backed away like deferential Orientals, and Loretta got her first glimpse of the man sitting resignedly in his silk foulard robe. He nodded to the Efficient One, acknowledging the surroundings, causing her immediately to collapse her face into a handful of Kleenex.

"You look like a day in the country, Chukker," Benton Hartman said, clasping a hand on Dunbar's shoulder. The others smiled and mumbled similar comments. Dunbar barely nodded in response.

The silence soon became so overwhelming that Dr. Hartman felt compelled to fill it and signaled to Loretta to approach the bed. "Loretta here is as good as we've got, and we got her for you."

Absolutely pathetic, thought Loretta. He's saying we've tried nearly everything and failed, and now we're trying our last resort. In a rare moment of disrespect, Loretta raised her eyebrows and rolled her eyes in Hartman's direction, just enough for Dunbar to see—or so she hoped. At that moment she spied a corroborating smile from someone whose name she had missed, the doctor who'd wheeled Dunbar in. She returned the smile as the pudgy doctor walked toward her.

"Michael Briggs," he said, holding out his hand. "I'm the resident neurologist. I've been with Dunbar since the beginning. It's not going to be easy," he said, rolling *his* eyes toward the ologists.

"I'm Loretta Worship. I can't believe I'm finally meeting you—I'm so glad to see you! I work with your wife at the museum—she and I work on a lot of the same research projects. I've been meaning to look you up." Loretta spoke softly, as she always did in a patient's room, and she hoped that Dr. Briggs could hear her through the thunderous greetings that continued to issue from the Dunbar medical team.

"Olivia's so glad to have somebody young working with her. So am I," Briggs said before moving back toward the door.

As ill as he was, Harrison W. Dunbar was a good-looking man. His salt-and-pepper hair was rich and thick, and his strong face was filled with kind creases. His prominent cheekbones still carried a splash of pink, and while the folds around his eyes seemed heavy, his eyes were a clear blue, reflecting the robe he wore. Only Loretta noted the tears welling in the corners.

He looked over at the framed picture of his son, then turned to the Efficient One and motioned with a single finger toward the tray table. She knew, as she always knew, exactly what he was thinking.

"No, H.W.," the Efficient One said. "Nobody's contacted Wilson, just as you wished."

Abruptly, he waved his arm to dismiss everybody, and then he closed his eyes.

As they departed, Hartman made it clear to the Efficient One that she too must leave. "It's been a big day for him. A good day, but enervating. Thanks to you, seeing his room was the best part. It's going to do wonders for him—just wonders," he repeated.

The Efficient One seemed near panic as she rearranged her tightly wound hair. Unable to decide what to do, she stepped forward, then back, then forward again, like a character in a silent film put alternately on forward and reverse. Finally she approached the bed. In what was probably her most intimate gesture ever toward her employer, she drew his hand to her cheek and lovingly said all the wrong things.

"This setback won't last."

Setback?

"No matter how many months you're here, I'll be here with you."

Months?

"That Dunbar fire can't die, H.W."

Die?

"Please, H.W. Please. You've got to get well."

For whom? Loretta thought.

It was like dragging a widow from a grave as Hartman threaded his arm through the Efficient One's and led her out. Returning to the room, he addressed Dunbar. "You'll be better in no time. . . . The room's the turning point we've been looking for. . . . It's always one step back after that many forward. . . . Loretta here can do more wonders for you than Annie Sullivan did for Helen Keller."

Again shocking . . . incredible. Loretta couldn't believe that Hartman, a doctor, had the stupidity to invoke Helen Keller. More encouragement like this, Loretta thought, and the part of Dunbar's brain that was untouched by the stroke would die of discouragement.

Dunbar shut his eyes to the excruciating monotony of Hartman's guarantees: the same overzealous promises that had turned hope into despair when, after weeks, Dunbar still remained partially crippled by paralysis.

To a man like Dunbar, whose whole life was power, to have none was tantamount to death. That's why the will and eventually the strength to tackle even the mildest tasks had gone. It seemed almost as if Dunbar were making sure that the unrealistic promises of his doctors proved untrue.

But since the hospital coffers would be more than replenished by a newly sparked recovery, the overpromising continued. It was as if Dunbar's fortune had become his worst enemy.

When Loretta finally closed the door on Dr. Hartman, Harrison Dunbar opened his eyes to make sure they'd all gone. When he closed them again, his breathing was deep and even.

Slowly Loretta looked again at everything the Efficient One had brought into the room. The museum had many fine sporting paintings, but none as fine as these. She wondered if he had any Landseer dogs; she loved how you could almost feel their fur and how they seemed always to be smiling. Loretta smelled the supple leather of his address book and rubbed her fingers over the worn gold letters: "Rosefields." She wondered who had named his house Rosefields. It didn't sound like a name a man would choose. He'd probably let his wife pick it: how nice.

Loretta had lowered the blinds to help Dunbar fall asleep, but slits of late-afternoon sun still slipped through. Examining each photograph in the weak light, she was amazed how little this man had changed through the years. Propped against the pillows, he looked scarcely different from the handsome man in the pictures: a proud man who cherished life . . . a man for whom the fresh boxwood at his bedside evoked pleasant memories . . . a man who cared.

Loretta sat in one of his green leather chairs reading and rereading his medical records. She noted that at the first slight sign of impatience and discouragement, "they" had immediately taken over and relieved him of even the simplest tasks. Didn't they recognize that for a man who'd never known restricted activity, even the tiniest loss of independence could have monumental repercussions? It was malpractice at its most insidious. What were they thinking of—how much money the hospital would lose if Dunbar died—or if he didn't die?

"He's got a whim of iron and a will of steel," Hartman had told Loretta. "Don't get the blood pressure going by getting him doing too much. That's all we need."

The charts gave no indication that his pressure had risen when he had first become active again: "tough" . . . "hearty" . . . "high-spirited."

Then the charts changed: "unwilling to do much for himself" . . . "just as soon be fed, wheeled, washed."

"For God's sake, don't take a chance with Dunbar's walking even with a crutch," one ologist had warned Loretta. "Not that his condition is really a regression. No, I believe it's just a pause that shouldn't be pushed." The doctor had fingered his stethoscope nervously. "This kind of thing is very common."

Very? Loretta wondered. Loretta had seen this happen only once: this time.

"We're lucky," Hartman had said, his voice indicating that he took personal credit for any encouraging sign. "No complications. No infections. No secondary clots. No tertiary disorders."

What about no will to live?

So caught up was Loretta with her thoughts about the charts that she was startled when Michael Briggs tapped her arm and motioned her to come outside. Leaving the door slightly ajar, they stood together in the corridor. Chubby Michael with his curly hair and dimples looked not only too boyish to be married but completely out of place as a top neurologist on Dunbar's case.

"You begin to think *you're* wrong, getting them to do what's right instead of what they think *he'd* think is right." Michael wiped his brow.

"I've seen those men perform miracles, and now I'm watching them commit murder." Loretta's anger burned. "And they seem so righteous in their wrongness."

"Whoa, now." Michael put his hand on Loretta's shoulder. "You're bein' a little harsh, Loretta. I'm not disagreein' that—"

Loretta whipped her shoulder free. "A little harsh? These doctors' brains are being stunted by greed and you say I'm a little harsh?"

Michael looked around; people were staring at them.

"I know where you're comin' from, Loretta, and I'd sure as hell hate to be your enemy. But you gotta understand that most of the others have been here long enough to watch this hospital grow to tops in the country, thanks to funds from people like Dunbar. To them they're redeemin' the world, not puttin' Dunbar to pasture. I'm not agreein' with them, understand. Just explainin'. I'm agreein' with you. That's why I'm here."

"Then I can call on you whenever?" she asked. "Anytime?"

"Anytime, Loretta. Anytime. Dunbar's just another case to me—not God, not even a new wing for the hospital."

"Thank you," Loretta said. And with a kiss on Michael Briggs's cheek, she sealed their newly formed friendship.

As the two together established themselves as Harrison Dunbar's new stroke team, Loretta realized she'd never worked on so unusual a case. Is this the care you get when everybody cares so much?

She wanted to ask Dr. Crestbourne's advice, but what could she say? It would be like reporting a crime, but then when asked for proof it would sound as if she were the one who should be put away. Summoning her courage, she called him anyway.

"Hello. Dr. Crestbourne? This is Loretta. Loretta Worship."

"Why, yes, Loretta. How in the world are you? Where've you been hidin' yourself? If it weren't for the hospital halls we'd never catch a glimpse of you. 'Course we're partially to blame—with the schedules Mrs. Crestbourne and I keep, it's a wonder we see each other. Tell me 'bout you. I hear great reports from the hospital. Just dandy."

"Thank you. I'm working hard. In fact, that's why I'm—"

"Still at the museum, too, I hear. Mrs. Crestbourne tells me you're doin' a fine job of research for them. Just dandy. Workin' with little Olivia Briggs, I believe she said. Come to think of it, her husband's over at the hospital, isn't he? You remind me to introduce you to him. They're nice young people for you to know. Fine people. Virginia people. That's some museum we have, isn't it? A privilege to work there. We were there just the other evenin'. Did you see about the dedication of the new Egyptian wing? Fine piece of architecture. Great to be able to make your money look so damn good. Hear from our Zinnia lately?"

"As a matter of fact I just got—"

"Mrs. Crestbourne mentioned her to me this very mornin', sayin' what a shame it was she isn't here. It's Zinnia's time of year, what with all those gardenias comin' full flower. Now, Loretta, you stay in touch with us, you hear? And not just by telephone, either, though talkin's better than nothin'. It's really nice hearin' from you, child. Sorry Mrs. Crestbourne's not here. Don't you worry though, I'll make sure to tell her you called. Funny for me to be answerin' for her, but I'm sure glad I did or we wouldn't have had this nice chance to visit."

With a warm yet distant chuckle, Dr. Crestbourne clicked away.

Loretta sighed with a smile.

# 8

In the weeks ahead Loretta, with Michael's help, concentrated all her energies on Harrison W. Dunbar. With each sign of improvement, no matter how small, Loretta made Dunbar believe he'd performed a miracle. What she never did was pamper him. If food fell from his mouth or he tripped with his crutch, she'd discuss how he'd improved since yesterday and they'd start again. And before he was "ready" for the next challenge she would applaud his clumsy progress as if he'd scaled Everest.

In little more than a week the adjustable bed remained permanently lowered. What once had been perilous excursions to the leather chair and the faraway bathroom became routine trips. After two weeks the crutch gave way to a cane, and even Dunbar's mumble was becoming intelligible. Though Dunbar didn't believe it, Loretta had no doubt that soon he would be managing the more complicated motions of putting on his shirt, jacket, and pants, and that such refinements as buttoning and buckling would not be far behind.

Her drive and optimism circulated fresh blood through Harrison Dunbar's twisted limbs and tortured brain. So contagious was her faith that even Benton Hartman admitted, "It's now just a matter of time before the head follows all I've done for the body." As Dunbar progressed, Hartman thanked his team, his man Michael, and especially Loretta, but he expressed his gratitude to her only when they were alone, far from Dunbar's hearing. If he sensed that Dunbar was enthusiastic about Loretta, Hartman would chime in and reaffirm how, of course, she'd been his idea from the start.

"Great morning, H.W.," Loretta said, entering the bright, cheerful room.

The Efficient One had asked Loretta to call him H.W. "It suits an important man like Harrison Dunbar. It sets the right balance between grand and familiar," she said, fingering her sapphire pin. Those who were truly familiar, or who, like Hartman, boasted of familiarity, called H.W. by his nickname, Chukker—something to do with polo long ago.

Dunbar's eyes were always open when Loretta came into the room, and as she pulled up the blinds, wetted the boxwood, or freshened the flowers, his eyes followed her.

"I'll bet you can't wait to see these roses growing in your garden," Loretta said as if only time, and just a little at that, stood between Dunbar and home. She bent to catch their full aroma, then held them out for H.W. "Roses like these make me think of what the countryside must be like in England, with big houses filled with highly polished furniture and chintz with roses and roses from the garden everywhere, even lavender roses." As she spoke she took his pulse, blood pressure, and temperature. "Perfect, H.W.," she said cheerily. After straightening the sheets she braced his back with his own down pillows. "Breakfast should be here in a minute." Even when Loretta wasn't smiling, her voice sounded as if she were.

When the tray came, she put it on the elegant bedside

table, fastened the monogrammed napkin around H.W.'s neck, and pulled her chair close to the bed. Then she placed the crested spoon in his stroke-paralyzed hand and folded his fingers around the shaft. Without moving a muscle Dunbar let the spoon drop. Again Loretta tried. Again it slipped away. And again. And again and again and again.

Was she mad? He hadn't used his left hand in weeks. H.W.'s stare was long and frozen and wild. "Uh . . . aw . . . ow." He groaned and grunted like an animal before turning his face to the pillow.

In a flash Loretta stopped and cleared everything away—the food, the spoon, the napkin—everything except her cheerfulness, which not only lasted through the morning but intensified as the rattling lunch tray was wheeled into the room. Once more it was time for the napkin, the food, the spoon. H.W. slammed his eyes at the approaching horror.

"Open your eyes, H.W., and listen. Listen to me," Loretta said, shaking him firmly. "Look at me, H.W. You can do this. Between the both of us *you* can do it."

Nobody knew better than H.W. that he couldn't. For God's sake, you look at me! Can't you see I can't? What the hell kind of nurse had they sent him this time? YOU *look, you blind fool!* Damn you! *You* look!

Dunbar's eyes became frenzied and his groans louder. Suddenly, savagely, with a surge of strength he lashed out. The tray flew, the food flew, and the dishes and glasses crashed to the ground. But the spoon didn't fall. It landed where he had thrown it. Barely missing Loretta, the spoon landed square in the middle of the room.

Loretta stared incredulously before hurrying to pick it up. In a burst of joy, the spoon in her hand, she whirled around the room, wanting to shout her happiness. Harrison W. Dunbar had actually thrown a spoon!

Now Dunbar was certain that she was mad. They all

were here. Maybe he was in some insane asylum where people were lied to and told they'd had a stroke. As loud as he could, he groaned over and over, louder and louder, "Ow! *Ow! OW!!*"

It was like lightning striking in the same spot, Loretta thought. First the spoon and now words. Without even seeing his arms sweep through the air she understood—OUT! OUT! OUT! But Dunbar wasn't going to make her stop dancing in celebration—not just yet.

Loretta made no immediate mention of H.W.'s progress to anyone but Michael. She didn't want the ologists' overenthusiasm smothering any of H.W.'s gasps for life. Only when the improvements steadied did she begin to talk about them, and even then she minimized their importance. Dunbar, too, knew not to show off during the endless sessions when the doctors discussed his condition.

In the days that followed, Loretta assumed the work of all the other therapists. Never had she had more faith. So hard to come by, so easy to lose, it flowed from her eyes, her fingertips, her smiles while she fought continuously against anger, frustration, and suicidal odds.


"Pay-per. Say 'pay-per'. Pay-per." Carefully, slowly, Loretta enunciated each syllable and pointed at the Richmond *Times*.

No answer.

"Pay-per. Say 'pay-per.' "

The lunatic was back. Was she trying to make a dummy talk? Or was she the dummy for trying? He'd definitely been incarcerated in the wrong institution.

"Pay-per. Look at my lips. Pay-per. Pay-per."

The idiot was smiling, even now. And as he acknowledged her unshakable determination, Harrison Dunbar knew more certainly than he'd ever known anything in his life that this dancing fool was never giving up on him. Never.

"Pay-per. Say 'pay-per.' " Loretta was nose to nose with Dunbar. "Humor me, H.W.—what have you got to lose? Can't get rid of me." Loretta wasn't sure, but she thought she saw a sliver of a smile. Again she repeated, "Pay-per. Pay-per."

"Ay-er" suddenly stumbled from Dunbar's lips. "Ay-er." He said it again to make sure the sound had actually come from his own mouth.

Loretta concealed her ecstasy. "Pretty good, H.W. But you can do better. Put your lips together. Pay-per."

"Ay-er. Ay-er."

Loretta's lips were almost on top of Dunbar's. Over and over she blew out the letter *P* like a baby puffing out its cheeks. "Puh—puh—puh—puh—puh—puh."

"Pay-er. Pay-er."

"Good. More. Pay-*puh*. PUH. PUH-PUH-PUH."

"Pay-er."

"All right, don't stop."

"Pay-er." Each time Dunbar said it louder.

"Good, H.W. Now let's get it all together. You can do it. Pay-PUH." Loretta's excitement mounted steadily. "Lips together. Pay-PUH."

"Pay-puh. Pay-puh. Pay-PUH. PAPER!"

"Read all about it! Read all about it!" Loretta yelled. "Harrison W. Dunbar has broken the sound barrier. Read all about it!"

As a mother would wrap her arms around a child, Loretta hugged a happy Harrison Dunbar. Then, racing to the bureau, she again grabbed the spoon and spun around the room. H.W. watched this whirling dervish and accepted it as the lunatic ritual part of his rehabilitation. Even if Loretta did turn out to be a witch, what did it matter?

\* \* \*

Over the next few weeks, Harrison Dunbar nearly tripped over his words in his eagerness to get them out. His growing ability to handle sentences as well as objects was staggering, and Loretta's mood was a constant high. Yet no matter how fast H.W. advanced, she never let up. Flexing and stretching, pushing and pulling, he had to relearn every physical maneuver.

"Stop," H.W. screamed, his leg unable to drag the weighted pully another time.

"One more."

"I can't. I can't. No more."

"Just one."

"No."

"Last one." Loretta turned her back to avoid seeing the pain on H.W.'s face. Finally she heard the grinding of the gears and the heavy thud as the weight fell one last time.

Immediately, the strain on Dunbar's face was washed away by triumph. He shook his head as Loretta helped him off the cushioned mat. "Bitch goddess!" he said slowly, a little slurred, but clear enough for Loretta to understand. "That's what you are. Henry James's name for success. God damn. He would really have hated you. About as much as I just did."

As his dexterity increased, H.W.'s depression abated. Guarded optimism replaced frustration, and gradually, vestiges of his old life returned. Friends came to visit and left smiling. Even the faces of Dunbar's Musketeers shortened. Eventually the day arrived when H.W. himself called a board meeting, to be held in the hospital the following Monday, the first of the month.

Knowing that the dozen dark-suited men before him had been warned about smoking, crowding the bed, taking up oxygen, and staying too long, H.W. succeeded in putting them at ease.

"Smoke, drink, and be merry, and after you've overstayed, don't talk to Hartman or you might be having permanent meetings here."

Chuckles and ever-so-tentative handclasps with H.W. followed. Then, in seconds, the men horseshoed around the bed on small folding chairs. Cases were unlatched, papers rustled, and the meeting began. So quickly did H.W. immerse himself in the business at hand that he didn't even notice when Loretta punched up his flattened pillows.

"We'll beat them at their own game. We'll be ready for any energy crisis." Only now and then was the slightest slur evident.

"What exactly are you expecting, H.W.? From where? And why?"

"As long as the Saudis believe we favor Israel over them, they'll slash their production. Prices will soar. So we buy now. Even the tankers."

"That's a hell of an investment, H.W."

"For a helluva return, if I'm right." H.W. loved to issue zingers with that "if" thrown in. "And as for Dunbar Discount Stores—no major cities. Everybody's in them. Walton's a genius putting Wal-Marts in towns under twenty thousand. He can have the first billion. I don't mind getting the second."

"What about the Toledo mall, H.W.? Our own employees sold us down the river after you got your . . . um . . . um . . ."

H.W. smiled. "As old Commodore Vanderbilt once said, 'Gentlemen, you have undertaken to cheat me. I won't sue you, for the law is too slow. I'll ruin you.'"

Loretta was astounded by this vital, chilling side of H.W. How she wished Mama could be here to see and hear all this! It was like *Mr. Smith Goes to Washington*—only it was real.

In the ensuing weeks, the hospital staff and H.W.'s Three Musketeers threaded through each other like a knotted prayer rug, and through them all threaded Loretta. She knew only too well that regression could set in at any moment, and she also knew how critical it was that any upswing in Dunbar's mood be maintained. "Keep the mind elevated no matter how slow the matter," she'd been taught.

What Loretta didn't know was that as Chukker Dunbar's condition improved, he began thinking more and more about Loretta, wondering about her enigmatic character, trying to imagine what made her tick.

Who are you, my pretty girl?

Why do you care so much that you defy the staff?

Why do they listen? Why do I listen?

How is it you know the Crestbournes?

Why do you look away when I'm in pain?

How did you get to be so tough? And how is it that you stay so soft?

Why am I so afraid that you won't be here some morning to continue my torture?

One day when the Efficient One arrived, as she did every afternoon, the first thing Harrison Dunbar had her write down were the titles of two books he wanted as soon as possible—rich, imaginative books about young ladies who lived in England's rose-covered countryside.

When Miss Collier brought them, gift-wrapped, the next day, H.W. almost grabbed the package from her hands. When he then held it out to Loretta, Loretta was annoyed. He was perfectly capable of unwrapping this present by himself.

"You can do that without my help, H.W.," she said, irritatedly.

"I would if it were for me," he replied gallantly, still holding the package for Loretta. He was smiling, and his eyes were a twinkling blue, again reflecting his robe.

Loretta smiled uncertainly. In all the months she'd been with Dunbar, this was the first time she felt that she was not entirely in control.

"Thank you, H.W.," she said. Like someone unaccustomed to gifts, she loosened every knot of the curlicued bow, peeled every inch of the Scotch tape before unfolding and refolding the shiny red paper. Her disbelief turned to pride when she saw that her present was books. "Thank you . . . thank you," she said as she kissed his cheek.

Miss Collier smiled as she gathered the ribbon and wrappings.

"Please, I want to save that," Loretta said quickly. "Please." She blushed deeply. She wanted to keep it all—to preserve the moment—but she was too embarrassed to tell them that.

"They're about England," Harrison Dunbar said. "About country ladies and getting married and prejudice and shallowness. Come to think of it, Jane Austen was a minister's daughter, too. And though she wrote a lot about marriage, she never did get married herself."

At times speech still came haltingly to H.W., yet now his words were clear and strong, and there was a new assurance to his tone. "Probably not much has changed about pride or prejudice in the years since that book," he continued, not wanting to embarrass Loretta by acknowledging her tears. "Probably not likely to in the next hundred and fifty either." As he smiled at her, he thought that he'd never seen anyone so beautiful. As Loretta smiled back, he wanted to tell her that she reminded him of those high summer days in the English countryside.

Loretta eagerly read whatever H.W. had Miss Collier bring: Dickens, Thackeray, Austen . . . Wharton, Joyce, and Dreiser . . . the French and the Russians . . . great, expansive tales where costume balls were frequent, where each night Loretta was the belle. She became Becky Sharp and Amanda Smedley, Emma Bovary and Lily Bart, the tragic Natasha, the languishing Camille. She was gay and vibrant, sad and saturnine. She spanned generations of families and family fortunes.

Added to Harrison Dunbar's list of unanswered questions was now the question of when: when did Loretta beg or steal time to read? In the morning her eyes gleamed, and when the day was gone they still glistened.

As Dunbar's daily strides grew into leaps, not only did he reclaim the long months since his stroke; he seemed healthier and happier than he had been in years. There could be no doubt that complete recovery was within reach. The once heavy creases in his face had folded into laugh lines, and the frozen lips became warm smiles. The once old, sad eyes sparkled anew, and even his thick shock of gray seemed more shot with pepper. While the team of ologists continued to pat each other's backs, Loretta and Michael Briggs smiled knowingly behind them.

Often Loretta and Michael would try to imagine the moment when they would tell H.W. that he was going home. Again and again they would set the scene, staging their various scenarios. The circumstances had to be special, tender, secure. Loretta would sometimes project the scene in her mind before going to sleep. Dreamily, she'd doze off with a mental image of the ecstasy of relief that would surge through Dunbar as they gently, easily delivered the momentous news.

And then it happened. Benton Hartman, followed by his team of ologists, burst through the door of room 1247. H.W. stood by the bureau, inhaling the scent of freshly cut roses, while Loretta stuffed yesterday's into the trash, proficiently avoiding the best-concealed thorns.

"Sit down, Chukker, young fella," Hartman said heartily. "We don't want our great news to bring on another attack. Ha ha."

One by one the doctors broke rank, each in turn walking over to where Dunbar stood near the bureau.

"You old sonofabitch, Dunbar," said the urologist.

"Takes a type-A-one blueblood like you," said the hematologist.

"Havin' us all fooled," laughed the pathologist.

"We never thought you'd be leaving so soon," Hartman explained.

Dunbar turned from the bureau and moved toward his favorite leather chair.

"Did you hear me, Chukker? You're leaving!" Hartman's voice carried into the hall. "Christ, I wish I had a camera. . . . Look at that face. He really can't believe it. Well, Chukker, we can't believe it either. It's a goddamn miracle." He clapped H.W. on the shoulder. "For Christ's sake, Chukker—smile! You look like a guy who's been given a life sentence, not a pardon."

Loretta and Michael were as stunned as Dunbar at Hartman's declaration. The same fear and shock that poured through Dunbar now flooded through her as well. Loretta seethed with a rage that she could not contain.

"Is self-serving shock a therapy that doctors should use on their patients?" she said savagely to Hartman.

"We were only trying to—" Hartman began to explain.

"Strip him of the only security he's had for months in order to clothe your own deformed egos?"

"Listen, young lady—" Hartman began again.

"No—*you* listen. The so-called miraculous recovery of this man had to do with this up here." Loretta's index finger nearly punctured her skull. "No matter what you think about your test tubes, you couldn't be more wrong. So *you* listen."

Hartman's voice was cold. "Aren't you speaking out of—"

"The heart and the head." Loretta's breath was short. She was frightening even herself, but she couldn't stop. Her hair whipped the air as her gaze swung from one bewildered face to another. "There are ways to tell a man he's better that make him feel great and ways to say he's great that scare him like crazy. We talked about all this. But all you heard was *you*. All you cared about was *you* getting the job done!"

"The first lesson a nurse should learn, Miss Worship, is never to discuss—"

"—anything about a patient in front of a patient." Loretta barely managed to keep her voice under any kind of control, but she had to fight for what she believed.

"Nobody knows better than Dr. Briggs and I that H.W. is ready to go. And nobody knows better than you what kind of preparation should precede any operation, including the one that you just botched."

From the doorway Michael applauded loudly, "Bravo, Loretta."

With a wild wave Harrison Dunbar semaphored the doctors to get out, then shook his head to indicate that Loretta and Michael should stay. He would be the one to calm her down—and to thank her.

Three weeks later than necessary, as fall snapped through

the air, Harrison W. Dunbar left the hospital. He had
begged Loretta to go home with him. The ologists, too, had
pleaded with her to go—anything to keep Dunbar happy.
But she couldn't; her place was at the hospital, not at
Rosefields.

Baines, H.W.'s driver, wearing a uniform the same
shade of green as the station wagon, held out a jacket for
H.W. the same shade of red as the small rose painted on the
wagon's door. Even the hood ornament was special: a fox
astride a hound. That's the way it should be, Loretta thought.
Wasn't it the fox who taught the Little Prince that real love
involved real commitment?

When H.W. walked with Miss Collier toward the waiting
station wagon, Loretta felt oddly isolated. Long after the
green wagon drove off, Loretta was still standing and waving. Maybe one day H.W. and Miss Collier would marry,
she thought. She'd be good for him; she adored him so. And
he needed someone.

So did Loretta.

# 9

In the autumn weeks that followed, an emptiness like nothing Loretta had ever known engulfed her life. It wasn't that she wanted H.W.'s stay at the hospital prolonged; it had been too long already. And it wasn't that she wanted to go home with him; she'd worked all of that out. She simply hadn't realized how much a part of her life he'd become. She hadn't considered that by cutting off contact she had cut off not only patient from nurse but friend from friend.

It had been Loretta's decision to make a complete break with H.W. She'd seen too many other patients succumb to hospital addiction, becoming dependent on the special treatment they'd had when they were sick. She didn't want H.W. to fall into that trap.

Although the hospital and the museum, the Briggses and the Crestbournes kept Loretta occupied, something was missing. Each time she'd speak with Miss Collier and hear again the words ". . . as well as can be expected," Loretta felt emptier. Christmas, when there was no report at all, was unendurable. The Efficient One had told her that they might visit Wilson in the Far East, but Loretta didn't believe

H.W. would travel that far so soon. When Loretta phoned and a maid told her that no one was home, she decided that Miss Collier and H.W. had gotten married and were on their honeymoon. Yet when Loretta received a call soon after the New Year, there was no mention of a wedding.

"Loretta?"

"Yes?" Loretta knew immediately who it was. "Happy New Year, Miss Collier."

"Thank you." She paused for a moment. "H.W. would like you to come to Rosefields, Loretta. Can you come for the weekend—Friday morning, say?" Her voice was without inflection.

"I'm sorry . . . what was that? I can hardly hear. We have a bad connection." Loretta needed to hear the words again to believe they were true.

"Can you come to Rosefields this weekend? H.W. asked me to ask you. He knows how you feel, but he thinks it's been long enough. Now has nothing to do with four months ago. It's a new year, and he'd like to say hello. I'll have . . . he'll send the car. The station wagon. With Baines." Miss Collier sounded so strained and awkward, so monochromatic. She didn't even sound efficient.

"Is everything all right?" Loretta asked. "Is H.W. all right? He's not sick, is he?"

"He wouldn't ask me to ask you if he were. He's fine. He's just fine." Silence. Neither hung up, nor did either speak for a moment. "Did you have a nice Christmas, Loretta?" The voice tried to be pleasant. "A nice New Year?"

"Yes, thanks. I was at the Crestbournes' Christmas and the Briggses' New Year's Eve. It was fun. Lovely." Now Loretta sounded strange, even to herself.

"Then I can tell H.W. you'll be here Friday? The car

will pick you up where it picked up H.W. At eight, all right? . . . What am I thinking of?—I don't mean the hospital. I don't know why I'm thinking hospital. I mean the residence, at eight. All right?"

It was now Tuesday night. That didn't give Loretta much time to find a weekend substitute. "Perfect," she lied. "I'm not on this weekend."

"Thank you, Loretta. Thank you."

"See you at—" Before she could finish, the Efficient One hung up.

Loretta didn't waste a moment. She threw on a coat, wound her scarf around her neck several times, and rushed out the door. Luckily, the bookstore was open late.

Sitting in the big backseat of the station wagon, watching the rolling farmland pass, Loretta felt small and lonely.

Baines turned out not to be the cheerful, chatty driver Loretta remembered calling for H.W. He was strictly one syllable to each of her comments and didn't reply at all when she remarked that the inside of the car smelled like the fine belongings in Mr. Dunbar's room at the hospital. In fact, at the mention of "hospital" Baines stiffened. Maybe the memory of H.W. being so ill was still too painful.

"Are we near Middleburg?" Loretta hoped the neutral question would change his tone.

"Yes'm."

Loretta couldn't bear the silence. "It's so beautiful here. It's God's country. Don't you think this is God's country?"

"Yes'm."

"I can't wait to see Rosefields. I hope Mr. Dunbar will show me around today." Loretta leaned forward as she spoke. Maybe the rutted roads were forcing him to concentrate on driving. Maybe.

"Ma'am."

Baines's vocabulary was even leaner than his pole-thin body. He reminded Loretta of something Zinnia had once said in exasperation. "More mules amongst my people than all the worlds together. Child, I could ask Mama somethin' till I was blue in the face, which ain't easy for me. And if she didn't feel like talkin' I could've just as easy been fillin' a well with a thimble. That's about how long it'd take me to have her say somethin' she didn't feel like sayin'."

Loretta pulled the lapels of her coat close together and turned the collar high. She felt uncomfortably chilly but was too embarrassed to ask for more heat. Nervously, she ran her fingers up and down the spine of the book she'd brought for H.W. She never thought she'd see the day when she would buy a book about Vietnam. In the years since Paul's death, her loathing for the war had in no way diminished.

Loretta was sure that H.W. would like the book, since it endorsed his favorite football theory of life. "Sure, you're ahead of the game," he had once told her, "if you're born on the fifty-yard line, with built-in defenses tackling the tackler out to get you. But the big score comes when you're there alone, when there's not only no help but no quarterback to sack."

Baines waved to the driver of a van that came lumbering toward them. As he'd done thousands of times, he pulled over to the side of the road, hugging the narrow shoulder until the van passed. From its half-open rear, two horses' rumps glistened in the morning sun, their tails swishing occasionally to flick away a fly. A bit farther on, Baines came to a complete halt behind a trio of velvet-helmeted riders. Upon hearing the car, and without glancing around, the riders broke into single file. Baines drove slowly past, and again he waved. Not until he had rounded the next curve and the trio was far from sight did he accelerate.

Soon Baines made a sharp right through gleaming archways of giant boxwood that marked the entrance to Rosefields. In the distance the snow-capped Blue Mountains seemed to start at the exact point where the miles of yellow meadows ended. Freshly painted fencing bordered the long drive to the sprawling main house, and thickets of pungently fresh dwarf boxwood nestled close to its white wood frame. Rosefields reminded Loretta of a Christmas card, with its giant wreath on the front door and a big, cozy fire blazing behind the leaded panes of the living-room windows.

As if by magic the front door opened as the station wagon pulled up. A heavyset black man in a white jacket, a small rose embroidered on its lapel, hurried down the steps for Loretta's luggage.

"This here is Miss Lawrettah. Miss Lawrettah, this here is Stratford."

"Thank you. Oh, thank you, Stratford." Before she had finished the second "thank you" Stratford had turned toward the house.

Stratford's family dated as far back as back went. They were slaved to the original Lee who had settled in Virginia three centuries ago. Old Leverett Lee had built a house called Stratford high on a bluff overlooking the Potomac, and with this new home rose a family of southern servants bearing the homestead's name. As Loretta would soon discover, the social distinctions among servants were even more finely calibrated than those among their masters.

As Loretta hurried to catch up to Stratford, she wondered why he had walked away at her greeting. And why, as she turned to say goodbye to Baines, was he already back in the car? Her anxiety increased when she saw the Efficient

One, standing still and somber. Was this the lady who'd hugged her and kissed her and laughed goodbye only months ago?

"Hello, Loretta." It was the same flat tone Loretta had heard on the telephone the other night.

"Hello." Loretta started to reach forward but stopped herself. A pit of fear began to open deep in her stomach.

The Efficient One turned brusquely to Stratford. "The Blue Room, please, Stratford." He nodded and carried Loretta's bags up the floral-carpeted staircase.

The entrance hall of Rosefields was large and square, and from the high, molded ceiling an enormous brass chandelier with dozens of tiny bulbs threw warmth onto the wood-paneled walls. A pastel Aubusson rug covered just enough of the floor to allow the parquet wood to glisten around its border. A painting of jockeys in the locker room donning their brilliantly colored silks hung above the marble console. And in the middle of the hall, a huge mahogany rent table held an exquisite Lowestoft bowl brimming with roses.

Walking on tiptoe, though she didn't know why, Loretta followed the Efficient One into a library with red lacquered walls, where a large log fire burned and the scent of pine filled the air. Near the hearth an old leather oats bucket with worn gold letters reading "Tomgirl" held cones to feed the blaze.

The room powerfully evoked H.W. Horse paintings were everywhere, and Loretta immediately chose as her favorite the one over the mantel, in which riders in scarlet jackets— nearly the same scarlet as the walls—flew over fences taller than their mounts. Sunshine poured in and onto everything— the worn leather chairs, the needlepoint pillows, the myriad photographs, and the overstuffed sofas covered in the same faded cabbage-rose fabric as the curtains were made of—yet a chill was everywhere.

Without warning, the Efficient One threw her arms around Loretta and started to cry. Unlike the last time, these were not happy tears.

As she watched the always dignified Miss Collier lose control, Loretta became terrified. Only when she noticed the Efficient One's large black hairpins falling onto the rug and her hair dangling around her neck did Loretta snap back to reality. Almost simultaneously Miss Collier herself grew calmer.

"Forgive me, Loretta. Forgive me, please—please, I'm sorry. You'll understand more after I've told you . . . I m so sorry, Loretta. Please sit down. Please."

Miss Collier walked toward the door and pressed a small ivory button set into a knot of the pine paneling. Before her finger left the button Stratford appeared. Had he been hovering outside as Miss Collier broke down? Loretta didn't want to think about it. She was grateful for the suggestion of tea; it might calm her racing nerves.

Soon Stratford wheeled in a double-tiered cart laden with a heavy silver tea service, delicate Meissen cups, and a small, gleaming salver of pastry. The Efficient One poured with a hand so newly steady that Loretta once again grew frightened.

After a few sips, some dabs with a lace hankie, and a quick twist to rearrange her hair into its bun, Miss Collier spoke. "It didn't start right at first, Loretta. No . . . not then. That was fine."

"What didn't? *What* was fine? Is something wrong with H.W.?"

"Actually, it was best in the beginning. Better than any time since."

The sentences were logical, but the words had no meaning. Loretta leaned forward and picked the pecans off a piece of pastry.

"It was gradual. It happened slowly." The Efficient One's eyes grew wide. "Of course, *I* knew. I knew right away." Without looking at her tea, Miss Collier took a sip; the cup was empty. She swallowed anyway.

Loretta felt as if she were living in some kind of a time warp. She wanted to speak, but she was afraid her words might forestall the news that she was so anxious to hear.

While the Efficient One gathered and refocused her thoughts, Loretta, trying desperately to calm herself or maybe just to forestall her worst fears, picked up a frame from the table next to her chair and stared at the black-and-white photograph of two couples posing in front of what appeared to be a hotel. The women, in identical slouch hats, wore their skirts high above the knee. The men, in double-breasted blazers, wore their boaters at precisely the same tilt. The man on the right looked a lot like H.W., yet the picture was at least fifty years old. Another time warp, Loretta thought eerily. "Who's this man?" she asked, pointing.

"It's H.W.'s father," the Efficient One answered without a glance. "His mother's on the other side of the other man. It's H.W.'s favorite picture. He took it in Palm Beach when he was a little boy. He couldn't have been more than ten. The other couple are the Murphys . . . friends of Zelda and Scott Fitzgerald."

"This photo was never at the hospital, was it?"

"Hospital! Hospital!" the Efficient One was suddenly shouting. "He can't go back! You can't let him! He can't! It'll kill him! He'll kill himself!"

Unable to contain herself any longer, Loretta grabbed

Miss Collier by the shoulders, forcing her to meet her gaze. "Something's happened to H.W.!" Loretta yelled. "What's happened to him?"

"He'll kill me," said Miss Collier, her eyes glazed with fear.

"No! I will, if you don't tell me what's going on!" In a last, desperate effort she shook Miss Collier with such fury she wasn't even aware that the woman was talking to her through her sobs.

"Setback" was the first word Loretta heard.

"Go on!"

"It wasn't at the beginning. Oh, God, Loretta! I wanted to tell you."

Her words were smothering each other. She was nearly incoherent as she released the agony she'd borne so long. "He became so much worse. He never wanted you to . . . after you said all that about nurse-patient dependency, he said he'd kill me if . . . It was around Thanksgiving when his arm started to . . ." She blew into her hankie and wiped her tears before continuing. "Still, every day he'd go to the greenhouse, to see the roses, then not so often, then not at . . . and he was really fine the time I called you and said he was all better and to come see him as a friend, and when he asked me if I told you he was really fine and I told him yes, he asked me if you wanted to talk to him. And I said you didn't because it wasn't time yet, so he decided that what he thought was a genuine friendship was just a nurse-patient thing and nothing special, and the torture began again. That was around Thanksgiving. But this time, it first came from his black mood and then it spread to . . ."

Loretta's heart beat so high in her throat that she thought she would choke. Though Miss Collier continued to talk, Loretta stopped listening. Walking to the window, she began to fit all the pieces together.

Of course Baines and Stratford wouldn't be happy to see her. Of course the Efficient One would be near collapse. And H.W.?—Oh, God! What had she done?

"That's why I couldn't tell you, Loretta. I've never broken a promise to him. I called so many times before Christmas . . . and at Christmas . . . even after. Each time I hung up before your phone even rang. It's not that he was in the room, but he made me hang up. Christmas, God! It was so awful." Miss Collier's head swayed with grief. "And through it all, he kept on with that awful scribbling, as if he were writing his epitaph."

Loretta pulled the bellows leaning against the hearth, knelt down in front of the fireplace, and started opening and closing the worn accordion belly. Sparks began to fly around the logs, and soon they stretched into flames. Still Loretta pumped the bellows, opened and closed, opened and closed. As if obsessed, she threw one, two, three more logs onto the smoldering embers. Damn you, burn! You can't go out on me! Burn! Don't die. You can't! I won't let you!

"H.W. didn't even want the curtains open for the sun to . . ."

Loretta walked toward the source of this sorrowful voice and placed a gentle finger on Miss Collier's lips. Tenderly, she took the Efficient One's hand and held it to the tiny Saint Christopher around her neck. With a powerful breath of determination and with a voice embodying all the authority she could muster, Loretta announced, "We're going to open those curtains."

What Loretta saw was an old man in a dark room with despair in his fading eyes. Those first days she stayed with H.W. for only a few moments, just to make him aware of her presence. Especially on Monday, because on Monday she wanted to prove to him that although she'd originally come just for the weekend, she now was there to stay awhile.

Without a moment's hesitation Loretta had called the hospital and told her supervisor that her aunt had died and that she was taking a leave of absence. She also called the Briggses and swore them to secrecy. A fully supportive Michael agreed that she should stay at Rosefields. Olivia packed Loretta's winter clothes, and Baines was sent to pick them up.

When days ran to weeks and H.W. remained determinedly morose, Loretta and Michael stayed firm in their resolve not to call in a specialist, believing that sort of healer could prove the ultimate killer. Loretta was certain that what the Efficient One had diagnosed as another stroke was in fact nothing of the kind. Her intuition and training told her that Dunbar's refusal to improve was just that.

Loretta realized, too, that someone as smart as H.W. might fear that his prolonged refusal might actually be irreversible. And she understood his terror of making any effort lest his fear be confirmed. Yet as her visits with H.W. grew longer and more frequent, a bit of brightness began to filter through, a flicker of hope nudging the rage and despair.

Whenever Loretta talked to H.W., she made sure that her tone was conversational, that they were actually talking to each other. "That's interesting. . . ." Loretta would pause as if for his reply, then continue as if he had responded. "Yes, incredible that Farland's been clipping away thirty years." Nod. Light laugh. "No wonder he never has to even up."

Once when she was sure that H.W. was watching, she unfolded a small piece of paper.

> Plant there some box or pine
> something in Winter and call it mine.

"That's just so beautiful," she said. Aware that he was still looking at her, she refolded the paper and placed it back in her pocket. Of course H.W. knew that she'd taken those words from the bronze plaque he had set in the path at the foot of the boxwood garden. She knew how he would like her saving them.

When Loretta finally decided to give him the Halberstam book about Vietnam, H.W.'s faint smile and hopeful eyes made her delirious. He was going to get well again; there was no doubt. And she would help.

A few days later, H.W. reciprocated by giving Loretta a specially bound edition that he'd bought months before and had intended to send to the hospital with a note asking her to visit Rosefields but to "expect only the aroma, not the aura of *Brideshead* as you go 'from scent to scent and climate to climate.'"

H.W. had completely forgotten the note he'd tucked inside. It pleased him, however, that it was there, and thrilled him that Loretta was really here to read it.

Anyone who saw Loretta with H.W. wouldn't have believed that their friendship had ever missed a day, or that their reading of each other's thoughts had ever skipped a page.

"No place could be more beautiful," Loretta said. "Not Brideshead. Not anywhere." She adored Rosefields, and she was amazed at how at home she was beginning to feel, how comfortable Stratford, Baines, and Miss Collier were making it for her now that they realized she was helping H.W. get well again.

When Valentine's Day arrived, Loretta gave H.W. a teddy bear like the one Sebastian carried in *Brideshead*. H.W. loved it, laughed at it, even cuddled it. "Hello, Aloysius," he said, with the first wide smile he'd managed in months.

Loretta was astonished and grateful. His speech was normal, his smile a miracle. Dawn had broken, and with it Loretta had ripped the curtains from H.W. Dunbar's darkness.

# 10

The weeks that passed seemed like no time at all, yet Chukker Dunbar not only recovered but got better than ever. The Efficient One, his household staff, even the mirrors attested to his return to form. In fact, he looked more a fit man of fifty than one who'd just turned the corner of sixty-three.

Though spring would soon arrive on the calendar, the more convincing outdoor thermometer had made Loretta and Chukker raise collars against the cold as they returned from a long walk on one of the trails surrounding Rosefields. Pulling her long hair from the neck of her coat, she shook her head much as a thoroughbred might toss its mane and went to join Chukker in front of the warming fire. Long and lean, Loretta stood as fine as any filly in any Virginia field. As she closed her eyes to the full pine bouquet, Chukker couldn't help admiring her bearing. It was a presence she didn't even know she possessed, yet one that others would recognize instantly.

"Should I put on something else?" Loretta asked.

"For what?"

"For tea. For the people coming."

"When they see you they'll be the ones to think about changing."

Loretta blushed. Always the kindness, the flattery. Chukker was a master at raising people's self-confidence. Even now, when Loretta was nervous about meeting people who knew so many things she didn't, Chukker could make her comfortable.

Putting his arm around her shoulders, he walked her to the wide bay window. The giant magnolia was in full bloom, its luscious pink blossoms defying the chill. "That was my mother's favorite tree," he told her. "Not just because it's beautiful but because it blooms twice and the second time is even more magnificent than the first. She used to say that if we could learn to bloom again we'd have life licked. I know what she meant."

Turning toward Loretta, he took her chin in his hand so that he could hold her face in his gaze. "You're so young, Loretta, so damn young. But you know far more than you think you know, and you're just beginning." Loretta picked a thread from the bold plaid of his jacket, and Chukker smiled. "You see, I'm the one who needs fixing."

As Stratford set out the china, he hummed gaily to himself, his smile whiter than any porcelain on the cart.

Today was important to Chukker. Since rumor mills in tiny towns grind coarsely, Chukker couldn't wait for his friends to see the "pathetic cripple" who hid behind his hedges. And he couldn't wait for them to meet the woman who had helped him recover.

Promptly at five the guests arrived. Some were still in their breeches and boots. Others merely looked as if they were. These were people whose big money made small noises, people who inhabited a world where delivering a foal might cost a quarter of a million dollars while delivering the heir to the entire stable cost a mere five thousand. Not only did these people keep their great wealth hidden; they kept their great houses hidden as well. All an outsider ever saw was the miles of fencing, not the vast expanses where derby winners grazed and farms stretched lazy miles against the distant mountains.

This was the world of tweeds and gracefully graying hair, where rouge was applied by the wind and outside adornment wasn't required for inside well-being. This was the sheltered world where everyone knew everyone else, where the Mellons and the Harrimans and the Belmonts were just the folks next door.

Loretta was fascinated by how they devoted the present to pursuing the past, how their main topic of conversation seemed to be everybody's background. Maybe, Loretta decided, it was just that they naturally categorized people like horses, where breeding is everything.

Not that they weren't warm and nice. They were. And most importantly, they were genuinely happy to see Chukker so healthy. And if Loretta was responsible, no matter who she might be, they were grateful to her. They were also, of course, surprised.

"Not at all what I expected."

"Chukker would never look that way if she were."

"Is that a ring she's wearing?"

"Hmmm."

"Knows about boxwood."

"And Jane Austen."

"And England."

"And Donina."

"Donina? Are you sure?"

"Hmmm?"

Although Loretta had been smiling since the guests arrived, her expression was only now, at last, becoming natural. The people she'd been so panicked about meeting were truly friendly. The Chenerys really wanted to tell Loretta about their horse who "could take it all." In the kindest way, Paul Mellon told Loretta that "all" meant the Triple Crown, of course. After toasts to Loretta, to Chukker, and to the Chenerys' horse, Secretariat, the guests departed in good spirits.

She had passed! It hadn't been a rousing, bosom-clasping welcome but a graceful acceptance because Chukker was so obviously well and thriving. Loretta was grateful the day was over.

What wasn't over, however, was the conversation she'd been planning to have with Chukker. She'd tried to tell him before today, but she knew she was right to have waited. He was happy about what had happened this afternoon. And now he would be happy, too, about her getting on with her own life.

When they re-entered the library in silence, each busy with his own thoughts, Loretta was dreading what she had to say, and Chukker was so eager to express what was on his mind that for one of the first times in his life he didn't know where to start. Thrusting his hands into his pockets, he looked from the fire to the window to the books, then back to the fire—everywhere but at Loretta. He took a stirrup cup from the mantel and poured himself several fingers of brandy. Looking again out the window and talking straight to the magnificent magnolia, he said, "Loretta, I want you to be my wife."

Loretta stared into the darkness all that night. She couldn't stop seeing his bewildered, hurt face as she ran to throw her arms around him while shaking her head in refusal.

She saw Big Luke and Mama, too, and Paul's face that last time they watched the sunset together. Yes, she'd grown to know and to feel for Chukker these past months—but was that love? She understood her love for Mama, for Zinnia, for all the patients she'd nursed back to health. But there was nothing with which to compare her feelings for Chukker.

Why, she wondered, did he see her as worthy of being his wife when she felt no such self-esteem? Loretta knew there were many parts of Chukker's life that she didn't understand. Where did he think she fit in? Where did *she* think she fit in? Marriage is so final, so certain, and she wasn't certain about anything.

In the morning it was easier than it had been the night before to tell Chukker that she loved him too much to marry him . . . that, although she adored him, she wasn't yet ready for the finality of marriage.

Chukker acknowledged that she was shocked by the suddenness of his proposal, although yesterday it had seemed to him so natural, so long in coming. He knew he would need all the patience and love not to mention marriage again. Thank goodness he'd at least persuaded her to stay a little longer . . . just until Wilson came home, so that she could meet him.

What surprised both Chukker and Loretta was the closeness they continued to feel after his proposal and her refusal. The nurse-patient relationship had entirely disappeared. Something more intimate had replaced it, and they were now far more relaxed with each other.

"You are a gift of life, Loretta. Long before I had the stroke, I needed it," Chukker told her. "You've probably made me too young." His staff would have agreed with that statement after finding Aloysius propped up against H.W.'s monogrammed pillowcases.

After Loretta confided in Chukker about her no-eyes teddy, she asked Olivia to mail it, along with her cherished picture of Paul. Loretta also told Chukker about *The Little*

*Prince* and was surprised that he had one, too, only his prince was *Huckleberry Finn*. "People really don't really read Huck right. All Huck's saying is that it makes no never-mind what you do if it's gonna make you lose sight of huntin' and fishin'."

"Like sunsets," Loretta said.

"Just like sunsets."

It was during their walks together, when Loretta wasn't face to face with Chukker, that she'd tell him about her life, about those awful times she herself could hardly bear to remember. She didn't tell him to get pity. She simply wanted him to know. At these moments Chukker would sometimes hold her hand so tightly that it made Loretta wince. Yet with all her confessions, she never told him the worst, because no matter what anyone would ever say or do, nothing could ever wipe away that horror and shame. She knew that she had to blot it out of her mind whenever she looked back, because every time it pushed its way in, it pushed everything else out.

Chukker rarely talked about his own life. Usually he said what he was thinking at the moment, or asked Loretta questions. Most of what she learned about him came from the scrupulously kept photograph albums that lined the library shelves. As she turned the pages on Chukker's world, so much reminded her of Mama's beloved movie magazines.

Of all the pictures in all the albums, Loretta was fascinated most by the photographs of Chukker's wife on their wedding day. She adored her straight, sleek gown and the way her train swirled like whipped cream around her feet. As Chukker had once said, "Class and the lack of it—both are impossible to hide." And there could be no mistaking that Kate Dunbar was class—not the wispy, porcelain kind but the sturdy sort that Loretta would have expected in

Chukker's wife. Kate looked kind, too. As Loretta stared at the pictures, she hoped that Kate hadn't suffered terribly, though she knew she probably had. "Two years," Chukker had said, and then he didn't say any more.

After Loretta had been through all the albums, she sat enthralled through the home movies, reel after reel of speeded-up figures playing polo and croquet, dashing in and out of waves, sipping champagne against backdrops of confetti and cruise ships. When the black-and-white became sharper and people moved more normally, she watched Chukker salute straight and center, throw his cap in the air, and smile the same warm, wonderful smile that lit up his face now as he watched, remembered, and held Loretta's hand. "Was I ever proud of those bars!" Chukker said, recalling his ensign's commission from the naval school in Newport.

Around the time of Chukker's marriage the movies pretty much ended. "It was my father's hobby," he told Loretta. There were only a few reels from when Wilson was little; they showed him on the same long lawns and private beaches where his father had played before him. Although everything looked lavish, especially in Palm Beach, none of it seemed intimidating to Loretta. Maybe it was because Chukker lived there.

Three weeks after the tea party and Loretta's unqualified refusal, she found herself still at Rosefields. Her old life now seemed the intrusion that Rosefields once had been. She'd extended her leave at the hospital, and telephone calls to Michael had become awkward.

"Don't worry, Loretta. Do what you have to do. It's just that we miss you and want you back."

"I know. Thank you for saying that. But he's so close. He's almost there."

"Don't worry. I understand."

"It should be any day now."

"Everything will be waiting."

"Thanks, Michael."

That night, a stormy evening in April, she dreamed that Michael called to say she'd been replaced, that the hospital didn't want to extend her leave anymore. He was crying on the phone. She begged him not to be upset, assured him that everything would work out all right. Finally, he promised to stop worrying. Loretta hung up happy. When she awoke, she realized that she'd had a nightmare—none of it was true.

Loretta resolved nonetheless to return. It was funny, she thought, how she divided her life into before Rosefields and now. Day after day she'd pick up the phone to call the hospital, to tell them she was coming back, and hang up before anyone answered.

The pace and pattern of life at Rosefields were lulling and romantic: huge fires giving off constant warmth, silver and brass polished with years of love, and heirlooms that served as reminders of beautiful times wherever one looked. And what could be more beautiful than greenhouses filled with spring all winter long? Loretta accepted the luxury because it was the life of the man she loved. It became a part of her because her acceptance of it made Chukker happy.

The forsythia, daffodils, and magnolias had bloomed and gone. Other new buds were breaking wherever the eye turned, and once sallow fields were becoming endless seas of green. Chukker snapped a small branch of lilac from a laden bush and held the tiny sprig under Loretta's nose. Its intoxicating loveliness hinted at the promise in the air.

As Chukker and Loretta pushed through the kitchen door, Chukker suddenly knew that somehow everything would be all right. Grasping Loretta's hand, he led her to see Aloysius.

It was not at all with the delicacy he'd imagined but with a trembling passion and a long-restrained desire that Chukker made love to Loretta. And with more ardor than she ever dreamed she could feel, Loretta responded.

The next day, as Loretta placed her no-eyes teddy next to Aloysius, she realized that Chukker wasn't the only one who'd never been happier.

# 11

As Chukker brought the green Mercedes to a stop and they watched the hunt cross the road, it was as if all the sporting paintings Loretta had ever seen had come to life. The wildly barking hounds with their feet just skimming the turf and the galloping steeds with their spit-and-polish brilliance were Sir Alfred Munnings at his most magnificent.

"It must've just started," Chukker said, smiling. "I don't see a single riderless horse."

When the last braided tail cleared the stone wall and the hunt passed safely on to the next field and the countryside was again at peace, Chukker pressed down on the accelerator. They were drawing close to the church, and Loretta turned to make sure that the station wagon carrying Baines, Stratford, Farland, and Miss Collier was keeping up. And that the Crestbournes' car, with Olivia, Michael, Wilson, and Zinnia, was right behind them.

To Loretta, Wilson had looked less like his picture than she'd expected. Although the blue of his eyes and his smile, when he flashed one, were Chukker's, Wilson was taller and stringier and much more disheveled than she'd imagined

Chukker Dunbar's son would look. Even though his clothes came straight off the rack at Brooks Brothers, getting them together obviously bored him. Yet even a rumpled Wilson had a certain indefinable air of self-possession.

"I'm so glad you're here," Loretta had said, uncomfortably, two days before. How else could she welcome Wilson to his own home? Even with the wedding so close, Loretta felt light-years from anything remotely approaching her impending status as mistress of Rosefields.

"I made good time driving," Wilson said. He meant driving from Washington. He'd flown to Dulles all the way from Saigon, where he'd been stationed since before Christmas, first covering the cease-fire and then the massive U.S. casualties. As Wilson's eyes registered Loretta's youthful, un-made-up beauty and her freedom from affectation, he thought how she was not at all what he'd expected.

Chukker had made sure that Wilson never found out how near death he'd been. Even if he had known, Wilson would never have believed that this child had saved his father. Yes, men fall in love with their nurses, Wilson thought, but what had ensnared his father? Realizing that he was still staring at Loretta, Wilson turned to Chukker.

"No wonder, Dad, you never sent me a picture." No one, including Wilson, knew exactly what that meant.

Chukker put his arm around Loretta's waist. "Think your father's a fool?" Gently he turned to kiss his bride-to-be as Loretta embarrassedly turned her cheek to his lips.

No, Wilson never thought his father a fool. He and Chukker loved each other and took pride in each other, even though they were little alike. Still, one of the few things Wilson thought they had in common was that neither was a starry-eyed romantic. Wilson had been in love, too, of course, but he'd never married. Actually, his relationships had always been as impossible as his father's seemed to him now. He was pleased that Chukker looked happy, but he wasn't quite sure he approved.

Over drinks, over dinner, over the next two days, Chukker and Wilson said few words to each other, because whenever they tried to talk Wilson felt obliged to reverse roles. "What do you really know about her?" he demanded of his father. "Are you really sure marriage is the right thing?" "But why else would she?"

Oddly enough, Wilson felt compelled to ask these questions mostly to convince himself, since the obvious answers didn't seem obvious in Loretta's case. There was an artless quality about her, a disarming naturalness that surprised him. The easy way she blended into his father's life seemed to bear no trace of a gold digger's wiles. Or could it all be a specious and conniving act?

Chukker knew it would take time for his son to come around, and he told Loretta that the good in Wilson would eventually love the same in her.

What a day to be married, Loretta thought. Everything was alive with fresh leaves, and everywhere one looked the early sun sprinkled shadows. Robins, fatter than they'd been all year, pecked through the softened earth.

The dress Loretta wore was soft and old-fashioned. It suggested more of Loretta's figure than it revealed, and the beautifully crocheted lace around the neck matched the lace on the cuffs. When Zinnia had arrived at Rosefields, only four days before, Loretta still hadn't found anything to wear. In pleased exasperation, Zinnia had marched Loretta to the "material store" and after much measuring and draping bought exactly four-and-one-third yards of ecru silk and half a yard of lace. After it was wrapped and Zinnia moved Loretta out the door, Zinnia rushed back inside and pointed to a bolt of blue on the bottom shelf. "I need just a scrap, just a nothin' piece of that there." Loretta lifted her hem and smiled at the tiny piece of "somethin' blue" sewn in the seam. It made her happy, too, that the modest décolletage exposed her tiny Saint Christopher and the roseate strand of perfect pearls.

> The luster, the quality, the perfection—
> when I saw them, I saw you
> > > All my love,
> > > Chukker

He had given her the pearls with that note after making love. When she had started to protest, he'd kissed the words away.

Any stranger who saw Loretta and Chukker on their wedding day would have said that they looked as if they had always belonged to each other—probably as father and daughter. Next to Loretta, Chukker looked every well-bred inch the proud patriarch about to give his daughter's hand to some chap they'd known from birth.

Chukker, however, was not concerned about their difference in years. Loretta might have gaps in her formal education, but she was schooled in ways no diploma could match, no degree could confer. She knew good, and she knew how to fight when others gave up. She was his own Huck Finn— not because of her crazed lout of a father or running away but because of her loathing of bias and what was bogus and because of the stored love she was ready to lavish. No, Chukker wasn't worried. If anything was missing, she'd find it.

Although the roads were rutted and difficult to maneuver, Chukker managed with only one hand, holding Loretta's with the other.

The small Norman church was a gem. The great oak doors, the elaborate grillwork, even the gray Virginia stone made it take on a jewel-like aura. Without doubt, the Trinity Episcopal Church of Upperville, Virginia, was proud testament to the eloquence of the discreetly rich.

Even before Chukker and Loretta got out of the car, the minister appeared to greet them. While waiting for the others, they spoke about the beauty of the day, the bounty of the rainy spring. Yet the more easily they spoke, the more Loretta's heart trampled out their words. When the tiny entourage finally entered the church, she could hardly hear the thunder of the Bach prelude on the organ.

As he'd done so often before, Chukker looked toward the choir of stained glass through which light poured into the chapel. Never had those biblical scenes seemed so extravagant in color. From Creation to Resurrection, these colored windows shone almost as splendidly as the woman about to become his wife.

Chukker held tightly to her arm as they proceeded down the aisle toward the altar. Loretta fought back tears as she gasped at what appeared to be more lavender roses than could possibly exist in the world. Oh, how she wished Mama could be here to see this! That was the only flaw in Loretta's otherwise perfect day. She'd written several times, and the Efficient One had even tried to place a call, but the letters had come back marked "Moved—No Forwarding Address," and the phone had been disconnected long ago.

With gentle authority, the minister raised his arms. Loretta and Chukker knelt.

"In times of trial . . . in seasons of joy . . ."

It seemed to Loretta as if she were in two churches. In one she was little, and a madman screamed from the pulpit. In the other it was now, this moment: her wedding. As the minister continued his benediction, his soft voice drowned out the voice from the past.

" 'Be not afraid,' said Joshua, 'the Lord thy God is with you. Love and faith can heal all hurt.' "

The humility Loretta felt whenever anyone mentioned healing seemed for the first time a source of strength as she turned and smiled at the man beside her.

" 'True youth dwells in the heart where true love . . .' "

An ebullient Olivia and a dour Wilson stepped forward holding the twin circles of gold. Wilson's face gave Loretta a twinge of sadness.

"With this ring I thee wed," Chukker said.

"With this ring I thee wed," Loretta repeated.

"I now pronounce you man and wife."

As Chukker kissed Loretta, the tower bell spread joy throughout the rolling hills. Arms around each other, Mr. and Mrs. Harrison Wilson Dunbar, Jr., ran through a hail of rice and the barrage of reporters and photographers waiting for them outside.

# PART III

# 12

Chukker and Loretta were in Venice when they read
that Secretariat had won the Kentucky Derby.

It was with great care that Chukker had chosen
Venice as their first stop. Unashamedly romantic, Venice
was part city, part nation, and entirely perfect for them
both. As the jumbo jet exchanged the Atlantic for the
Adriatic, Chukker read Loretta the words Thomas Mann had
written obviously with only them in mind: "How can anyone
repress the secret thrill of arriving in Venice for the first
time—or returning after a long absence and stepping into a
gondola?" Ecstatic with happiness, Loretta squeezed Chukker's arm and snuggled close to him.

The fat-bellied gondolier who helped Loretta and Chukker into his ornately carved sliver of black presented a jolly
contrast to the sleek craft. As they glided through the
breathtaking streets of water, he sang with lusty exuberance.
Loretta was completely unaware that Chukker's largesse of
lire was responsible for the "O sole mio" that issued from
those off-key lips.

The huge orange sun, more enormous in Venice than

anywhere else in the world, was just falling beyond the silhouettes of towers and domes. Chukker, who knew this skyline well, had never before seen such fire. Not even Turner had captured a moment of such blazing brilliance.

As they passed one splendid sight after another, Chukker softly whispered the names to Loretta. He didn't want to break the sorcery of the shimmering palazzos, the pigeoned piazzas, or the fairy-tale bridges. It was not until they floated between San Marco and Santa Maria della Salute that Chukker spoke in anything near a normal tone. Even then Loretta didn't move her eyes. Everything around her was enchantment; even the trails of strung-up laundry seemed washed with gold.

Before they reached their hotel on the tiny island across from San Marco, they passed the Palazzo Barbara, where Henry James had lived, and where Cole and Linda Porter had entertained Chukker's parents and the Murphys at parties with floating jazz bands that thundered into early dawns. As Chukker identified the place, Loretta remembered the photographs in the albums: people sprawling atop the same stone lions, lying along the same sinking steps. The more Loretta saw, the more she repeated, "It's a dream. I can't believe it," hardly able to take her eyes away, just in case.

The Cipriani Hotel was small and grand, and the graciousness of the staff was constant. As Loretta and Chukker sat on the terrace overlooking the lagoon, a waiter lifted glasses from a bucket of crushed ice and poured a sip for Signor Dunbar. With a nod, Chukker acknowledged the wine's perfection.

He covered Loretta's hand with his and told her how old Giuseppe Cipriani used to sit at this very table, pounding his chest, boasting to any and all who would listen that he, Giuseppe Cipriani, was the only "real live in a Papa book" in all of Venice. "The truth was," Chukker said, "it was the truth. In all the stories Hemingway wrote about the bars and bordellos of Venice, Giuseppe Cipriani was the only real person he used. I wish you could have known Giuseppe. I wish you could have known it all." Chukker clinked his glass on hers. "You will, Loretta. You will." His eyes misted as he repositioned the candle on the table to read about Secretariat and the Derby.

The papers had arrived that afternoon with the other mail. Since they had been away so short a time, Loretta was surprised that there was anything for them at all. She would have been more surprised had she seen the cables Chukker had intercepted at the hotel desk. Chukker had not yet revealed to Loretta the vast scope of his business affairs, his interests, his monies. That would come in time. It would be too overwhelming, too frightening, for her to digest at once. And for now, Chukker wanted her all to himself.

At their wedding, Loretta had been caught unawares by the flashbulbs and reporters crushing in as they left the church. Chukker's explanation—"It's a tiny town and anything's news"—had sufficed only until the next morning, when Loretta awoke to the shock of seeing their picture on the front page of the Richmond *Times*.

"Front-page news?" Loretta had asked in disbelief. For a moment, Chukker was furious with the paper, but when the anger faded he was glad. At least the article told Loretta some of the things he hadn't. It didn't say it all, because everybody knew it all already—everybody but Loretta.

The gentle May air heightened the honeymoon pleasures of looking and learning and loving. Venice was one of the few places he knew where the outside world didn't intrude, where cares, like so many dandelion seeds, floated away on the wind. As they followed the footsteps of Ruskin and Wagner, wined and supped in the manner of princes and popes, no man had ever been more in love than Chukker Dunbar. Although Loretta was the one filled with wonder, Chukker was the boy in the candy shop.

There was no church too far, no piazza too crowded or palace too dark for Loretta to explore. And from Giorgione to Bellini, from Titian to Tintoretto, the glories of the city seemed even more glorious as Chukker rediscovered them through Loretta's eyes.

What amazed Chukker was how the glass blowers of Murano, the lace makers on Burano, even the pigeons on the square made him want to sing. He couldn't believe he was patronizing hawkers and vendors, occasionally even handing perfect strangers his camera so that he could get pictures of Loretta and himself together. When the two of them shopped, it was for each other, and when they made love it was that way too. Chukker wanted to buy Loretta the world, but all she wanted was something small as a keep-sake. She decided to add a charm from each place they visited to the gold link bracelet he'd bought her on their very first day in Venice. And from Venice, the charm had to be a gondola.

Loretta tugged Chukker into the nearest souvenir shop. He laughed as she pored over the tiny charms as if they were uncut diamonds.

"The enamel will peel on this one—don't you think? Yes, I guess it will." Loretta answered her own question much the way Mama used to do. She put the charm back on the counter, then pointed to another. "This one with the gondolier will catch on everything, don't you think? I'm sure it will." Finally, she decided on a charm that she'd seen in the window of nearly every jewelry shop. Its practicality was assured. It wouldn't peel. It wouldn't catch. It matched the bracelet. It wasn't overpriced.

The shopkeeper rolled his eyes. When a few moments

later he returned with the gondola soldered onto the bracelet, his eyes flashed with triumph. "This one," he said as he tried to pull the barge from its moorings, "it never come off. Never!"

The honeymooners left Venice in a shiny black Fiat that they drove along the northern lakes to their rapturous night in Milan. There, seated in a box at La Scala, they listened as "Celeste Aida" rang up the curtains on Milanese society. At the exact moment that the aria began, Chukker and Loretta looked lovingly at each other and reached for each other's hand.

Through the following weeks, as they traveled the miles from Padua to Parma to Pisa, the history-laden black dots on the map opened like microfilm—although when Chukker suggested a detour to Montecatini, Loretta wanted no part of its baths and muds and cures: they were too reminiscent of her own unforgotten healings.

The unblinking sun made the tumbling Tuscan hills and the rambling Po river sparkle with illusory magic. Chukker hoped he'd be rewarded with at least a few photographs from all the times they stopped to snap one incredible view after another.

Chukker thought how much his father would have loved Loretta. He thought, too, how important it was that Wilson love her. He knew it would take work. And time. Time Wilson would have to spend with Loretta. Then Wilson would see what she was really like. Chukker would work it out. He had to.

Chukker and Loretta were in Florence when they read that Secretariat had also won the Preakness. Record time again, and more than ever people were talking Triple Crown, the first in a quarter of a century. Secretariat, "the wow horse of history," was being compared to Citation, Man O'War, Native Dancer. "Bloodlines—The Riches to Riches Story," one newspaper headline screamed.

Chukker had his own theory about bloodlines. "Have the dam's virtues cancel the sire's flaws and vice versa," read the carving above the door on the old breeding barn at Rosefields. Chukker liked the idea of the dam canceling first. He liked it even more that almost every man had called him on it. It got so that he was disappointed when one didn't. Looking at Loretta now, Chukker wished he knew her breeding brilliance. She was so unlike most of the women he knew—so many of them merely society spear carriers who out of necessity put lineage before looks.

Secretariat's Preakness win wasn't the only news the papers held that day for the Harrison W. Dunbars. They had just returned from an afternoon of sightseeing—Ghiberti's bronze doors, Botticelli's bare maidens, Michelangelo's David. It was a day when Loretta's enthusiasm was so infectious it seemed to inject new life into every old church Chukker had sworn he'd never go near again. Before entering the hotel lobby, Loretta turned to cast a last look at the shimmering marble bands of the Duomo.

While Chukker checked at the desk, Loretta went ahead to their suite. As a frock-coated porter handed her a corded packet of still more papers and mail, the cord suddenly snapped, and the Palm Beach *News* unfolded at Loretta's feet. The paper's cover featured the same wedding picture that had been on the front page of the Richmond *Times Dispatch*. But the headline this time bore no resemblance:

### MYSTERY WIFE WHISKED TO EUROPE

The words so startled Loretta she didn't realize she was still stooped as her eyes flew over the page.

MOUTH speaks . . .

Harrison W. Dunbar, for many years one of Palm Beach's most prominent residents, has whisked his mystery bride of nary a month right from under our curiosity. Rumors are rife that $$$$$$$$$$$$$$$$$ion-aire Dunbar, who was crippled by a massive stroke and felled by another before recovery, has already settled a hefty handful of those $$$$$$$$ on his young nurse-companion-wife in return for continued services. MOUTH learned from friends who have seen the couple in Paris and London that tanker tycoon Dunbar looks frail and wan, while Mrs. Dunbar looks more nubile than nurse. MOUTH's same sources say she is proficient at being proper especially when prompted!

Harrison W. Dunbar is one of the few Palm Beachers who has added to an inherited fortune. Nobody knows the $$$$$$$$$$$$$ controlled by Dunbar Enterprises, which of course is Harrison Dunbar. And now Nanny's???

Loretta's tears made welts on the shiny page. And each tear that fell made the words look bigger and meaner.

When Chukker entered the suite, he had only to glance at the headline to have read the entire story. Kneeling next to his wife, he gently pulled her arm from over her eyes. Like a coiled spring, the tear-wet sleeve sprang back as she tried to cover more tears.

Chukker wanted both to kill and to console. He was a madman and lover gone wild. So many words pounded in his head that he was lost for a single one. That oracle of the gutter had swilled it all. He knew as he skimmed Mouth's column that he would have to explain to Loretta somehow.

To have at his command everything except an antidote to the poison pen was devastating to Chukker.

Maybe he should have told Loretta more—more about his money, about outsiders wanting in. What should he tell her now? Where should he begin? She already knew that he was important, that he ran an immensely successful corporation. He couldn't expect her to understand the oil market any more than he could expect her to appreciate the intricacies of mergers and acquisitions. But to tell her only part would be meaningless. Perhaps he would sit her down with the Musketeers one day. They were masters at making complex issues seem simple.

But it wasn't so much the business aspect that worried him. It was the money: what he owned, what he earned, who wanted it; what money bought; what it could never buy.

"Dollars? Dollars? What do they mean? Do they mean I cured you so that I can kill you?"

He looked at his sobbing bride with a pity so intense that it created desire. Agonized, he tore at the newspaper, unintentionally ripping their picture down the middle.

Loretta grew calm as she began to grasp the implications of the Palm Beach *News*'s story. If the place was as wicked as its newspaper, then that's what it would do, tear them in two. "It says 'resident.' Is that true?" she asked without looking up.

Chukker wasn't quite ready to say yes. "Loretta," he said, holding her tightly, "I love you."

Loretta nodded. She understood that. But what she also understood was that something could destroy their love.

"Why didn't you ever say you lived there?" Loretta broke away from his embrace.

How could he explain that he hadn't told her because he was afraid he might frighten her? Only Chukker knew what

Loretta would see with her own eyes once she was there and how much good Loretta could accomplish.

Chukker folded his arms around Loretta's body once more. "Loretta, darling. Listen to me. Listen closely." His voice was soft and solid, his sentences short and measured. "I have never mainly lived 'there.' Besides, I never *have* to live anywhere—ever." He kissed her ear, her neck, her hair, but when he moved to turn her head toward his, the sudden set of her features told him not to try.

"How can you live around people who lie like that? Why?" Loretta's voice was hoarse.

Seeing her so fragile, like some sapling against the wind, an erotic energy again surged through Chukker's entire being. He suddenly realized that the very same toxins flicked by Mouth could be used to prove to Loretta that all the gossip was entirely without foundation. Hadn't Mouth claimed they'd been to Paris and London? A blatant lie.

Gently, he raised her head from his chest. Unable to bear the sorrow on her face, his eyes traveled past Loretta, through the room to the wide-open window. He had been aware that the day was almost gone; he thought to switch on the lamps, then decided against any intrusion on their nightmare, knowing that interrupted dreams were the ones remembered.

Pulling Loretta up beside him on the sofa, Chukker took her limp hands in his.

"Loretta, listen to me. I must show you that the lunacy and lies of 'Paris' and 'London' are not for us but for people who can't touch us."

"Why do they care? Why?"

He rested his chin on her hair and ran his fingers along her back, tracing her spine through the hot silk. "You find good and evil all over," he said quietly. "Just because Big Luke is bad doesn't mean that God is." Chukker knew if

Loretta was distracted by her own thoughts and only half-listening, he could reach her more easily by saying something she'd heard before.

"Those lies, Loretta, have nothing to do with you—nothing, my darling. They would have been said about anyone I married. And not because these people are against me, either." Chukker took the foulard from his breast pocket and wiped it across his face and neck. He wasn't used to perspiring.

Loretta moved closer into Chukker's embrace. The more he said, the less she seemed to understand.

"Tell me why, Chukker . . . ?" she asked again.

To say that the reason was simply that he was extraordinarily rich, with a name extraordinarily well-known, was not enough. To say that he was news merely because there was never any real news about him would confuse her more. It would all sound the way he felt at this moment: crazy. To tell Loretta she would one day make midgets of the gossip-Goliaths around her could hardly reassure her. God damn it, Chukker thought. "Why?" is right. Why? Somehow, Chukker's dream of having Loretta walk into his world with a sense of security she'd developed for herself was not going as he'd wished.

Chukker began to tell Loretta a little bit about everything. He told her that he was rich, without revealing the extent of his wealth and power. He told her how he was part of several different worlds, although he didn't really live in any of them. He explained how his family was "in land," in "the land's resources," and how he had started a tanker business with friends from Athens to ship those resources. He described some of what John Carstairs and Tony Minetta and Peter Nicholas, the Musketeers, did for him. He told her of the buildings he owned, the malls he'd developed, the discount chains he ran.

"Like K mart?" Loretta asked.

Chukker smiled yes.

"K mart was Mama's favorite place for makeup," Loretta said from the middle of her thoughts.

Chukker rocked her slowly as he continued. "Palm Beach is an extension of my youth, my past. It has always been a way of life, for some. Especially for those who took early retirement from Princeton." That made Loretta laugh, finally. Chukker stifled a huge sigh of relief.

"Listen, darling," he went on, "the Palm Beach routine of doing nothing successfully for a living can be helped by the Lorettas of the world." He smiled tenderly as she gave him an incredulous look. "You'll see what I mean, I swear it." Picking up the torn Palm Beach *News*, he slapped it with his hand. "Soon this trash will not only be endangered but extinct." Chukker crumpled the paper into a hard ball and hurled it at the wall.

Once more, he told her how much he loved her . . . how proud he was of her . . . how he always would be.

Then he told her about Donina.

"She has lived in Italy for years—since the war. She's American—not quite apple pie, but you'll see." Chukker grinned. "You'll love her, and she'll adore you. She's like you. Courageous and smart."

As he continued to talk, the tension slowly eased from Loretta's body. Caressingly, Chukker lifted her chin and again kissed the dried tears from her cheeks. He was overjoyed as her mouth opened into a smile beneath his lips and she leaned forward to encircle him with her arms. Still entwined, they rose from the settee and led each other to the turned-down sheets, to the bands of colored marble bathed in moonlight.

When Chukker called Rome he was told, "The contessa

has already gone to Capri. To Villa Donina." He rang her there.

"You and Loretta must come after Rome," Donina insisted. "And you know, I know no 'no.' "

Chukker knew. "Good, then. It's set. Couldn't be happier."

"I cannot wait to see you, to meet Loretta."

Donina hung up, abruptly as always, so her caller wouldn't have time to reconsider. Chukker could just imagine her racing to the guest room, throwing the windows open to the sea, making sure that all would be perfect for them.

As it happened, it was better that the Pope and not Donina was in residence while Chukker and Loretta were in Rome. Since there were so many sights to see, Loretta wouldn't have had much chance to be with Donina. Also, her time alone with Chukker gave them a new closeness in the wake of what had happened in Florence. As Loretta kept her shutter finger clicking, she wondered how anyone could ever really have believed "the glory that *was* Rome." In fact, the present glory so moved her that she lit a candle in Saint Peter's and prayed to the *Pietà*.

# 13

**M**oments after Chukker and Loretta arrived at Villa Donina, Sergio, the butler, bowed and handed them fluted glasses of champagne. Loretta felt giddy before even taking a sip.

Contessa Donina Caldoni looked anything but a contessa to Loretta. Contessa! Not that Loretta had ever met one, but those she had read about never looked like Donina. Donina resembled an incredible, wonderful gypsy. It wasn't so much what she was wearing as how much of it she wore. Her hair was the color of a layered sunset, and her makeup was a splash of each container on the many trays that crowded the marble counter in her dressing room. There was enough silk in her long, flowing caftan and enough jewelry jangling on her wrists for two Doninas. Especially fascinating, Loretta thought, were the mismatched features that together became something marvelously appealing, and the theatrically husky laugh, still so sexy. It was impossible not to be entranced by Donina. She embodied an aura of immediate fun; an attitude toward life that invited emulation. It was her searching eyes, however, darting and circling like dragonflies on a quiescent pond, that lured Loretta. Casting about, Donina's eyes caught everything, even as they managed to avoid being caught themselves.

Although there was a bit too much flesh underneath the yards of shimmering brocade, Donina moved the way a cherub might waltz from a Veronese canvas. Her tiny feet, balanced on impossibly high stilettos, almost danced their way to Chukker.

Villa Donina was much like its namesake: alluring, exciting, alive. Built high into the hills above the Mediterranean, the large, high-ceilinged rooms opened into each other as well as onto balconies, making the house feel much more expansive than it actually was, while the distinctive mixture of palettes and patterns, blended by man and by God, recalled Capri's grandeur in Tiberian days.

In the corners of the sun-filled rooms, plants in giant faience vases bloomed nonstop and on the walls gold-framed mirrors reflected paintings of mischievous monkeys nibbling from tables laden with Flemish feasts. Everywhere Loretta looked there was some entrancing object to pick up, to touch, to feel, to look at again.

Moroccan archways led to a tiled terrace surrounding a rock-hewn pool. Loretta gasped as she looked down at the cerulean sea and watched transfixed as luxury ships, looking more like white dots, moved lazily around the marina.

When the champagne glasses were nearly empty, they were discreetly refilled, their bubbles rising to just the right height. Delectable hot tidbits filled with something or other were passed around, and before Loretta had time to swallow, whatever it was melted on her tongue. The exquisite, undersized napkin with an embroidered *D* and lace border couldn't possibly be meant to be used, Loretta thought. Appreciatively, she smoothed the cloth with her hand.

Suddenly, Donina held her champagne glass high and clinked it with her rings. "To the first Triple Crown in twenty-five years! To Secretariat! *Salute!*" Her long, satisfying sip left perfect red lips on the thin crystal. "Can you believe, Chukker, that I still know the name of the first Triple Crown winner? Not because of so fine a memory but because of so good a teacher." She looked at Chukker, then laughed her intoxicating, ageless laugh. "He is impossible, you know?" she said to Loretta; then, "Ask me the name, Chukker. Please. Ask me who." Afraid he might not, Donina went on. "Sir Barton! I am right, no? I have not forgotten." Like many Americans who haven't lived in America for many years, Donina spoke with an indefinable yet unmistakable accent.

Sergio, seeming to appear from nowhere, handed Donina a large lacquer frame. "Loretta, come," Donina said. "I have something I want you to see."

It was a photograph of an American sailor with his arm around the waist of a small, exotic woman. The woman didn't look young, but it was obvious that Donina never really looked young until she got older.

"We have not come through badly, hmmm?" Donina asked, turning the picture to Chukker. Then she looked at Loretta again. "My darling, this picture was taken before you were born. Here. Right here, down there." She pointed. "There were different ships there then. It was horrible, but wonderful—the beginning of the end. Of the war, not us. No?" Again the laugh. Donina squeezed Chukker's hand.

Loretta stared at the picture. She had recognized Chukker immediately—not simply because she'd seen so many of his old photographs but also because the strong features and firm build were still so evident. She had also recognized Donina at once. The smile, the confidence, the aura of fun that were here now were there then. Even the eyes, those all-seeing eyes, had been there back then.

"We'd landed with the limeys in Salerno, almost thirty

years ago. 1943. Thirty years . . ." Chukker said, his voice trailing as he looked at the picture, seeing instead the ships and exploding shells, the red beaches and endless sea of bodies.

He also saw a pretty redheaded woman whose junk-laden necklaces swayed heavily over her peasant blouse, pulled daringly low. She was yelling at a man in a bib-top apron who at the same time was yelling even louder at her. Each was shaking with rage, each oblivious of the patrons at the street-side tables behind them. As the man raised his hand, the woman's eyes flashed, and instead of backing away she moved toward him. When his palm struck her still-railing mouth, she moved even closer so that her gathered saliva would hit its target. The man moved toward her again, but suddenly Chukker pushed between them, and the white-aproned body sank between tables.

The gypsylike woman stuck her spiked heel into the man's crumpled ribs, then rose on tiptoes to kiss the chivalrous sailor. "Thank you," she said. "It's inadequate, I know, but thank you."

Lieutenant Dunbar wasn't positive, but he thought that what he heard was perfect English.

"If you're here on leave, I'm sure this wasn't at all what you had planned for Capri." Although she was clearly undone by the man who'd slapped her, and who was now groaning on the pavement, there was a spark of humor in her eyes and a tugging quality to her laugh. Lieutenant Dunbar couldn't take his eyes off her.

Born poor, born Polish, born somewhere near Detroit and sometime between the Model-T and the Jazz Age (but nearer the time of the Model-T), Donna Pitowski had acquired an unheard-of divorce and an unequally unheard-of college degree before she met and married Mario Latta. Like his "Donina," Mario too was self-made, a successful oil geologist at the time the war broke out. Just a few months after their marriage, Mario learned that his parents had been killed while working for the Italian resistance. Within days, Mario left for Italy to take up where they had gone down. And then when the ultimate happened, when Donina learned that Mario too had been killed, she felt that she had nothing to live for but liberation, nothing to do but continue Mario's cause. That was a little more than a year before the day she first met Chukker.

Obviously, Chukker was not aware that the man whom Donina had screamed at, spat upon, and spiked had failed an urgent mission for the Allies. Since the whole world was mad anyway, this yelling American misfit with her flawless Italian made at least as much sense as the lunacy of war.

Even in that first wild encounter, Chukker saw a sympathy in Donina's toughness, a dignity in her tartiness. Therefore, weeks later, when they were lying in bed and Donina leapt up in the middle of the night, Chukker wasn't really surprised when she begged him to help her. "We have to find a boat. Any boat. But please don't ask questions," she pleaded. "Just believe it's desperately needed. Please, Chukker, you must help me." Although her tone had turned from lover's to warrior's in seconds, he was relieved rather than upset. It helped him locate what he thought might be misplaced feelings, and made him less fearful of their depth.

Donina lit the stump of a cigarette, put on a robe, and began walking about the room. She looked from the window to the sea as her mind scrambled to understand why this man was different, why she was reluctant to use this one, knowing that he of all of them could probably be the most useful. And this time she hadn't really wanted to leave his bed; but she was afraid not to. Huddling into herself, she blew trails of smoke out to the dark sea. Religion, she knew, often made a sin out of love. But suddenly all her own goals, all her reasons for being in Italy and doing what she was doing, were forcing her into the same kind of sin. Wars may bankrupt morality, she thought, but by God they don't stop whatever she was feeling. Yet like the others, Chukker would soon go, and she must remember that all that mattered was the resistance.

"The man who must escape," she told him, "is a leading American intelligence agent. Your assistance could make you a great part of history. That's exciting, no?"

He wanted to say that becoming a part of her was the only exciting thing he could think of now. "Yes," he said.

Chukker knew that it was absurd even to dream of finding, let alone camouflaging, a boat. The shore wasn't exactly crawling with high-speed Chris Crafts waiting to whisk fugitives to safety.

But Chukker's desire for her was great, and if it is true that desire is father of the deed, then Donina's indomitable will would surely be done. And so it was. And after the impossible mission was completed, when Donina again lay in Chukker's arms, she remained there. Her feeling for him was stronger than ever. And it was at that moment that she told Chukker something he would believe his whole life long.

"Chukker, my darling, somebody's more than somebody else only after he's done more." How akin, Chukker thought, her street smarts were to the manor smarts of his father, whose wisdom he would never forget: "Princes can learn no art truly but the art of horsemanship. The reason is, the brave beast is no flatterer. He will throw a prince as soon as a groom."

Although Donina's and Chukker's backgrounds were as disparate as could be, Donina, like Loretta, was a woman born to be anybody. Therefore, when Donina and Chukker's friendship turned to love, a love of never not needing or wanting the other, it was a true love that could have happened anywhere, anytime, with or without a war to inspire it. As it happened, the war made their love into a series of constant partings and passionate reunions. Chukker almost didn't mind, because he knew they would one day marry. Donina knew they would not.

It felt as if the whole of Italy were crowded into the Grand Piazza when the giant loudspeakers roared the news of capitulation. Hugging, kissing, sobbing, all Capri reverberated with an instant insanity. Imprisoned emotions thundered loose, and the frenzied mob cried with joy. But the tears flowing from Donina were different.

"Don't ever be ashamed to be wrong," she said into Chukker's ear, unable to face him. "It's the only way to learn." And suddenly, as Chukker clutched her frantically, she broke from his embrace and disappeared from sight. Chukker, crazed, searched futilely through the raging hysteria in the Grand Piazza.

Once he was back home in America, Chukker desperately tried to contact Donina's family. Somewhere near Detroit, she'd said. But she had lied about their whereabouts to protect her own future. In the end, she had continued to lie for Chukker's sake. It wasn't until much, much later that Chukker realized that Donina had been right to leave him.

Wilson was ten when Kate and Harrison Dunbar took him to Europe the first time, and it was during that trip that Chukker had his first postwar reunion with Donina.

A dog-day heat had swallowed most of Italy and was beating mercilessly on the pebbled beaches, vineyards, and sagging olive trees of Capri. The carnival of characters fuming and fanning under Cinzano umbrellas were worlds away from the scene Chukker had last witnessed in the Piazza Umberto.

Although the thought of running into Donina had flashed through Chukker's mind, it was Donina, with obviously no such thought at all, who spotted him first. Upon hearing that voice laughing out his name, Chukker assumed it was his imagination, and that this little rift with reality was fit punishment for wanting to revisit the past when the present was so wonderful. Hadn't Donina told him, "You can never walk through the same garden. Never again will the same flowers bloom"? Yet as the voice came closer, Chukker realized that this was no fantasy.

"It is the lieutenant, no? Yes! My God! *Chukker!* CHUK-KER!" Donina's parasol fell as she ran to plant those perfect red lips on Chukker's. For the first time since she could remember, Donina was unable to believe her eyes.

Breathlessly, amid tears and hilarity, introductions hurtled forth. In mere moments the war, the boat, the resistance, nearly the whole story was recounted, and an awesome happiness had settled on the entire group.

Donina raised her hands to the heavens. "Madness. Sheer madness, no? Like the war. Like everything is. *Impos-SI-ble*. Like everything that happens every day." In no time they all found themselves at Villa Donina for lunch . . . for dinner . . . for a week.

Donina, it turned out, had not returned to America after the war; she had remained in Italy to rebuild the rubble, repiece the lives—and to marry an Italian count so rich and noble that the Vatican came to *him*. She had met him during the war, when he too had been with the resistance, and Donina had known nothing about his background until after their marriage. So like Loretta and Chukker. So like Loretta.

In the years that followed that chance reunion, Chukker and Donina never again lost touch. When Count Caldoni died racing his red Ferrari in the Grand Prix, it was Chukker who came and comforted Donina, and when Kate passed away, Chukker's extended business trip never would have been possible had he not first found solace from Donina's returning his words of "Live for the living."

It didn't surprise Donina at all that Chukker, unlike so many of his generation, who squandered their inheritances, had not only left the family fortune intact but had increased it more than tenfold. Hadn't he found a boat when there was none to be found? And as Chukker's business affairs forced him to travel farther and farther around the world, it was at Donina's that he would stay en route. And what kept their friendship perpetually in bloom was that they both knew better than to walk in what was no longer their garden.

How lucky for Loretta that Donina was in Capri! Only Chukker knew what good friends they were bound to become. Donina had already experienced and survived many of the same fears that Loretta faced—yes, Donina could do much to help Loretta, without Loretta's even realizing that she was being helped. To Donina it didn't matter what people didn't know; what mattered was that they cared to learn.

Even in the few days Loretta had been at Villa Donina, little escaped her focus. In the same way that she was making Chukker feel a young man again, he was making her a woman. Slowly, she was beginning to collect the attention of those around her. It was her frailty as much as her strength, her awkwardness as much as her grace. Sometimes when she spoke it was as if she knew where every word was going; yet whenever she asked for assistance, the world reached out to help.

There wasn't any doubt in Donina's mind that the faux tortoise mats, carved salad crescents, and thin-stemmed wine goblets that set her own table would one day adorn Loretta's—just as the Italian high-tie sandals, halter sarongs, and basket bags were quickly beginning to become Loretta's own style. It wasn't just that Loretta knew what style was but that she instinctively knew what was style for *her*.

One morning after Loretta had been at the villa almost a week, Donina asked, "My darling, please do lunch today. I forgot, I must visit a friend who is sick. Sergio will show you what cloths, mats, silver. Whatever. And he will cook whatever you want. What your appetite says, mine will agree." She looked up at the sky, then counted her fingers. "We shall be eight." With a double kiss in the air and a clanking of jewels, she was off.

She wanted to be gone before her all-seeing eyes registered the panic in Loretta's face. And it was *important* that she hurry: even though she had no sick friend to see, Donina must quickly round up five healthy friends to bring to lunch.

Loretta was unable to move or think. She didn't have a clue what or how to order. Like most people, she confused experience with worth and inexperience with inadequacy. It was all the more disorienting to think that she was helpless in a world where the living was easy.

All at once, as if she had rubbed a lamp, adoring hands cupped her frightened face. "I thought Donina was up to something when she raced out of here," Chukker said, shaking his head. Loretta couldn't see that his smile was indulgent. "What did she do?"

"Nothing."

"Tell me the nothing."

Knowing that he would think it really *was* nothing, she didn't want to seem to be overreacting. "Nothing," she repeated. "She just wants me to do lunch. Everything."

"Cook it?" Chukker's voice was mildly mocking.

She didn't notice. "Order it. Do the table. Pick out everything. Do everything. She said *eight people*. Then she left. She went to see a sick friend." Probably not as sick as I am, Loretta thought.

Chukker walked her to where they could sit. "Only dummies have all the answers. And I didn't marry any dummy." Chukker hugged Loretta hard. "I love you so, Loretta."

It was then, at that very moment, that Loretta first felt the enormous power of a woman who is vulnerable, first understood the great strength of a wounded bird.

When Donina returned with her guests, everything was ready. Although it seemed as if Donina hardly bothered to look—as if she never entertained any thought of Loretta's inability to manage—her experienced gaze took it all in.

After introducing her straw-hatted, sarong-wrapped, gold-chained quintet of friends, all with multisyllabic names, Donina motioned Loretta to a quiet corner. Lacing her arm through Loretta's, she spoke in an airy, offhand way. To one without instinct, her tone would have made the words inconsequential.

"I just want to show you, my darling, my way. My idea. Who knows really right or wrong? All we know is what *we* like." Sometimes Donina smiled. Now and then she would laugh. Always she watched Loretta listening. Always she spoke slowly, remembering how people had sometimes spoken too fast when she herself had been learning.

"The dahlias, the stock, the phlox are perfect—just a little high for anyone to see anyone across the table, especially anyone as little as me. Though I may not like who I see, I like deciding myself." Her eyes sparkled as she squeezed Loretta's arm, as if what she said was confidential.

The height of the flowers *was* ridiculous. What had she

been thinking of? What hadn't she been thinking of? Donina had to prevent her from removing the entire arrangement.

"Stop! Darling! Stop! I am not saying this for today. I am saying something for tomorrow. Heaven knows, I had many more tomorrows than you before I knew how to put a leaf in a bowl." Donina changed her tone to one of apology. "I am sure in all this mess you could not find luncheon napkins— and, of course, once you found these, they are so beautiful with the flowers, why look more?"

"I thought at first that they were too big. It's just that the colors, as you . . ."

Donina lifted the red wine from the coasters. "Every Italian," she said, feigning annoyance as she tossed her hennaed curls toward the noise in the next room, "goes crazy if it is not a little chilled. It is their hot blood—the wine must be chilled to help keep the temper cool." Her brows arched heavenward as she pushed the kitchen door with her hip, a bottle in each hand.

Before lunch was announced, Donina refreshed her curls, her scent, and her lips. When she sat down, she looked coquettishly around the flowered centerpiece into the eyes of the man across the table.

Even though lunch consisted of all the wrong foods, it was all right with Donina, since Loretta told her she'd ordered what Chukker had ordered throughout Italy—for dinner, however, not lunch. When Loretta saw that most of the food had been left on the platters and the small portions that had been taken had mostly been left on the plates, she knew for sure she was no dummy, although she wasn't sure that being a dummy wasn't better.

Several days and dinners, luncheons and lessons later, Loretta and Donina were sitting atop the polished teak deck of one of the luxury yachts that they had so often seen in the sea below the villa. Watching the geyserlike spray of the ship's wake, Donina clasped Loretta's hand between her own palms.

"I never had any children, Loretta. It seemed that when I wanted to, it was the war, and when the war was over . . ."

"You would have been a great mother, Donina. The best—the very best!" Loretta was surprised at the sudden strength of her feelings. For whatever reason, she had assumed that Donina was one of those women who had a nephew somewhere who every so often, around the holidays, came home and collapsed into Auntie's arms—and vice versa.

"Loretta, you are the first—child-woman? woman-child? whatever you are—who has ever made a regret pass through my mind. Of course, had you been mine, I would have shielded you from everything that makes you you." As she squeezed Loretta's hand too hard, Donina let out a laugh that filled the air. But it wasn't her usual laugh. This laugh could just as easily have been tears.

Whatever Chukker had told Donina about Loretta, Donina knew that there was still much more to know—more than even Chukker suspected. Nobody understood better than Donina that Loretta was no ordinary orphan. Besides the extraordinary instincts, there was an intelligence no school could teach, and a strength that could be gained only by passing on one's own the toughest course that life has to offer: survival.

As their host crisscrossed the decks delivering introductions, an oiled flex of muscles came to stand near Donina and Loretta's chairs. Making sure that his jock bikini got as close to Loretta as possible, the stranger kissed the air above her hand and thudded bare heels. As he squatted before her, he positioned his heavy-link chain to dangle between Loretta's breasts. His error was groping to retrieve it.

Before the man knew what had happened, he had toppled into a contorted heap. As he started up, a similarly swift, sharp movement drove him permanently away.

"Brava! Brava, Loretta!" Donina hailed, as she watched Loretta fight as she herself had fought years before.

When Loretta's immediate anger subsided, she became nearly as frightened as the stranger who'd dared to insult her.

"He was insulting Chukker too," Loretta said. She thought about what he had wanted and what she had done, and her breath began to come in gasps.

"You are loyal, but a bit too brave," Donina said. "They don't always limp away."

Yes, Donina thought again, there was much about Loretta that she didn't know. Much more than nice and good and smart. Whatever Loretta's past had been, her future would be much more interesting because of it.

On Loretta and Chukker's last night in Capri, after the rest of the villa had gone to sleep, Donina and Loretta sat alone under the stars, above the sparkling marina below. As they talked, Donina's face and body stiffened. Her voice grew tense. An urgency entered her tone, as if she had only a few moments to impart a lifetime.

"The beauty of growing old, Loretta, is a myth," Donina said. She wasn't sad; simply honest. "When I was like you, I would look at older, experienced women and believe that if I were like them I would know and have everything. So much time I wasted wanting! Never waste time wanting, Loretta. You above all, Loretta Dunbar, you must behave rich from the start. Show them from the beginning. Anyway, my darling, do not waste time wanting, and know that the only good thing about growing old is that the alternative is worse." Again, Donina's laugh sounded teary.

As the moon freed itself from the clouds, Donina's face, though tired, looked stunningly beautiful. The crags and valleys of her friend's world seemed to Loretta deeper than the moon's and even farther away, but it was a world Loretta wanted to explore. A breeze, cold as sand after sundown, made Loretta draw her shawl close. Then, as the moon disappeared once more, she again felt safe in the darkness of the night. Staring straight ahead, she spoke haltingly but clearly.

"When I was seventeen . . . my foster father . . . he was a monst—. . . a minister . . . not a *real* minister . . . real, but not really . . . he was evil . . . he lied . . . he drank . . . he pretended to heal . . . he didn't heal . . . he made *me* heal . . . I didn't heal ever. . . ." The jerked words were flat, uninflected. Loretta saw the altar, Luke's crazed hulk, his drunken stumbling toward her, on her . . . her voice grew as chilling as the night breeze.

"I begged him . . . he'd have killed us . . . I begged him to . . . or he would have killed us . . . Mama . . . me . . . us . . . but all Mama heard was my begging . . . begging him to . . . pleading with him to . . . begging . . . then he was on me . . . at me . . . in me . . . *Mama!* . . . MAMA!"

When Loretta said "Mama," her voice was like that of a child pleading for help.

Donina opened her arms and Loretta, exhausted, huddled into them.

The horror had come out. It had, hadn't it? She had told Donina, hadn't she? Please, God, these *are* Donina's arms, aren't they? Please.

Still cradling Loretta, Donina spoke to the same darkness. "During the war, Loretta, I did many things . . .

many, many things. The doctor in the emergency room told me it was fortunate that I lived. I did not think so. Not for a long, long time. Not until Roberto. Happily for me, Roberto was so much a child himself that he never wanted the child that I could never give him. You are much luckier, my darling . . . much. You will see."

Already Loretta felt stronger. The judgment she had expected and had feared so long had instead taken the form of a special bond that now existed between her and her confessor.

Capri was just awakening and the sapphires in the sea barely rising as Loretta and Chukker stood amid luggage and farewells. Loretta knew that there would never be a right time to say goodbye to Donina, never a time when she would want to leave her.

As the sun continued to unwrap the early dawn, Loretta felt uneasy standing next to the woman whom she had told the worst about herself. It was as if they were lovers from the previous night, whose secret could be spoiled by the growing light of morning. Loretta stared at her own too-long feet, then tugged at the sides of her too-short skirt. Fingering her blouse, she checked for open buttons.

Donina walked over to Loretta and lifted her chin. Precariously perched on tiptoe, she gave Loretta a kiss. Yes, Donina knew everything: every feeling . . . every thought.

She crooked a single finger, and Sergio appeared with the tray. She took a champagne glass for herself, handed one to Loretta, and waited for Chukker to take his.

"As you arrived, so you shall leave. Celebrating! To you, my darling Loretta. To you, my other darling. To Capri. To our meeting in Paris. To your meeting each other. To all of us meeting at all. To today—always to today."

Compared to Donina, the contents of any glass seemed spiritless even at dawn.

Although Donina's ample girth and layers of weaponlike jewelry made hugs difficult, Loretta encircled her friend as much as she could. "I love you, Donina."

Donina hugged back. Swallowing hard, she struggled to control herself. "No claiming race for her, Chukker," she said. "Not quite Secretariat." Then slowly, "Not quite yet."

Before Loretta got into the car, Donina pressed a tiny drawstring pouch into her hand. "For your bracelet," she said. "They say he's the saint of the impossible, and I say between the two of you the word might cease to be. Anyway, my darling, everyone needs a little push. And remember, you always have me, the really impossible."

The motor roared . . . pebbles crunched . . . kisses and waves were thrown back and forth. And over it all rode Donina's laugh.

# *14*

As Loretta sat cross-legged on the picture-littered floor of their stateroom, pasting almost a year's worth of photographs into albums, she heard that laugh again. It roared from a blown-up print of her and Donina watching Chukker dance with the star stripper at the Folies-Bergère.

Loretta laughed herself as she pasted it in.

### HARD-CORPS DE BALLET & CHUKKER
### PARIS

"When was this? November?" Loretta mumbled, the pen in her mouth.

"It never was," Chukker said.

"Too bad it's just black and white. God, you were red!"

"Typical frame-up. Didn't take you two long."

Rising from the floor, Loretta carefully threaded her way through Austria, Germany, Switzerland, France, Britain. Luckily, the rest had already been put between the plastic pages.

"Frame-up?" Loretta said, miming the stripper's motions as she kissed Chukker. "It's all here. All in these expensive albums." She meant to say "exquisite." Like a shot she remembered. She hoped she hadn't triggered Chukker's memory too.

It had been one of those rain-mad London days, the kind that fill shops with customers.

"Why, I can't believe my eyes, but it's indeed a sight for sore ones! Mr. Dunbar—my word, I'm happy to see you, sir!" Mr. Drew, the stocky, gray-haired salesman, pumped Chukker's hand. Asprey had been serving Dunbars for as long as both the firm and the family had been in existence, and Mr. Drew had been helping Mr. Dunbar since before "Master Wilson" was born. Mr. Drew was not only delighted to see Chukker but delighted to meet the lovely new "Missus."

"Please, this way," he said, leading them toward leather goods in response to Chukker's request for photograph albums. In a moment the counter was filled, and in seconds Chukker had made his choice. Mr. Drew smiled. He had known without looking the one Mr. Dunbar would select.

When Loretta opened the cover she recoiled at the price. "Two hundred pounds!" she said without thinking. "That's crazy! Why so expensive?"

"Exquisite, not expensive." Chukker's voice was low and flat.

Mr. Drew took a chamois from the drawer and wiped the immaculate leather.

"How much is two hundred pounds exactly?" Loretta asked.

"A tenth of a ton," Chukker said.

"Tell me, Chukker."

Chukker snapped the album shut, and at the same moment something snapped inside his head—an absurdity that he had to tend to, deal with once and for all. Loretta's confused attitude toward money was largely his fault, and he was determined to change that. It had gone on far too long already.

Before they left Asprey, Chukker ordered not one album but four, of the larger size, in bottle green. Mr. Drew would have them sent straight over to the Connaught.

On their way back to the hotel, a relentless downpour drummed on the roof of their car. Chukker remained silent, lost in thought about what Donina had said: "Make her behave rich."

Loretta was thinking about Mr. Drew. She thought of how he had talked about Wilson, reminisced about the old days, stirred Chukker's memories. This was obviously the explanation for Chukker's mood. She thought, too, how lucky it was that no lettering had been ordered for the albums, because when Chukker came to his senses, the albums could be returned.

Chukker chose to head for the Connaught bar rather than return to their suite. He wanted to have people stop by their table. For the first time since their marriage, he wanted friends and acquaintances to emerge from the high-gloss mahogany woodwork. Instant enlightenment was in order.

"A Beefeater martini, stone cold and straight up." Chukker placed this uncharacteristic order and then turned to Loretta.

"I'll have coffee. . . . No, I'll have tea. . . . No, wine . . . white wine with soda and ice."

Loretta was relieved that Chukker had ordered a drink, for it precluded that his mood had anything to do with feeling sick. And when Chukker pulled his hand from under hers, it was only because he wanted his drink, she told herself.

Loretta wondered who all the people were who kept coming to greet them. Why were they all approaching, and

why was Chukker so willing to be cordial and have them
linger? And why did they all seem so deferential? "Money
likes you, my friend," said a dark young man with a long
last name and an English-educated accent, his smile accompanied by a knowing nod.

"We respect each other," Chukker said, smiling back.
"And we're smart enough not to fall in love."

The young man didn't budge. He wanted to hear more.
"Ari is sure you are Greek," he laughed.

The two men talked about how Chukker's tankers held
an unreal quarter-of-a-million tons . . . about how Chukker
knew to fill them before the embargo . . . about how he *was*
actually probably an Arab. They laughed together.

Only when a couple approached with effusive greetings
did the awestruck young man finally leave. With all these
important-sounding conversations going on, Loretta couldn't
understand why nobody ever mentioned Watergate. It had
been front-page news in all the papers since they'd arrived
in London, and now, with the possibility of impeachment so
near, this silence on the subject seemed impossible. Only
later would Loretta learn about Chukker's links to the Re-
publican party, about his family's generations of generosity
to the elephant's trunk. Chukker Dunbar had been among
those who had accompanied Nixon to China. And if Chukker had wished it, he could have been receiving those same
visitors as ambassador.

Interrupting the flow of names and faces and the efforts
at vibrancy, Chukker ordered another martini, straight up,
and then another. By the time they left the bar, he was
tighter than Loretta had ever seen him. In fact, he almost
tripped over the package from Asprey that had been placed
inside the door of their suite.

"What you have been witness to, my dear Loretta,"
Chukker said thickly, misjudging the height of the sofa as

he plunged down, "is a part of Chukker Dunbar that you have not seen. This is to some extent my fault . . . possibly all my fault. Maybe I've gone too far in protecting you from what I know you don't want to know."

The way he spoke made her tense. It was altered and wobbly, as it had been when he was in the hospital, yet he sat stiff and erect, trying to frame his next words.

"Sit, Loretta. . . . No, don't—first pour me a gin." He was glad she wouldn't. He managed to get up and fix the drink himself; he wanted it just in case.

"I'm a very rich man, Loretta—you have no idea how rich. Therefore, *you* are very rich. *We* are very rich. I live rich. We live rich. But it takes up here to enjoy it"—Chukker tapped his head. "It's like roses. Like horses. After you have them you must use this"—again he tapped his head—"to enjoy them. Listen to me, Loretta. Listen to me very hard. Only after the poor get rich do they tell you the most important thing in life is love."

Loretta thought she knew what he meant, but she wasn't sure. The only thing that was sure was that she couldn't understand how to deal with this. Her thoughts shot back to Asprey's. She was embarrassed at what she'd said. Yet she couldn't help having that gut reaction. The last time she remembered seeing a price on a photo album was when she was with Mama. The album had roses on its laminated cover and cost a dollar ninety-eight. Seeing a price four hundred times that much made her recoil. She had no idea what their trip was costing because bills were never discussed. In fact, they were rarely presented—just sent on. The immense sum would have been unintelligible, anyway. And even though Chukker was now telling her how rich she was, in her head she was still poor.

"Donina told me she talked to you about how to behave. Do it!" Chukker swallowed his drink. "God damn it, Loretta! Do you know what I'm talking about? Ask me something!"

"How rich are you?" Loretta blurted, running her hands through her hair, digging in with her nails, knowing that what he said wouldn't make any difference, for how could she compare this to anything she'd experienced?

"Rich enough to have time for flowers and for love. Rich enough to make people jealous and envious and greedy. Rich enough for money to be a responsibility—which is not to be confused with a liability. Do you understand at all? Do you?"

Loretta pressed the Saint Jude medal Donina had given her and squeezed her eyes shut. For the first time since she'd married Chukker, she began to wonder, to doubt, to question not only her own values but Chukker's. Just who was Harrison W. Dunbar, Jr., and why did he love and need her? Opening her eyes, she pushed those thoughts out of her head.

She looked at the big package from Asprey and turned to Chukker. "I'm going to take these all back tomorrow afternoon. I'm going to have our initials put on them before we go to dinner with the Chatfield-Taylors."

As Loretta brought her comic yet sexy mock striptease to an end, the heel of her shoe punctured a large, glossy photo. It stuck like a piece of newspaper on a sanitation man's stick, but she didn't move to take it off.

"But as we know, my darling Loretta, not too expensive for us," he said as he kissed her. "Right?"

Loretta threw her arms around Chukker's neck. "As London rain. Right-right-right." She nipped his ear and hugged him again.

Not until their last night on ship were the albums finished and packed away in their boxes. As Loretta gazed at the other boxes lining the walls, her eyes stopped at one of Chukker's hatboxes, and she winced as she thought of the difference between Big Luke in his Stetson and Chukker in those tweed caps he wore at Rosefields. She remembered their trip to Lock's in London. Loretta had never seen so many men's hats. How Mama would have loved this store where the bowler was invented, whose biggest customer had been Charlie Chaplin!

Loretta grew excited thinking about the bird cage, the rent table, and other purchases she'd made the times Chukker had gone off for business and she'd decided to roam London alone. The first day on her own she'd passed the bird cage in Mr. Reffold's window on Pont Street, and for almost the entire morning he'd described how the wooden, steepled house had been in the Brighton Pavilion, how it was a unique triumph of Regency design, and how she must visit the Pavilion before she left the country. She remembered feeling proud when Mr. Reffold told Chukker about her good eye and her swift grasp. It was Mr. Reffold who had mapped out the stately homes and who had instructed her that "a room starts from the rug up." And after seeing the stately homes, Loretta knew what he meant.

Even Chukker was startled by her eye and urged her to buy more. Although her purchases remained modest, to Loretta it seemed as if she were acquiring an impossible amount. "When we redo the other house in Palm Beach" —Chukker was careful not to say the "big" house—"you'll see it will all fit. I know you can't believe it now, but one day that home will be more than just *my* dream, darling. It may be even more yours than mine."

Loretta smiled. This house in Palm Beach was not only Chukker's dream but also another way of his being kind. She knew that if it weren't for Chukker she'd never have the courage to set foot in Florida again.

Chukker told Loretta that they would be in Palm Beach for Easter, after a brief stay in New York to meet with his Musketeers, his Wall Street gurus, and, he hoped, to see some theater. He needed time, too, with his old friend Randy Hearst; there had to be some way he could help with Patti.

Although he said she could see forsythia, dogwood, even magnolias from their Fifth Avenue apartment window, somehow Central Park still sounded foreign. He said, too, that before they tackled "the other house" they'd stay in the beach house, "where the Atlantic pours through the door and sunsets come hand-blown from Venice."

"Let's never be too busy," Loretta murmured.

"We won't," Chukker said, knowing that no one, not even Donina, had warned her sufficiently of the Palm Beach trap that can close out the outside world.

As moonlight filtered through the porthole, Chukker lay awake, gazing at Loretta. Who was she really? What was it about her that was so constantly compelling, so naive yet far wiser and better equipped than she knew? Where was it he wanted her to go? After nearly a year of flowers and love, what exactly had Loretta cut and pasted?

# PART IV

# 15

It was the kind of day that Palm Beach real estate agents would have you believe lasts forever. As Loretta took her sneakers from the closet, she threw one up in the air out of sheer joy.

Yesterday the tennis pro had told her again he couldn't believe she'd never held a racket before. She wanted so much to be good, to improve, to make Chukker and herself proud.

Although more than a week had passed since the Carristas' Easter party, Loretta still had trouble sleeping. Images kept whirling—the carousel, the fountain, the people—while she saw herself somewhere in the middle, pushed and pulled, held back and suddenly released. It was blindman's buff, and only Loretta could see. And what she saw was an orphan.

As she drew a white polo shirt over her head, she could hear Chukker shouting on the phone. "Embargo! And what about Arco, and those gas lines we'd planned?" His conversation was spliced with "sonofabitch," "screw the bastards," and "blow them out of the water." The classy fighter was at work, using every punch but the low blow.

With a last look in the mirror, Loretta decided to wear

her shirt outside her shorts the way Angela Seagrist did.
Loretta didn't wear a visor, because she didn't yet know that
in Palm Beach only tourists get tan.

The slap of the papers against the kitchen door brought
an immediate response from Essie. Servants were always the
first to scavenge for gossip and were as fiercely competitive
about "their" people as "their" people were among themselves. One society daily even came wrapped in plastic in
case an errant gardener might misdirect his hose. And, as
legend has it, that paper's only rival had switched from
rough to shiny stock lest any ink blacken milady's linen as
well as her brain.

Today was indeed a day for celebration in the Dunbar
kitchen. A photograph of Mr. and Mrs. Harrison W. Dunbar, Jr., filled the entire front page of the Easter issue of
Palm Beach's bible, the same glossy rag that had once
caused a flood of tears in a hotel room in Florence. But not
today. Mouth knew that Loretta was here to stay, and since
Mouth wanted to do the same, her words dripped honey.

Essie, still wearing her slippers, scuffed into the living
room, smiling broadly as she spread open the picture of
"her" people.

Chukker's immediate reaction was to grab the newspaper
and rip it to shreds. Then he realized that Loretta hadn't
connected today's edition with the paper in Florence. She
simply stared. Essie began to babble.

"Good-lookin' people, my people. Some good-lookin'
couple." Essie removed her wire-rimmed glasses and squinted
so close that her nose touched the print. "How often I tell
you, Mr. Dunbar, no need you whippin' the devil 'round the
stump, just come out with it. If you'da said how mad you
was 'bout them takin' your picture, you'da had it out and
woulda been smilin' when they took it."

How right Essie was. Chukker remembered nearly exploding at the bursting bulbs.

Loretta didn't even remember the picture being taken. As she looked through the other pictures inside, she wondered why she'd ever worn that orphan dress. She had other clothes. So what if it was Easter Sunday.

"I'll know better next year," she said aloud to herself.

"Not to go?" Chukker asked.

"Not dressed like that."

"You lookin' like a young girl should—don't she?" Now Essie's nose was in Chukker's face.

Like a teenager wanting to look older, Loretta was angry she looked so young. How embarrassed Chukker must have felt! But why hadn't he told her that her clothes were wrong? He knew Palm Beach.

"Why didn't you tell me not to wear that?"

"Wear what?" Chukker seemed amused. At least he wasn't still upset.

"What's in the picture."

"Why would I have done that?"

"Because it's wrong. It's awful. It looks funny."

"*You're* funny," he said, patting her shorts. Such displays of innocence made her as exciting to him as she'd ever been.

"I mean it," Loretta said, again studying the other pictures. "See. See what these women have on. Why didn't you tell me?"

"Come here."

"I'm here."

"No—here." Reaching from his chair, Chukker tugged at her waist. "Here, to my ear. I want to whisper."

"Don't mind 'bout me," Essie said.

"Do you want to make love?" Chukker whispered.

"I love you."

"That's not an answer."

"You haven't answered me yet."

"Forget what they're wearing. You're best with nothing on."

Loretta noticed a blinking light on the phone. "Chukker, do you have someone on hold?"

"My God! I can't believe I did that! See what you've done? Give me a kiss and a rain check." He won't believe it either, Chukker thought. Then again, maybe *he* will. "Hello, Nelson? God, I'm sorry! Jesus Christ. Sorry, but you'll under—"

Loretta began to apologize, then realized, to her own astonishment, that she wasn't actually sorry. That her questions seemed superficial to Chukker didn't make them any less real or important to her. Sometimes they seemed even more important.

Loretta threw the white sweater around her shoulders and looped the sleeves the way Christina Knox did. Then, ever so gently, she pulled Chukker's mouth away from the receiver and brushed his lips goodbye.

The maroon Mercedes convertible, Chukker's Palm Beach present to Loretta, glistened with a Beaujolais brilliance as it stood before Dunesday. Loretta loved the name of their beach cottage. And she loved its coziness, especially compared with the formality of the big house, which had been boarded up since Kate had died. You could hardly see the long barrel-tile roof of the old stucco house behind the high-hedged and whitewashed coral-and-limestone wall. Although a two-lane road separated the mansion from Dunesday, an underground tunnel made walking across the road unnecessary.

As Loretta drove along South Ocean Boulevard toward the club, sunshine splashed against the waves on one side and floodlit the mansions on the other. It was a sight at which Loretta would never cease to marvel. Though some of the houses along the road were hidden like Chukker's, most could be seen awakening to the gardeners spraying the lawns and butlers walking the dogs.

Another visual wonderland was Worth Avenue, Palm Beach's main shopping street crammed with elegant boutiques, grand galleries, and the Spanish flavor of winding vías. Loretta loved watching the women in their daytime linens link arms as they went from shop to shop, trailed by chauffeurs waiting to carry their purchases.

Before going to the club, Loretta stopped to buy Chukker something that she'd spotted in a window the day before: a teddy bear with a flashing heart.

"I'm sorry, Mrs. Dunbar. It's only for display. It's not an item we stock. It's a display for our animal carrying cases."

"Please?" Loretta asked. "I'll buy you another. I just want this one with the heart." Her voice was pleading, but not in a spoiled, rich way. Anyway, rich ladies didn't plead; they demanded.

The salesman smiled indulgently. "We'll gift wrap it for you and you can stop in for it later."

As he took it from the display, Noreen Newirth tapped on the outside window. Standing beside her were Michael and David, Julietta's decorators, who often accompanied Noreen when she showed houses. Loretta waved them all in and gave Noreen a big hug.

Loretta was truly happy to see Noreen. It would have surprised her to know that Noreen was just as glad to see her.

"All right then," the salesman said, holding up the flashing bear, "when would you like to pick it up?"

Loretta blushed crimson. Noreen and Michael and David were seeing what a dumb thing she was buying. "It's kind of a joke present," she explained. "It's sort of a thing that Chukker and I—"

Spontaneously, Noreen kissed Loretta. "Look," she said, laughing. She unwrapped a box containing a leather thermos with a label that read, "Press Lord for Holy Water." "See, you press the word 'Lord' and the spout pours. I just this minute got it for my saintlike husband, whom I always kid about the holier-than-thou editorials in that newspaper of his. Now tell me that's not stupid."

Loretta was delighted by it, and delighted Noreen liked her. "I adore it."

"Going or coming from tennis?" Noreen asked.

"Going. Do you play?"

"Never enough time."

"Want to come to the club for lunch?"

"Thanks. Too busy today. But let's do have lunch. Soon." She knew Loretta didn't have a clue about the club.

"Anytime," Loretta said. "I mean it. Please." Again, the same pleading.

"You bet." As she had at the Carristas', when she'd first seen that young face with the prematurely aged eyes, Noreen felt a kinship with Loretta.

Loretta wondered if all the people who drove past the club knew it was there, if they realized what lay beyond the simple black sign with gold letters spelling out "Private." She wanted them to know, because she wanted them to know that she belonged.

As she waited for the light before turning into the club grounds, Loretta again got that alien feeling. She tried distracting herself by making believe that she was one of those hardhats strapped to that giant palm, pruning coconuts from its royal column. But she knew that when she drove inside, beyond the guard, beyond reality, she would be anything but one of them. Once, just once, she wanted to feel that she really belonged somewhere. If only she knew how many of this particular club's present members had pasts that would tarnish those golden letters with but a breath.

The guard, so used to spotting the club's sticker on the windshield, seemed as if he weren't looking. Loretta immediately interpreted his lazy nod as rejection.

As she drove by, she listened for the sound of tennis balls from the courts and anticipated the scent of lavender from the locker room. She loved using the talcums and creams and the extra-thick, extra-large towels. She was still too new not to be seized by the urge to take one of the club-crested towels home, never quite believing she would come back.

Loretta adored wandering through the clubhouse itself, into the vast parlors filled with the oversized grandee furniture, floor-to-ceiling tapestries, and thick Oriental rugs. She craned at the tree-high plants soaring from giant tureens and wished Mama could see the abundance of fresh flowers that gave everything a sense of luxury.

Before leaving the locker room, Loretta again checked what she was wearing. She didn't want today to be another Easter.

"Great picture, Mrs. Dunbar!" Max, the pro, called out. "See you in a couple of minutes, okay?"

Damn. Even Max had seen it. "Okay."

Loretta watched the girl Max was teaching. God, she was good, her strokes so long and clean—like Loretta wanted hers to look.

Christina Knox removed her feet from a chair so that Loretta could sit. "You'll play better than that," she said truthfully.

"Thanks."

Loretta wondered why Christina was wearing her sunglasses on the top of her head, especially since she was squinting.

"You and Chukker looked super in the paper."

"I hated what I wore."

"I didn't notice."

I'll bet, thought Loretta.

An ambulance wailed to a sudden stop near the courts. The first time Loretta had heard this all-too-familiar sound she had instinctively run to help. Then she learned that if she ran every time she heard a siren at the club, she'd be doing nothing but running, since the average age of the members was deceased, or so it seemed.

After her lesson, Loretta met Angela for lunch on the patio next to the eighteenth green. "If it's a choice between watching the old farts putt out or going to the beach to see a lot of people as hung over as you, give me the farts." Angela had been referring to the other club, a beach club, where the daily luncheon ritual seemed to center on how many "bloodies" they needed transfused into them to get them through the day.

Angela was already sitting with Nicola, a dark, youngish man with strong Mediterranean features. When he jumped to his feet and planted a lingering kiss on Loretta's hand, she guessed that he was one of those "working men" she had met in Capri, about whom Donina warned, "Beware—their kind have branch offices."

Maggie and Jamie Pearsal, visiting from California for a week, were also at the table. Somewhere along Angela's mother's marital mile, Maggie had become Angela's half-sister. To Loretta, it seemed that everybody in Palm Beach had more halves than wholes. It also seemed that what everybody really wanted was to be once and forever removed.

Both Pearsals were in their early thirties, but alcohol had covered just enough of Maggie's youth to make her ponytail cuteness sadly out of sync. Still, there was no denying the Pearsals had that look—class. Had Loretta ever seen them on the streets of Tampa or any other city, she would have been struck by their looks and would have reflexively watched them. What Loretta didn't realize was that they would have singled her out as one of them.

"I hope I get lucky when I'm that old," Jamie Pearsal said, referring to Chukker. He held a chair for Loretta.

"You are that old," Maggie answered.

"Please, please. All morning. All night. Stop." Angela sighed, motioning to the waiter.

"How did you hear?" Maggie asked, jabbing Nicola.

"Were you aware that your sister was a wit?" Jamie asked.

Angela blew three perfect smoke rings. "Rhymes with 'it.' And imagine her, with all the discrimination of a Hoover. Until you, of course, Jamie."

Loretta couldn't believe that such private matters were made so public, and all so lightly.

"Now that you've met a bit of my family, Loretta, how about drowning them with a north wind?" Angela asked.

"What's a north wind?" Again, Loretta felt the outsider, even though few of the club's members could have told her the drink's contents were light rum, lime juice, and that special dollop of honey—a recipe imparted to the club bartender by John Ringling himself.

"Witches' brew," said Jamie, Groucho Marx–ing the blond eyebrows that nearly melted into his skin. "A little rum-a-dum-dum and magic."

"Wild as the wind," Nicola said, whirling his *w*'s.

"He's funny too," said Jamie, raising his glass.

Angela let the ash of her cigarette fall on the zipper of Jamie's flowered pants. "To help your garden grow."

"Family wit runs rampant," Jamie smirked.

The north winds came and went and came again. Even just half a north wind was enough to make Loretta feel the blast. Although two full glasses stood on the table in front of her, still another round was ordered. Crayolas kept coming over to the table too, each of them staring at Loretta, wondering what she'd really done to get Chukker.

As hands flew and crest rings collided, Jamie gagged at Angela. "For chrisssake, Angela, you're blowing enough smoke to screen Miami."

"Remember Father's definition of Miami? 'Palm Beach without us'?"

Loretta knew that the "us" didn't include her. She slowly finished her first drink and moved on to the second.

"Who do you think finished Miami?" Jamie asked. "Give up? The Castro pervertibles."

"You're disgusting," Angela said.

"I'm disgusting, yet all anyone here says is how the Jews and spics are ruining Palm Beach. Christ, a Jew can't even come to this precious club to eat its rotten food! Your wonderful guest rule: Don't bring anyone who won't be welcome as a member. Salk and Sabin can stop their kids from having polio, and then those same kids can stop those same Jews from coming through the gate. If a member were dying inside the club, would his Jewish doctor be allowed in to save his life?"

"Nice, isn't it, Loretta?" Angela asked.

Loretta didn't answer. She couldn't believe Jamie's words. She prayed that it was liquor lying, because she wanted to like this place, and the people here seemed to want to like her. "What's it like living in California?" she asked, looking at the Pearsals and hoping that no one would notice her attempt to change the subject.

"Our state of the golden poppy?" Jamie replied, leaning back to launch forth. "Could you ask for a more appropriate state flower? Where else could you find so many body-beautiful, vegetarian health nuts stoned by noon?"

"Right here," a new voice boomed. "And if I may be so uncouth as to drop a name into this smart little group, I'm Sam Bayberry." Sam managed to drag a chair over from the next table without spilling a drop of his drink.

"Invitation only," Jamie said, moving to make room.

Loretta was delighted to see Sam. His vagrant charm seemed especially appealing now.

"Reckon it's right, what Jamie says about California," Maggie said, her southern accent stronger by the sip. "I worry so for the children. What are they anyway but little mirrors?" From the way she listened to her own words, one could tell that this was the first time she'd had this brilliant thought.

The more that was said, the less Nicola understood, and the closer he moved toward Angela, caressing her, kissing her.

"What Mrs. Pearsal is trying to say," said Sam, enunciating each syllable, "is that it's she who pays the schoolmaster, but 'tis the schoolboys who educate her sons. She *is* the one who pays the schoolmaster, isn't she?"

Even if it hadn't been poor old Sam who'd said those words, Jamie wouldn't have responded. Anything short of physical assault, anything as unimportant as an attack on his character, didn't bother him.

"Jamie, honey," Maggie said, "tell them what Reagan said. Tell it straight, word for word. Go on, say it. Tell Angela. Tell Sam."

Why didn't Maggie say, "Tell Loretta?" Loretta had even leaned forward to catch Maggie's eye.

"Listen. Listen, everybody, to Jamie. Listen t'him tell how our great Governor Reagan answered those Symbionese Liberation people."

Jamie tilted his chair back. "Remember what they asked for—food for the poor? Know what our genius governor came up with? You're not going to f-ing believe it. 'Too bad,' he says, 'we can't have an epidemic of botulism!' "

"The higher the monkey climbs, the more you see his ass," Sam Bayberry said, his fingers scaling the pole in the center of the table.

"And they're talking about running him for President!" Maggie screeched. "If California's the edge of the hor-ri-zon, give me the brink of diz-aster."

"So let's hear it for sunny Florida, famous the world over for its sweet-talking state bird, the mocking-. Now that's even more appropriate than your flower." Sam made more sense drunk than most people did sober. "And to make it really big in the land of sunshine," he continued, turning to Loretta, "to really be able to fit into those velvet slippers and rounded heels, you gotta follow that fine, sentimental tradition of the broken promise."

To be part of the conversation, to join in at last, Loretta heard herself say, "My father used to tell me, 'The only way to keep a promise is to never give it.' " So what if she was really quoting Jane Austen?

"You're in the garden spot for that advice." Sam laughed, lifting his glass. His bitterness made Loretta sad.

"You know, Loretta," Jamie said, "I'd've liked you poor."

"Don't get carried away," Maggie said.

When at last it was time for lunch, they ordered the kind of food that people who like to drink eat. Tempty, spicy things: chili, welsh rarebit, steak tartare, anything with Tabasco—and always prepared differently from the way it was on the menu.

"No beans."

"In wine."

"Not toast. In a potato shell—crispy."

"Tell him it's for me. Then he'll know no anchovies."

Loretta was in the habit of lunching with just one person, Chukker, and lunch usually lasted no time at all. No one here ever finished until the day was already well into the afternoon. As a waiter loaded the last tray, Sam grabbed somebody else's half-filled drink and gulped it so fast it was back on the tray before the waiter even noticed.

"Did I ever tell you," Jamie said, "about the Pope's niece? The no-a-nice-a niece. Not-a nice and sweet like Loretta. She gave her vow and kept it, but not to the church. That's what made her a no-a-nice-a Pope's niece."

"You know, Jamie," said Sam, "you oughta drink more, before that western weed strangles instead of just tangles your brain."

Loretta knew that Sam was trying to protect her, but she didn't want him to do it in any way that might make Jamie and Maggie angry at her.

None of them saw John Murphy and his trio of geriatric annuities approach the table. For Murphy afternoons spent on the course were always more lucrative than those spent in his office. And who knew better than Angela that Dr. Murphy's emergencies seldom had anything to do with hospitals?

"How's the nineteenth hole doing?" Murphy asked.

As usual he was the only one to think himself funny. Loathing pounded in Angela's head when she heard his laugh.

Loretta would never forget the gold fox-head buttons and yards of pink blazer he'd worn on Easter. But the outfit Murphy wore now was special: it redefined "preppy." Murphy caught Loretta staring at the club-seal cap, the emerald-green club-shield shirt, and his cornflower-blue pants embroidered with pheasants.

"You know good taste, Loretta," he said, nodding approval. To him stares always meant either admiration or jealousy, depending on the sex of the starer.

"If it isn't our mating call to the jaded," Sam said.

The others in Murphy's foursome were members of the vanishing old guard, gentlemen whose whole lives had been made up of better days. Still, they were savvy enough to know how to use a John Murphy while letting a John Murphy think he was using them. A midday golf game assured a midnight house call. Only John Murphy believed it could be a wedge into dinner.

They were more than friendly to Loretta. After all, most of them had married women like the woman they assumed Loretta to be, and therefore she belonged among them more than a John Murphy ever would.

Maggie cupped her hand to her lips. "Loretta, see the man with the hole in his shirt? That one there?"

The hole, Loretta thought, was nothing compared to the parts: the enormous paunch, the at least day-old stubble, the colorless madras trousers.

"His granddaddy set up a railroad six miles long just to carry the marble for the bathrooms in a castle he was building in North Carolina. They say it took an army almost five years of work before the place was good enough for the whore he married."

"And that one there just married some kraut who's supposed to do more tricks with a prick than Heinz with a pickle." Jamie's brows arched double-time.

"Howdaya know?" Maggie drawled.

Loretta didn't care what they said. She cared only that they were choosing her to confide in.

"Anybody dined yet?" Murphy asked as he parked his haunches next to Loretta, an arm dangling around her shoulders.

There was a time when Angela would laugh whenever Murphy misused words she'd taught him, but now his gauche stupidity merely reminded her of her own for ever having had anything to do with him.

Only Loretta replied with a yes. The others couldn't believe that he had the nerve to stay at their table.

"Want some good Palm Beach advice?" Murphy asked Loretta. Without waiting for an answer, he said, "Try to be just like Angela. Do everything she does."

Angela's good breeding prevented her from making a scene. And Murphy knew it.

"Nothing could make me happier," Loretta said, pleased at the comparison.

John Murphy patted her head. "Smart girl. After all, who better could you be when you grow up?"

Angela's eyes were wild with rage, and her jaw was so tight her teeth hurt. A swizzle stick snapped in her fingers.

John Murphy put his other arm on Loretta's shoulder and gave it a squeeze. "Here's my last word. Forget the old wives' tale about Palm Beach doctors being too busy for house calls. Anything, anytime, anywhere—Triple A, that's me." He looked directly at Angela as he spoke. "Nothing I wouldn't do for Chukker, and especially his wife." He kissed Loretta's cheek, touching the corner of her lips, as he straightened.

"Whore!" Angela Seagrist said—more a grunt than a word, pushing their wrought-iron table so hard the ashtrays crashed on the terrace stone. Hurrying away, she sent a chair flying as her purse strap caught its arm. Maggie rolled her eyes toward Jamie, then ran after Angela.

"See you in the office, Loretta?" John Murphy called, loud enough for everyone to hear.

Loretta had no idea what had happened, but she knew that suddenly her world had dropped away. She was too shocked to follow Angela and Maggie—to apologize, to explain. But to apologize for what? Explain what?

"Angela's nuts," Sam Bayberry said to her. But Loretta knew that Sam was being nice again, like one cripple to another.

"No insanity like a woman scorned. The whole family's a little—up there," Jamie said, touching his head with the ash end of his cigar, assuring Loretta that he had married into the right group.

Maybe they were all sick, but at the moment nobody felt sicker than Loretta. The thought that she might have done something awful to someone she liked, and without even being aware of it, frightened her. A web of perspiration dripped down the back of her neck. All she wanted was Chukker to hold her, to take her back to Europe, to Capri, to Donina.

With Sam limping at her heels, still begging her to believe that Angela hadn't meant her, Loretta walked in a daze to the parking lot. If she waited to have the car brought up front, she might run into Angela and Maggie.

The late-afternoon sun was low in the sky, and the mottled sliver of the moon was newly visible along the ocean. The mist through which Loretta drove had nothing to do with the sea. Wiping tears from her eyes, she remembered the bald patches on her no-eyes teddy, patches that had been flattened by just such tears.

# *16*

"Yes, whore! Whore!" Wilson shouted at his father. While Loretta lunched with Angela at the club, Chukker had called for Wilson at the airport. Only a few days earlier UPI had summoned Wilson Dunbar back from Buenos Aires. After brilliantly predicting the Allende coup in Chile, Wilson had become the agency's numero uno in South America. Now, however, with the story of Nixon's impending impeachment not just hot but wildfire, Wilson's experience and energy made him a perfect Watergate ferret.

Although Wilson had been raised in Palm Beach, the only time he'd been back since Harvard was when his mother had died. Not that he was some renegade of the rich, sitting at John Galbraith's knee disdaining "private affluence." Chukker had taught Wilson well the importance of money, how "wealth will always summon the knife to carve a slice of social conscience." And what better place to do it, Wilson had always thought, than Palm Beach—Palm Beach, the only city in the world where the charity ball reigns as the leading symbol of culture? Wilson wondered how long before Loretta would become its queen.

Chukker knew early on that Wilson had no inclination toward Dunbar Enterprises. Wilson listened; he understood; he was proud of his father. But even as a little boy he had squirmed on his father's lap whenever Chukker had talked business. The excitement of the deal provided no thrills for Wilson. He believed that writers saw the world a little more clearly than anyone else, and that it was his own duty and privilege to make other people see it that way too.

Chukker Dunbar was not disappointed that the twig never bent toward the tree. Failure would have disappointed Chukker, but not the fact that his son wasn't like him. The purpose of Chukker's life was not to perpetuate his name through his business. Through Wilson, yes; and through whatever good Wilson and Wilson's children might do.

"It's standard operating procedure for nurses—especially one with her history," Wilson said, frustrated not to be getting through.

A happy surprise was turning into a nightmare. What Chukker had hoped might be the occasion for Wilson to get to know and love Loretta was already a disaster. He could barely listen to, let alone look at, the lanky, pacing figure. Wilson was actually beginning to look as ugly as his words. Ordinarily, Chukker would hardly have given the rumpled reporter's garb a second glance, but his son's constant railing against Loretta made him appear disgusting.

Wilson hated having to tell his father about Big Luke, but seeing Chukker so fooled into happiness created the same despair in him as his words created in his father. "For chrissssake, Dad. Look! Listen! Her own father threw her out! You yourself told me you were almost dead when you took her in. Dad, I know when you—"

"Don't 'Dad, look' me! Don't tell me that you know, because *I'm* the only one who knows. I *was* a dead man. Not *almost—dead!* And when *she* never wanted to see me again,

I died again. Not because I was sick—because I was well, that's why! And I'd be dead now if it weren't for her. This is no mercy marriage, rescuing some orphan from a storm. This is love. And *I* was the beggar! Do you understand? *I* was the one who pleaded! And I'd do it again now. Harder. Better. Because I've never been better. Ever!"

Again Wilson slapped the decade-old poster featuring Loretta's picture. "Then tell me about this. Tell me about what her own father told me. Tell me!"

That Wilson Dunbar had even spotted the poster with Loretta's picture was proof that destiny is controlled by coincidence. Back only one day from Argentina, he was on his way to a Key West motel where Nixon and Bebe Rebozo were secretly meeting to decide which members of the White House staff to make sing in order to keep "Hail to the Chief" for themselves. Instead of driving on to Bill's Marina, Wilson took a left into Big Luke's Miracle Mass.

The poster was of a much younger Loretta than the woman Wilson had met, but there was no doubt it was his father's wife, just as there was no doubt in Big Luke's twisted mind that Wilson was an undercover agent investigating child molesters.

Before Wilson even had a chance to utter a word, Big Luke looked to heaven, made the sign of the cross, and began. "Only He knows how I snatched that poor babe from the streets, and only He knows the suffering I've endured all these years, fearing the day I'd have to throw her back where she belonged. Poor soul, just never was any good. The only reason we use the old poster, and if you'll forgive what I mean, is that it still pulls 'em in. And once they're in, I figure the good Lord'll take over where the devil left off. . . ." As the words tapered, tears fell and Big Luke sobbed. "After her young years, after she got grown—I guess you'd say 'developed'—there wasn't a town where she didn't make more money outside the church than she'd collected in His own house. Finally, things got so bad I just couldn't hide it from her dear Mama, and that's when I did what I had to do." Again, Big Luke squinted through tears. "And now, if you'll excuse me . . ."

At the wedding, Loretta had seemed almost shy, but Wilson was now convinced that his suspicions were true. For his father's sake, he'd wanted to be wrong about Loretta. Talking to Big Luke convinced him how right he was. He was aware that women like Loretta were not new to his father. Even today, Wilson could hear the special voice his father had used on the phone when talking to women he knew weren't his mother. It was something many children know, just as they also know that their fathers will never marry these women—unless those fathers are desperate, are about to die.

"For God's sake, Wilson, don't you think I know about that lying, cheating, sonofabitch father?"

For a grief-filled moment the eyes of father and son locked. Each of them sensed the impossibility of reconciling their differences about someone each knew the other didn't really know. So involved were they in their thoughts that neither of them heard the door. So involved was Loretta with hers that at first she didn't notice Wilson. All she wanted was to see Chukker, to be with him. Gratefully she threw her arms around him. Ever so gently he turned her around.

"Darling, you missed the surprise."

As far as Loretta knew, she didn't know the surprise. She stood stone still as Wilson tried to smile. Then all at once the eyes and grin told her. Not that there was much of a grin, but the eyes were so like Chukker's.

Embarrassed, she smiled back. "It's the beard," she said. "You didn't have one at the wedding. It's almost as big a shock as seeing you." She couldn't decide between a kiss and a handshake, so she offered neither. "When did you get here?"

Wilson stared at Loretta, at those almost noble cheekbones and at the grace with which she moved. And the—yes, God damn it—class. It wasn't what he remembered from the wedding. And she looked nearly as young now as she did on the poster—almost childlike in a way. He noticed how his father's eyes fixed on her with the same protective look he'd used when Wilson himself was little and wounded.

Wilson tugged at his left eyebrow. "I've been back a couple of days. Since impeachment rumors started going wild."

Loretta smiled politely, barely listening. She wanted desperately to have Wilson like her, but at this particular moment she wanted even more to be alone with Chukker. She wanted him to tell her what she'd done to upset Angela. She ached to call Angela right now and invite her to something grand to see if she'd come. She wanted to behave rich. What could she have said or done to make Angela call her a whore? The only other person who had ever called her a whore was Big Luke.

Chukker knew Loretta was upset, but he didn't want to ask about it in front of Wilson. He grew even angrier at his son—not just because of the lies, but because Wilson was rendering him powerless as well.

"With a million stringers on Watergate, why do they need another?" Chukker asked Wilson. "Why take the hottest journalist from the hottest spot in the world and drop him down as an also-ran?"

"Because the hottest does the story best. Only the best *can* do the best. You know who taught me that? You." Wilson knew his father's tactics, and he knew how to respond to them.

Once more Loretta realized something was happening that she didn't understand. Today, it seemed that everything was beyond understanding, or at least beyond hers. She looked from father to son and became so frightened that she hugged her arms around her body to stop it from shaking.

Seeing her so helpless, Chukker couldn't resist going over to her, holding her. "Whatever it is, my darling, it isn't anymore," he whispered.

"But you don't know. You have no idea what Angela—"

"Angela? I don't know Angela? I have no idea?" Chukker forced a laugh, to soothe her anguish.

Wilson saw the way they touched and talked, the ease with which their emotions entwined. Loretta seemed so natural, so unaffected. She seemed the kind of girl every man wants, the kind of companion his father had needed long before his stroke.

Suddenly the door burst open. Never before this moment would any Dunbar have believed that the arrival of Mary Dodd could provide a welcome release. Balancing a martini in one hand, she clutched a leash in the other, trying to restrain a high-stepping poodle who held a thick vellum envelope between his firmly clamped teeth.

"Van Cleef and I just took the chance," which she pronounced "chaunce," "but that of course is what life's about. Well, I do hope you'll forgive me—us." Her layers of cheeks shook with each precise syllable. After kisses to the room, Mary Dodd sank gracelessly into the sofa. The chiffon of her hat mismatched the garden on her dress, which in turn caught not a single color of her strapped stilettos, making the sum effect that of an international bazaar. Van Cleef seemed adequate proof that four-legged Palm Beachers had the town's best pedigrees.

"By the most incredible coincidence I knew that Wilson

was here—not that I would have recognized him with that camouflage."

Wilson barely stifled a smirk. There were few coincidences in Mary Dodd's life. Her informants were legion. Loyal they were not, however, and her profligate spending was beginning to make Mary fear that she wouldn't be able to keep them paid off forever.

"My camouflage is especially for you, Mary." It had taken only a moment for him to be reminded how she embodied everything he hated about Palm Beach. "But I would have recognized you anywhere. Like Ol' Man River."

"Thank you, Wilson. I accept the compliment, and believe me, I'm grateful still to keep rolling."

"And getting a cut from the house." Wilson's smile was overly disingenuous.

"You should keep that spark for your writing, dear boy," she retorted, smiling back.

Again, Loretta didn't understand. That everyone in Palm Beach knew everyone else was clear. So far, however, she had hardly experienced what one might call a sense of neighborhood.

"How about a drink, Mary?" Chukker asked. Always the gentleman, he refrained from saying "another."

Mary extended her glass, and as she did she noticed Loretta eyeing her gloves. "My good friend, the queen mother, who at the time was queen, of course, warned me about those nasty little sun spots. You know the English and their skin." The longer Mary Dodd lived, the more regal she became. Her real reason for wearing gloves was that her hands, unlike her surgically lifted face, looked as though the queen she referred to might have been Victoria.

"You just know that mother was a queen," Wilson lisped.

Tossing her head, Mary Dodd called to Van Cleef and freed the cream-colored envelope. "This is no ordinary invi-

tation, my dear Loretta. This is an urgent appeal. This is a
We Want Loretta! A We Need Loretta to Co-Chair Our
Feather Fantasy!" She lowered her eyes as her voice faded
away. "Sadly, the lady who was going to do it died."

"Not for the cause, I hope," Wilson said.

Chukker held his smile as he watched Mary roll on.

"You were demanded by our other co-chairman. Naturally, you were also my first choice. And, Loretta, when I
say 'demanded,' I mean, my dear, nobody else will do."
Mary Dodd's speech was now almost feverish. Delivering
Loretta Dunbar would be a coup almost worth having killed
the lady who died. "You know, many people never realize
that underlying our marathon of gaiety is a whole world of
philanthropy. And it's those poor pitiful Indians who'll be
the lucky beneficiaries of our Feather Fantasy. Isn't that just
a wonderful name for those sad little Seminoles?"

As Loretta unfolded the cream-colored vellum, a tiny
red feather fell to the floor. Her eyes read no further than
the name Angela Flagler Seagrist. Unless she was the one
who'd died—and that would have had to be within the last
hour—Angela had never demanded her. Loretta felt sicker
than ever.

"And since Angela knows I'm here, if you'll say yes now
I'll call her with the good news."

"When did you last talk to her?" Loretta asked, the
invitation shaking between her fingers.

"Angela'd be with me now, only the silly girl's undone
over some scene with that Irish vulgarian at the club." Mary
Dodd's head shook with disgust.

Over the next few minutes it was made clear to Loretta
who had done what to whom. Once she understood, Loretta
was ecstatic about the Feather Fantasy. And Chukker was
thrilled that Loretta was happy, as well as relieved that
Wilson had shifted targets.

"Mary," Wilson said, wishing his pointed finger were an arrow between her brows, "you know I think of myself as a cause-fighting journalist, but next to your good deeds I'm a hack copy boy. So today it's the Indians, is it? First we scalp them, rob them, and pump them full of fire water to burn themselves out, then our Mary saves them. How? Let me count the ways. Two for Mary and one for Sitting Bull.

"Actually, Mary, given the opportunity you'd probably have had the same generous spirit to offer them twenty-four dollars and some of your shiny trinkets for *this* worthless island. Although, considering the present populace, they'd be better off selling.

"Now tell Loretta," Wilson continued, enjoying himself, "about your Good Samaritan good deed. About that fiasco— excuse me, fiesta. About that fine event you once organized to help the poor, the sick, and the needy. And tell Loretta about the ambulance that rushed our old cook, Thelma, to the emergency room because she was sick and needy and, oh, yes, dying. Tell how they wouldn't admit Thelma because she was black. No blacks allowed into Good Samaritan Hospital, Loretta. Good Samaritan! The perfect name for that place!"

"Things are changing," Mary said, trying to maintain her composure.

"But you're not. And you're on the board, Mary, same as you were then."

"Is that true, Chukker?" Loretta asked, imagining Zinnia on a stretcher being turned away at a hospital door.

"Yes," he said. He was sorry it was true, and upset that it might make her dislike Palm Beach, make her unhappy with a world he accepted as part of his life.

"Blacks are no better off here now than when they pedaled their old wicker afromobiles," Wilson continued calmly. "Another great name. Right? Can't you just picture those old, sweating blacks as they pedaled their white masters from one watering hole to another?"

"I'd love a chance at that hospital board," Loretta said coldly.

"You've got your chance," Chukker said, seizing the opportunity, seeing how Good Sam, instead of driving Loretta away from Palm Beach, might be the very thing to hold her, make her stay and fight.

"And after you get the blacks into the hospitals you can get the Jews into the clubs." Wilson turned to Mary again. "A lot of people say that Mary here shouldn't be in the clubs, but then that's just a mean rumor about a birth certificate torn up many moons ago. Right, Mary?"

Wilson was right. Mary had been born Miriam Wolf and grew up at 1347½ Mosholu Parkway, The Bronx. When she first came to Palm Beach, there had been so many times when she had wanted to send Mama and Papa her pictures, to know that it was really their "plain" Miriam with that beautiful new nose and chin and teeth. So she had the urge to send her stuck-up Aunt Sarah clippings showing her with the duke and duchess, Winston and C.Z., Mimi, Brenda, Sonny, Jock, Rosie, and Dolly. She had wanted desperately to tell them all, "That's me in the middle. *Me*, Miriam—the good-for-nothing with the big-shotitis!"

"You know what I'm thinking, Mary?" Wilson asked. "I'm thinking about my grandfather and Joe Pulitzer. Would it surprise you to hear that they were the best of friends? I'm thinking what old Joe might have printed had he discovered that he couldn't get into your clubs because of his brilliant heritage. A good thing those clubs didn't exist then, because they wouldn't have existed for long. But how lucky for me they exist now. You know, Mary, I may win a Pulitzer yet! And if I do, I might have you to thank."

"I hope I have inspired you, Wilson," Mary said, still

smiling stiffly. Since she had no conscience to haunt her, she was hardly threatened by Wilson's churlish tone. She was also years beyond worrying about being discovered, although she never let any new churchgoing crossovers forget that she was on to their secret. Their pathetic lives, like her own, depended not only on constant denial but also on being the type of friend who'd kick the ladder away once on board.

It had been just such a friend, by the name of Langston Thomas, who had taken Wilson aside at the beach club to give him some sound advice about the "nice young man" he'd brought as his guest. Wilson was home for Christmas vacation. His Harvard roommate, Bernard Strubelman, was staying with the Dunbars. Wilson and Bernard had just come from the courts, hot and happy, after beating the club's number-one doubles team. Unexpectedly, the kindly old man with the deep, even voice of a radio announcer and the same frightening matter-of-factness banished his friendly smile and issued the false sigh that always precedes the words "What I'm about to say is very difficult."

With great ease, he continued. "Wilson, my boy—and you are like my own boy—why, I've seen you grow from a tad. . . ." He faked a small cough and another one of those sighs. ". . . What I'm about to say is something I don't like to say any more than you're going to like to hear it." A blue-blazered arm reached around Wilson's shoulders. "Rules are rules like laws are laws. I'm not saying I agree with all of them, but what we all have to do is . . ."

As he spoke, he walked Wilson out of earshot of his target. With words such as "incident" and "embarrassment" he explained how it was up to people like Wilson to change what was. "But, son, since it isn't yet changed, I'm just so, so sorry, but I'm afraid, my boy, you just won't be able to bring . . . um . . . well, actually his name doesn't matter

. . . here again. What does matter, though, Wilson, son, is I'm just so, so sorry. But let me say, I can't impress strongly enough that you never . . ."

Wilson couldn't believe the words spewing from this one-time two-bit art dealer, whose selling of frauds—himself the biggest—had consumed his life. By the time his sickly mouthwash-heiress wife had discovered that his own origins were as spurious as those of his old masters, it was too late to throw him back to the gutter.

Wilson wrenched himself free, anger surging through his body. As the smug Langston Thomas started to walk away, Wilson thrust out a leg and never once turned back as he heard the crash, the cry, the crunch of bifocals. The movement was so fleet that only Wilson ever knew who was to blame.

Riding home with Bernard, Wilson behaved as if nothing had happened. But as soon as they arrived at Splendido he went to his room, locked the door, closed his eyes, and clenched his teeth. Then, with some crazed, summoned force, he twisted his ankle until the pain was unbearable. Limping to unlock his door, he screamed for help.

"Damn! God damn, Bernard! I have no idea what happened. My foot just went from under me, and—Christ, look at the size of it! God, I'm sorry. What a fuck-up! We could've won the whole tournament, too. Wiped them off the courts." There were tears in Wilson's eyes as he hobbled toward the best friend he'd ever had.

Later Wilson had raged at his father, who in turn had raged at Langston Thomas. But even Chukker lost to City Hall. After all was said and nothing done, Wilson never again stepped his sprained foot inside the beach club.

An ironic smile now crossed Chukker's face as he watched Mary Dodd and Van Cleef prance out. Through the back of her overbleached head, he sensed that she too was smiling.

Even Loretta and Wilson wore tentative smiles. Amazing how one little ecru envelope changed the color of everyone's mood. Chukker pushed his hands into his pockets and turned toward Wilson. "Mary, whoever she is, is what your grandfather would have called a piece of work."

"Close," Wilson laughed.

"Chukker, will you get me on the board?" Loretta asked.

"You bet I will."

"And Wilson? You'll write about it? The hospitals and the clubs?"

"You bet I will. And when I'm finished, they may ride me out on the same rail that Granny's parlor car rode in on."

"I can't believe all this ugliness in all this beauty," Loretta said. "When I tell you what happened today at the club . . ."

"The club? Sweetheart, don't worry about anything at the club." Chukker smiled. "You don't have to fight there too."

"No. Maybe *I* don't have to. But why hasn't anyone else?"

Wilson's anger and resolve grew right alongside Loretta's.

"You know, darling," Chukker said evenly, "we have to live in many worlds we don't agree with, and so just try to fall in stride with those that don't lean too heavily on our day-to-day existence."

"You do, Chukker, not me. I'm not a child anymore, taking somebody's hand because it's easier than walking alone."

"And Loretta, I'm not to blame for a system that existed long before I did."

Chukker suddenly realized that he was shouting at Loretta while at the same time pushing his nails so hard into his palms that he looked down to see if the skin was broken. Why the hell was he arguing with her for all the same reasons that he loved her? Especially since the one thing he'd always wanted was for her to grow—hadn't he?

When Loretta went to give him a hug, she sensed a sadness in Chukker. It filled her too, perhaps because she felt Chukker had also realized that she could no longer rely on him for everything.

# 17

No matter how many hours she devoted to organizing the Feather Fantasy, Loretta's energy never flagged. To her, the work wasn't work, and the ball itself paled in comparison to the cause. With Angela's main involvement being Angela, and with most of the committee members' contributions no more than their names, Loretta had free rein to let loose her enthusiasm. She had no idea about the customary workings of charity functions—nor did she understand that when they were successful, their proceeds also lined the pockets of florists, caterers, tent raisers, orchestras, and the Mary Dodds who'd hired them.

And so when Loretta started comparing the prices of a Worth Avenue florist with others, she was completely unaware that she was disturbing a well-oiled cottage industry. Suddenly, the tradition of big names lending only their names while others lent cunning and greed was being challenged.

Noreen Newirth waved as the maroon Mercedes pulled up outside her office window. She watched Loretta lock the car door and smiled. It was a habit that Noreen herself still had, but something that one who'd never known poor would never think about.

The excitement with which Loretta told Noreen about her latest money-saving coup wasn't met with the plaudits she'd expected. Noreen remembered how she herself had been imbued with a similar resolve to bring changes after she'd first arrived in Palm Beach, how her background had triggered the determination to make seas part. Yet through the years, even as she watched the ethnic balance become equal, nothing that she or anyone else tried had ever changed anything behind the high hedges, the walls of bougainvillea, and the club gates marked "Private."

Noreen had suffered many hurts learning that society was the business of Palm Beach and that most of the invitations she received were because of her husband's *Pictorial*. How well she understood Loretta's intentions, her starry-eyed belief that Palm Beach was just a sweet, sleepy town rather than the drowsing monster Noreen knew it could be.

"You don't think it's great," Loretta asked, "about West Palm Planters doing the flowers at half-price? I can't believe the difference between them and the florist the committee wanted me to use. I'm already ten thousand under budget."

"Great," Noreen said, not knowing how to tell Loretta how costly these savings could turn out to be.

"You don't think they'll think it's great?"

"Who?"

"The committee."

She knew what they'd think.

"Chukker can't believe it. He's even told Wilson."

Noreen knew that the committee would hardly believe it either. As she watched Loretta now, pushing her hair back and relooping her sweater around her shoulders, it seemed ironic how much Loretta projected the Palm Beach image.

Attempting to change the subject, Noreen handed Loretta an elaborate four-color brochure featuring one of the fabled Palm Beach oceanfront villas. "Sold and signed this morning." Almost imperceptibly she shook her head. "I must say, though, the owner's twenty-year ride was longer than most Detroit legacies get before hitting the scrap heap." Again, Noreen held back. What she didn't say was that the new owner, a self-made jillionaire who would restore the derelict mansion to its old Palm Beach grandeur, wouldn't be allowed beyond the club gates that his twice-jailed, once-convicted predecessor still passed through with impunity.

Chukker had once pointed out the house to Loretta as they'd driven past. He told her how he'd visited it as a boy, when Palm Beach was an overnight train ride from New York and the Palm Beach station was the middle of town. He told her about the dinner party where a malachite sandbox served as the dining-room table's centerpiece and where during dessert and champagne guests were given tiny gold shovels to dig for seashells containing diamonds, emeralds, and rubies that they could keep for souvenirs. He told about the neighbors next door and how relieved everyone was when they finally built their Mizner extravaganza, because not until the Stotesburys came did Palm Beach arrive. He remembered his mother talking about the wedding of Mrs. Stotesbury's daughter, more like a coronation with the parade of royalty and braid—all for that social-climbing West Pointer Douglas MacArthur. All this in a town that only years before had been a wilderness of man-eating alligators and rattlers—many of whom, Loretta thought, had returned in human form.

"Should we celebrate?" Loretta asked Noreen. She couldn't have been happier for them both. "Pick a place. I have a hospital meeting at two. Chukker managed to get me on the board of Good Sam." Noreen wasn't at all surprised.

The power that came from being Chukker's wife was not squandered on Loretta. Strange, Loretta thought, Big Luke had once had power but not a clue how to use it. Now it was her turn, and she was learning from watching, from reacting, from trusting her instincts.

Her mind flew back to the Chatfield-Taylors' dinner party in England, when the chalk-skinned trophy wives had replied with arpeggios of laughter to everything the men said. The talk had centered on sanctioning the improprieties of the ruling class and sloughing off such inconsequentials as "buggering" or, as they said, "kicking with both feet." The speech, always precise and cultivated, made the conversation sound much more profound than the content deserved.

Their thin, jolly host dismissed as jabberwocky the absurdity of a woman becoming prime minister. "To quote Father," Lord Chatfield-Taylor said, " 'Their place is the home, not the Home Office.' " He looked quite pleased with himself as "hear, hear!"s and arpeggios filled the room. "Can you imagine a woman pressing the button? The women I know can't even do shirts." Again the arpeggios—but not so much as a grin from Loretta as she set down her glass of claret.

"Why wouldn't a woman press the button?" Loretta asked. Noticing that no one had paid her any attention, she began again, louder. "Why wouldn't a woman press the button?" The dinner guests suddenly looked as if they'd been unpleasantly disturbed by someone they hadn't realized was there.

"If my survival were based on the enemy's knowing that I *could* press the button, why wouldn't I?" Fired by conviction, Loretta lost her customary shyness as the other tongues fell silent. "Wouldn't you?" For Loretta the boneless fish, the undercooked game birds, even the crumbly Stilton were easier to digest than her dinner companions.

"Not quite the jabberwocky one might think," Chukker said, winking at Loretta.

Lord Chatfield-Taylor tried to smile. He couldn't allow himself to forget Dunbar's position with the World Bank, his ability to open British markets for world trade. Lucky chap, that Dunbar, building his tanker fleet at the wrong time and then having the market turn right around. Damned lucky. The Americans were becoming luckier and luckier, he thought. For the present, however, without Dunbar Enterprises, England might be forced into a nasty go with the unions, unemployment, inflation. Then God knows what might happen. There could (heaven help us!) even be a woman prime minister.

"Things are cyclical," Chatfield-Taylor said, ever so slowly nodding his head as if continuing his thoughts aloud, attempting to steer the conversation away from Loretta's question. "The old tradition of genius and inventiveness seems gone from Europe for the moment. Not Britain, but Europe."

"Gone with the Jews," Chukker said.

"W-w-with the Jews?" James Hornby asked, incredulous, squeezing his fingers over his lower lip, making his stutter even more incomprehensible.

"Yes, with the Jews."

"W-w-where did they take it?" Hornby said sardonically.

"To the grave."

Loretta often thought of that night—especially of the warmth and closeness she'd felt toward Chukker as they sat at opposite ends of the table.

On her way to the hospital, driving past the old Stotesbury place, Loretta played the game of imagining how it must have been with fifty servants, a private zoo, and handpainted menus for every meal. Then she imagined herself on the *Sea Cloud*, the world's largest private sailing ship, with perfume spray flushed from the guest-room toilets. But even her imagination could hardly conceive of Addison Mizner soaking tons of stone in the sea for months in order to give Mrs. Horace Dodge's palace a built-in touch of age. That was when Palm Beach had been just one happy little social register. Loretta wondered what kind of small minds had lain behind those huge fortunes. Had their purse strings tied them to bigotry as well as idleness? Were the inhabitants of Palm Beach merely Big Luke in fancy dress?

In the hospital parking lot a light breeze suddenly stirred the heavy air, and Loretta gratefully drew a deep breath. She turned at the sound of clacking heels and the excited voice of Julietta Carrista calling her name.

When Loretta first met Julietta that Easter Sunday, Julietta had pulled her aside. "Eet won't be easy, but eet will come. They still look at us Cubans like we're not whole. But in your eyes I see you will make it." Then she threw her waving arms around Loretta and hugged her hard.

Julietta had been the first to ask Loretta to lunch. They had driven to the beach club in Julietta's electric-blue Rolls, and Loretta had wondered how someone as tiny as Julietta could see over the steering wheel and if people driving behind her ever thought the car was driverless.

"Loretta, today most of the upper crust is just crumbs and no dough—like there, those three weetches," Julietta had said when they first sat down and she dismissed a certain trio of women with a flick of her tiny bejeweled fingers toward the bar.

"Every day those women seet there, drink there, be mean there, and wish to be the people they hate. One inherited cold cream, but her jar's been empty for years. The middle weetch was a model, now a bum. Now she calls all models bums. And weetch number three is the nicest. She doesn't talk because she cannot afford another leeft— you know, when you talk your face makes lines."

The more Loretta saw Julietta, the more she had fun yet also became aware of the seriousness, the generosity, and the kind instructiveness that lay beneath the accented voice.

Now as the clattering heels drew closer, Loretta realized that Julietta was more than excited.

"Loretta! You must hurry! Sahm—Sahm Bayberry is in emergency, and the doctor on duty is nowhere. Sahm's going to—" Loretta was through the emergency doors before Julietta finished her sentence.

The stretcher, the IV, and the stone-faced paramedics were all horribly familiar to Loretta. But this was Sam— poor, godforsaken Sam. His terrified eyes implored her, and though his lips moved, he hadn't enough strength to make a sound. Loretta held his limp hands while his hysterical housekeeper babbled on.

She'd arrived at work late. Sam was on the kitchen floor. She didn't know how long. She thought he was passed out as usual. But when she touched him it was different. So cold. Blood was on his lips. She called the firemen. The ambulance came.

Loretta's training kept her from panic. She knew that the paramedics couldn't do any more than they'd done and that Sam desperately needed a doctor. Since Good Samaritan wasn't a teaching hospital, there were no interns or residents. Where the hell was the doctor on duty? Sam's hand became ice as the minutes ticked by. "You're going to be fine, Sam. Everything's going to be great. Better than ever. God's here, Sam. It's just His warning—like the one He gave Chukker. And look at Chukker now." In quiet terror she whispered to a helpless nurse, "For God's sake, get *any* doctor—anyone. The man is dying."

Loretta's heart pounded as she watched in horror while the paramedic listened to Sam's heart, then slowly removed the stethoscope from his ears. His eyes caught Loretta's for a second, and he shook his head.

She refused to let go of Sam's hand. Her tears fell on his pallid face; tenderly, she kissed them away before she closed Sam's eyes on a world that had shut its own eyes on him long, long ago.

As shocking as the circumstances were surrounding Sam's death—the doctor on duty, John Murphy, never showed up—even more shocking was Murphy's appearance at the funeral. Loretta watched as he stared solemnly at the minister, and she knew that if narcissism were a corporation John Murphy would be its CEO.

At first the authorities were only going to censure him. Some even thought they shouldn't do that. Anybody could get a flat, get tied up in traffic. Why all the furor about Sam Bayberry, anyway? Wasn't he better off than when he was falling down drunk and insulting everybody he fell on?

Loretta, however, could not remain silent. For a new broom, she sure was shaking up a lot of dirt: first the blacks, now this. The pressure against John Murphy mounted in direct proportion to that exerted by Loretta. When the Dunbars were invited to a dinner, the Murphys were not. Club dining rooms had no table for the Murphys if the Dunbars were on the grounds.

And so the arrogance in John Murphy's voice when he asked Chukker to meet him at his office roused Chukker's wrath all the more. The only reason Chukker agreed to the visit was because he thought it must have something to do with Loretta's health.

"Hi there, Chukker, old boy," Murphy said, all smiles and enthusiasm as he clapped Chukker on the back. Murphy's large corner office, done up with the usual diplomas, family pictures, and bookshelves lined with thick medical texts, was as much of a fraud as Murphy himself.

Chukker's face, creased with character, contrasted sharply

with the bloated features of John Murphy, evident even in an old wedding picture that Murphy thrust in front of Chukker's eyes. "He's my brother-in-law, you know," Murphy said, pointing to the man standing next to Murphy's wife.

"No, I didn't," Chukker said, suddenly uneasy. He knew Murphy hadn't called him here to show him a picture of Randy Byrd.

Murphy's eyes registered Chukker's discomfort. Only in bed had Murphy ever enjoyed himself more.

"I know a lot of people say I married real good, getting into such a nice southern family. I know, too, some of those same friendly folk say my not being from so fine a family is the reason for my wife's overpartiality to the juniper berry. As a doctor who knows at least a few things about genes, I think it's just a little weakness that sometimes happens to those fine families." Murphy didn't try to hide the sneer in his voice. "It seems a lot of those aristocrats have little quirks: some for booze . . . some for boys . . . some for whores. Some just get a bigger thrill if they gotta pay."

"Pick it up, John," Chukker said coldly. He knew when sleaze was wallowing in its own slime for kicks.

Again, Murphy pointed to the picture. "Now, my brother-in-law, Randy here, has as his particular weakness tarts. He gets what you call jollies by paying and treating them the way they should be treated. As he says, 'Indecently!'"

Chukker pressed his hands on the arms of the chair, getting up to leave. "Either it's out or I am."

"Chukker, you and I know those ugly armies of gossip that seem to gather here in Palm Beach. And I know you certainly wouldn't want them launching any attack on Loretta, especially because of some weakness a weakling like my brother-in-law might have." Murphy knit his brow, shook his head, and wrung his hands in mock concern. "Sad the mistakes we make when we're young. Yet chains we forge early on shackle us the rest of our days."

Chukker's hand was on the door. Murphy, seeing the foreplay was over, came forth with the details in seconds.

Seems Randy Byrd was in Palm Beach—just a few days; family business. And if he didn't pick up the Easter *Pictorial*! Why, nobody alive could have been more shocked than Randy to see Loretta on the cover! Imagine, *his* Loretta on the cover of the *Pictorial*. At least she had been his back then. The same Loretta that *the* Chukker Dunbar had married. Of course, Randy had to tell somebody. "Lucky," Murphy said, "I happened to be the one around. Otherwise, those armies would've fired the proverbial shot heard round the world." John Murphy chortled at his own cleverness.

"Who do you think'll believe that lie?" Chukker asked, with great conviction in his tone. Steeled in board-room bluff, he also knew how to make the worm squirm before threading a hook through its heart.

Dr. Murphy tugged at his socks to avoid Chukker's narrowed eyes. "It's not me, Chukker—not me. It's Randy—a blue blood, blue grass, blue Byrd. It's your fine feathered friend from that old state of seven presidents who's the one singing."

"Would you mind getting him on the phone for me?" Chukker said, as if he were asking a waiter for a glass of water. Moving from the door, he looked again at Murphy's wedding picture. "You know, John, you've put on some pounds since then. A doctor should know better than that, but then they always say doctors never do what's good for them." Chukker slid the picture across the desk onto Murphy's lap. "Did you hear me? Would you call your brother-in-law? He's still staying with you, isn't he?"

With all the cards so clearly against Chukker, Murphy couldn't understand why he suddenly felt that it was he who wasn't dealing with a full deck. "I think so."

"What's the matter, Murphy? Forgotten your own number? Want me to dial?"

Murphy shook his head and dialed. Without a word, he handed the receiver to Chukker.

"Hey, Randy old boy. Chukker Dunbar here. . . . Heard you were in town. Sorry not to see you, but glad to catch you before you pulled out."

John Murphy watched in disbelief as Chukker smiled, then laughed into the phone. "Hear you're up to your usual tricks, old boy—tying one on and telling tall tales. Bragging, like. . . . Anyhow, that's what your brother-in-law, the good doctor, tells me. Even says you knew my wife in Washington. Someone running for the Senate should have a better memory than that, don't you think?"

Again, Murphy watched Chukker laughing and nodding into the phone.

". . . Of course, Randy. I can understand being confused by a similarity in names—especially after you've had a few. . . . Forget it, Randy, and I will, too. . . . Right. . . . I wish you a lot, too. November'll be here before you know it."

Chukker left the office without a glance or a word for John Murphy. All he wanted was to hurry home, take Loretta in his arms, and say how sorry he was if such a secret had ever tortured her.

# 18

The town talk was not only Loretta's success in swaying the board to get blacks into the hospital but also her ability to involve Chukker in these disruptive moral issues. He saw them as challenges, and when Harrison W. Dunbar saw anything as a challenge, action was taken. Weeks before the Feather Fantasy, the committee also bestowed on Loretta the dubious honor of chairing next year's ball. As usual, the women previously approached hadn't wanted to part with their time or money. And at least Loretta ensured their not having to ask a Jew.

The unlikely friendship of Loretta Dunbar and Angela Flagler Seagrist was also another favorite town topic. Although Loretta was also friendly with Noreen and Julietta, that was understandable. Mary Dodd, deprived of most of the kickbacks she counted on during the charity ball season, spread the word that Angela's friendship with Loretta was a John Murphy payoff. As Mary always said, "After all, a common hate is much stronger than a common love."

Mary even invented the scenario. Angela and Loretta had hired a call girl, paid her big money, set her up in a rented Rolls, and arranged for her to have a flat on John

Murphy's route to the hospital and to waylay him, so to speak. Of course, they didn't plan on Sam dying that day.

Lennox Knox told his Crayola cronies that of course Angela and Loretta were lovers. How active could Chukker be after a stroke? And everyone knew about Angela being a "free spirit." Nothing normal had amused her for years, and a tart like Loretta could turn anyone on. Fort craved a piece of Mrs. Dunbar himself, especially since she reminded him of his daughter.

Yet however much of Palm Beach remained a house divided, Julietta, Noreen, and a lot of others knew how lucky Angela was to have Loretta as a friend.

Loretta's face shone in the sharp sun as she and Chukker breakfasted on the terrace. The air, redolent with orange blossoms, intensified Chukker's love and desire, if indeed that was possible.

"Darling, you not only made the shiny sheet, you made the *Post*. And not only the *Post*, but the page opposite the editorial. In fact, you *are* that page," he said, proudly handing her the folded-back newspaper.

BLACKS ADMITTED TO PALM BEACH HOSPITAL
Special to the Palm Beach Post
by Wilson H. Dunbar, UPI correspondent

Good Samaritan Hospital, in a distinct departure from tradition, announced today that it would henceforth admit black people as patients. The vote of the board of directors to discard the ban on blacks was unanimous. "We decided to live up to our name and at the same time acknowledge the twentieth century," said a hospital director who requested anonymity.

Insiders credit Loretta Worship Dunbar, a newcomer to Palm Beach and the board of Good Samaritan, for spearheading the anti-discrimination movement. Mrs. Dunbar was not available for comment. Meanwhile, the South Florida NAACP hailed the move as a "unique reversal of Palm Beach bigotry that will set future standards for all aspects of life in the community."

"What did you tell Wilson?" Loretta asked, reading the words over and over.

"Just what happened. And if you think *I'm* proud, you should have heard the dauntless crusader."

"It wasn't hard. The people were ready."

Chukker couldn't believe that Loretta thought so lightly of what she'd done. "Loretta, darling, how many people would use their power to make changes that wouldn't bring something good for them? Getting blacks into the hospital is not going to do whites any good. What if whites need the space? What you did was far from simple. It's not easy to make people change portfolios knowing their dividends will decrease." He leaned over to brush his lips against hers.

"I don't know what that wretched girl is thinking of," Mary Dodd said to Walter and John, "her" florists. Her fingers curled like claws as she pulled irritatedly at a lace hankie. "Girls like that usually have the stars shot out of their eyes by the time they're twelve."

"You've got to think of something today, Mary," Walter hissed. "It's not like you to be so wide of the mark."

"We hear she's doing next year's gala as well," John added.

Mary paced back and forth, her feet sinking into her sculptured pink carpet, Van Cleef bouncing at her heels.

"I never thought her stupid," Mary said. "Nobody stupid could have gotten Chukker Dunbar. No matter how dotty they say he was, he wasn't. I simply don't understand why she's not more interested in being in."

"What you don't understand," John sniffed, "is that she already *is* in. Unlike you, Mary, who's still trying."

Mary Dodd had had to deal with tradespeople all her life, and she hated doing it, especially with bitchy old queens like these. Walter and John might still share a house, but they were no longer sweethearts. Where years ago they'd have been in each other's arms laughing about rising to the occasion for some old dowager in exchange for the promise of a fortnight at her Positano villa, the best they could hope for now was the worst slice of the pie from Mary Dodd.

"Nastiness isn't going to help," she said, tossing her headful of curled wig. "I still don't understand what motivates her."

"Mary, you couldn't possibly understand her making the old coot happy instead of just killing him off," Walter said, looking straight at John.

Mary paid no attention to comments unrelated to the situation. "There must be something we can do."

"It's not going to be easy," John said, tapping his foot. "Our problem is, she's nice. We never had to deal with that before. Even that pinko son of his is mad about her. Did you ever read such shit?"

"How do you know she's nice?" Mary asked, knowing it was true. "Are you going soft in your dotage?"

John looked at Walter. That at least gave them both a laugh. They'd heard enough of Mary's bizarre monologues with Van Cleef to know who was going soft.

"I've got to think of something, and it should have something to do with those stupid Seminoles, so we're safe for next year."

"I'm sure you will, Mary," John said, "your mind has always functioned well along these lines."

Only a few days passed before Mary Dodd was able to call Walter and John and tell them she'd found her poisoned arrow.

## 19

A hallucinatory brilliance surrounded the night of the Feather Fantasy. The great ballroom of the Breakers Hotel had been transformed into the world's most magnificent tepee, and feathers fluttered everywhere with a grace and splendor that rivaled the most extravagant Hollywood musical.

Standing back to gaze at the beauty, Loretta marveled as if she herself had had nothing to do with it. Chukker beamed with a glow that made him look ten years younger, especially seeing how his young wife looked in the white chiffon dress he'd selected himself at Martha's. The trimming, however, she'd done herself: all around the low, portrait neck she'd painstakingly sewn the fluff from three feather dusters to frame her shoulders in a sensual glow of crimson. Her hair, done in a French braid, was intertwined with even more red feathers.

Loretta, Chukker, Angela, the Seminole chief, and his reigning princess stood at the end of the double row of cigar-store Indians between which the guests entered.

The poles supporting the giant tepee were carved and painted like real totems, and the centerpieces on each table were in the shape of war bonnets. Special hand-beaded key chains from Gucci and an Indian Love Call fragrance conceived by Estée Lauder had been donated as favors. People crowded the dance floor and each other as Neal Smith's orchestra played its rain-dance heart out. Tonight was the last hurrah of an ever-lengthening Palm Beach season, and Loretta seemed to have succeeded in making the entire crowd as excited as if it were the opening gun.

Even the Lennox Knoxes, the legacy Crayolas, the boozy broads who'd seen it all hadn't seen anything like this. Handsy Hormel, once Revlon's most-photographed matching-lips-and-fingertips model, reacted to the scene with particular vitriol. She'd wanted Chukker for herself, and if she'd ever gotten those nails into him, she'd already be a widow. Although only weeks had passed since people had wondered who Loretta was, tonight there could be no doubt.

Mary Dodd did not need the pink boa and cockatoo headdress to convince people that she'd made an effort. Her usual war paint would have been more than appropriate. Her imperious smile and impervious manner was beginning to make her escorts, Walter and John, grow increasingly curious. She'd never revealed her plan to them, but as they looked around, years of experience told them that tonight would be difficult for Loretta to lose. They did notice, however, that the usual press coverage had been stepped up. The Newirths had noticed it, too. Jack thought Chukker must be responsible. He must have done it for Loretta. Noreen knew that that wasn't Chukker's style. She wondered whose style it was, and more than that she wondered why.

Loretta didn't feel she deserved so much praise. All she'd done, with everyone's help, was to have fun giving a party and to feel great giving the proceeds to the Seminoles.

Loretta was seated between Chukker and Chief Lightning Bolt. Noreen sat on the Chief's other side, across from the Carristas. Loretta and Chukker had danced nearly every dance, and whenever they took the floor they took all eyes with them.

A vague but growing sense of unease filled Noreen as she watched a group of photographers position themselves at the door. It made her even more uneasy that Mary Dodd and John and Walter should be among them. Although the mood was high, the orchestra at fever pitch, and enough champagne had been poured for even the most regal pretender to have mislaid his elegance, something ominous gnawed at Noreen. After fifteen years of Palm Beach politics, she'd learned to trust her instincts.

When it actually happened, Mary Dodd was nowhere near the door. Neither were Walter and John. Flashbulbs were—fireworks of flashbulbs to herald the grandest entrance so far this evening.

The orchestra stopped in mid-beat, and couples ran back to their tables. People climbed onto chairs to get a look at the man screaming his way toward the mike. Noreen Newirth was the only one who kept her eyes on Loretta. It was as if a tornado had blown in, obliterating even the slimmest ray of light.

Big Luke didn't need any more light. The neon cross he held between his swollen hands was enough to illuminate his debauched features and wild eyes. His tar-and-feathers robe, brought from a nearby Klan rally, was the best costume Big Luke could manage on short notice. Holding the cross high and looking, as he had so many times, toward the top of a tent, he launched into the most expensive sermon of his life. Little did he realize that his booming voice, always capable of selling in a ruthless marketplace, had never found, and never would find again, more welcome buyers.

"What might seem like luck, like good fortune always does to heretics, was God's hand on my heart. To think, after all these years, it was only yesterday that He got to helping me discover the whereabouts of my long-lost daughter, my poor baby Loretta—yes, still just my poor baby Loretta. Sinning makes you poor. The Lord makes you rich. If she had only come to God, instead of running from Him, when we all knew it was her dead half-brother's unborn child she was carrying, she'd be truly rich today. But imagine my happiness, nonetheless, in finding her, after all the years of not knowing if she was dead or alive. Imagine my joy in knowing she's living under all your blessings.

"Being a man of God, a father to my flock as well as to my lost baby, I take her discovery as a sign from the Almighty to forgive her sins right here among her mama's people, her good mama being descended directly from you good Seminoles. And although her mama has gone to her happy hunting ground, the Lord has sent me here to forgive our baby for sending her there." Big Luke stopped and squinted into the whispers and semidarkness, waiting for the eerie stillness to return.

"In the name of the Almighty, I want to thank every last one of you for taking my little Loretta—though I guess she's hardly little anymore—into your hearts, those who so generously let her blend into the foliage of your souls."

Suddenly, spotlights from the back of the tent knifed to the dance floor, harshly illuminating a cardboard-backed montage of Baby Loretta posters. Gasps from the stupefied guests were louder than any applause could be. Big Luke's frantic eyes searched through the crowd for Loretta, just as every other eye in the room fell on the empty chairs where only seconds before Mr. and Mrs. Harrison W. Dunbar had sat. Only Mary Dodd had seen them leave, since only Mary Dodd had been expecting it.

Noreen, fleeing to the parking lot with her husband, heard the orchestra race into a desperate upbeat. And as the ship sank, Noreen prayed that that one special girl would make it safely to the lifeboat.

Noreen and Angela arrived at the Dunbars' just as the morning newspapers were hitting the door. They had said little to each other on the way over; there was no need. They were Loretta's friends, and they were coming to offer whatever they could.

Noreen, always immaculate, still wore last night's makeup. Angela, so protective of her beauty sleep, had never closed her eyes.

They weren't there for explanations. They knew what was wrong wasn't Loretta. Something was insane: that man . . . whoever staged it. Last night had been another unfortunate stay of execution for what should have died long ago in Palm Beach.

Essie was still in her nightclothes when she came to the door, looking confused and bewildered, as if she expected Angela and Noreen to explain.

"Can we come in, Essie?" Noreen asked, forcing a smile. "Can we see Mrs. Dunbar?"

Essie looked from Noreen to Angela. "They must be halfway to New York by now," she said. "They left in the middle of the night. I never saw anythin' like it. They didn't pack or nothin'. Just left."

"Did they say they'd be back?" Angela's voice was tentative. "Did they say anything about coming back?"

Essie shook her head. "Didn't sound anythin' like comin' back. After Mr. Dunbar hung up the phone about gettin' the plane, he didn't say much of anythin'. Mrs. Dunbar, she couldn't stop cryin'. My heart's just broke for her and after how pretty and everthin' she looked. Mr. Dunbar, I never seen him so upset. He shouldn't be gettin' that upset. Each of them tryin' to tell the other not to be upset. Somethin' terrible musta happened. But not between them. That's what's so sad. They love each other." Essie shook her head again.

Noreen felt like screaming, "Loretta, just you wait! You'll see, Loretta!" It was now Noreen's turn, after all this time, to muster forces. Angela, beside her, was just as determined to fight.

The Feather Fantasy's mood of moonlight and magic seemed worlds away from the tarmac of La Guardia Airport as Chukker's chartered Lear set down its wheels. Hurrying Loretta into the limousine that by special permission was waiting on the field, Chukker felt a sense of relief. Not that he wouldn't fight to the death whoever was responsible; for the moment, however, it seemed best to put space between Loretta and Palm Beach.

For Loretta, far more upsetting than seeing Big Luke was hearing that Mama had died. Poor Mama! Loretta was going to make her so proud and happy. She was going to take her to Hollywood to introduce her to the stars and to the *real* Loretta, not this miserable failure sitting beside a man who, because he thought he owed her his life, had convinced himself that he loved her.

Another limousine was waiting at Kennedy, with luggage Chukker had called to have packed with clothes from the New York apartment so that they'd be ready to go when the plane arrived. They'd taken nothing from Palm Beach. Loretta could have worn her ballgown across the Atlantic, so paralyzed was she by the image of Big Luke.

# 20

The few weeks spent in St. Moritz reminded Loretta of *The Magic Mountain*, but it wasn't until weeks later that she could joke about it. With nature's unexpected opulence, dalliance took on new meaning as Chukker, their roles reversed, nursed Loretta back to life. Yet as calm as Chukker appeared about the Big Luke incident, a fire wilder than any of the preacher's insane gospels burned in his heart.

"It's probably blown over," Chukker said, as they walked through the gardens. "Storms are short. Rains are long." Taking her hand, he wondered why the hell he hadn't heard from Wilson, and where in God's name was Cardinal Downey now that his cathedral was built with Chukker's money? Chukker wanted that lunatic Luke defrocked—yesterday for chrissake.

As always Loretta asked, "Why? Why did it happen?"

As always, Chukker explained. "A payoff. Somebody gave Big Luke what to him was big money."

Loretta understood that. She didn't have any illusions about Big Luke. "But why would somebody do it?" That's the "why" Loretta didn't understand.

Patiently, over and over: "Jealousy."

"Who?"

"I don't know." And he didn't—although when Chukker stopped to consider, it horrified him how many there were who might have done it.

Loretta's worst fear was that it might be a friend. She'd trusted those she'd grown close to. It would be better that a whole outside group be responsible rather than one friend.

After what amounted to a clinical rest in St. Moritz, Chukker suggested that they fly to Capri. It proved the perfect elixir. Loretta's best friend in the world, for always, would be Donina. And for the first time in a long time Loretta made an effort to look good, to have her hair and clothes just right. She wanted to be what Donina expected. Chukker was exuberant.

The faience vases, the gold and silver icons, the Flemish feasts, even Sergio pouring champagne—all were sights that Loretta in her wildest dreams never thought would make her feel at home. And right in their midst, the happiest sight of all: Donina. There, with her sunset hair, curb-high heels, and arsenal of jewelry, stood Mother Earth. As they embraced, what Loretta remembered best was what she heard first: that wonderful laugh.

Loretta looked better than Donina had been led by Chukker to expect. She couldn't say the same for Chukker, though. Consumed with uncovering the party or parties responsible was clearly getting to him. It was that same boat mentality he had exhibited thirty years ago.

Luncheon on the terrace seemed more unreally beautiful than ever. Yet as the boats danced across the water's shiny surface, Loretta sensed that this was a much more real world than where she'd been. Donina watched her, noticing that in spite of her recent shock Loretta displayed a new resolve, a new security. Whatever strength she had built up before the Feather Fantasy was staying with her. Donina had once told Loretta never to waste time on tomorrow, and now Donina realized that Loretta knew exactly where she was going—and that that was more important than where she'd been.

"Why do you not have babies?" Donina asked, wanting to make Chukker feel young and also to make Loretta understand that her life was really just beginning.

In the time they'd been married, it was a subject that Chukker and Loretta had never discussed. Somehow they knew that they both felt the same, and that talking about it might alter the feeling of "whatever happens happens."

But Donina's raising the question at this unlikely time achieved its intended goal and drew Loretta and Chukker even closer.

"At this point I guess some people will think we're unfit parents," Loretta joked, pulling Chukker's head down to kiss him. "Or at least one of us."

"I not only shall be godmother," Donina continued, "but possibly his . . ."

"I'm sure you will," Chukker laughed.

"Why a he?" Loretta asked.

"Look at Wilson. Is he not something?" Donina asked.

It struck Chukker at this moment how truly ageless Donina was. She possessed that quality Proust wanted as his only gift: "an unlimited resistance to fatigue." Something Chukker was feeling more and more.

"Remember, Chukker, that time you told me, 'Old money does not need to make a statement.' I notice, though, your new tankers are making quite a noise." It fascinated Loretta that Donina not only remembered so much but kept up with every detail of Chukker's world.

During the weeks that followed, Chukker worked incessantly, while Donina and Loretta spent almost all of their time together. The gray men, Chukker's shadows—the Musketeers, directors, lawyers, and accountants—called and came as he became involved in one oil deal after another. Those who showed up seemed oblivious to any atmosphere other than that of a boardroom, never taking on the clothes of resort or relaxation. Their dark colors traveled from airport to airport and country to country, while their attaché cases opened and locked in fortunes.

World leaders sought not only Chukker's advice but also the floating gold that filled the bellies of his supertankers. The cover of *Time* pictured him at the helm of the largest one as it stretched the eastern seaboard from Palm Beach to Wall Street. The press likened Chukker to the Rothschilds when their corner on gold had decided wars and kept nations solvent. Yet amidst all the deal making, what Chukker Dunbar wanted most was a pipeline to the truth about the Feather Fantasy incident and fuel enough to have whoever engineered it burn in hell.

As Donina and Loretta sat beneath the stars, Loretta was reminded of the night she'd told Donina about Big Luke, when Donina had cradled her in her arms. Now as then, Donina's heart reached out, but this time the anger in Loretta's hurt had more fight than fragility. Not that the softness that made people want to protect Loretta had diminished. She'd just grown. Living with Chukker and absorbing his world had made her more confident to tackle life head on. Having new friends had helped too. Without even noticing, Loretta had learned to behave rich—rich in ways of sensitivity as well as of power. No, you couldn't be Chukker Dunbar's wife and not have some of his strength rub off—not with Loretta's instincts.

"I didn't know what was happening," Loretta said. "We were on the plane before I had a thought. I know Chukker was right, but those people will always believe that I did something wrong." Until Big Luke could be discredited, Chukker had used his influence to assure that no further mention was made in the press. Still, he couldn't stop the gossip.

"They will not think anything of the kind when Chukker gets through," Donina said, clasping Loretta's hand between bejeweled fingers. "This is a man who saved lives that could not be saved. A hero who refused to wear the war on his chest."

The cool night breeze blew Loretta's hair across her face. With an almost childlike gesture she brushed it past her ear. "Donina, things that I tell Chukker because they upset me seem to bother him now. I think I tell him too much. He's had enough of my problems," she said, explaining about the hospital, Sam, the blacks . . . about Noreen, the Jews, the clubs. . . . She showed Donina Wilson's article. "These are my battles. He's fought his war."

Donina smiled in the dark.

The call from the Cardinal came during lunch. Chukker's morning had been spent giving an interview to a journalist from *Il Messagiero*. It wasn't that he wanted publicity; but his anti-Arab views were of significant interest, because only by agreeing with the Arabs did Chukker himself stand to gain. His disagreement, in the face of diminishing returns, carried uncommon weight in the Common Market.

Cardinal Downey called from just outside the Oval Office and gave an even worse account of the situation than Chukker thought possible. "And don't worry about defrocking him. He's never been frocked. A hundred percent snake oil, thrown out of every parish he's ever preached."

"Thanks, Francis. And thanks for letting me use your name. . . . Right. . . . Of course. . . . To him, too—and to Pat and the girls. . . . I know. I can't imagine. . . . I don't know what to say except a big thank-you to you, again, Francis." Immediately upon hanging up, Chukker called Wilson in Washington. He was thrilled to get through right away. Chukker knew he'd share his joy. He knew, too, what Wilson would do with this information.

Back at the table, a tired but exultant Chukker told Donina and Loretta about his conversation: how the Miami police had Big Luke in custody and how they would probably put the sonofabitch fraud in an institution rather than the electric chair. Big Luke told the court stenographer that he had been paid five hundred dollars for his performance by some friends of a sister of God. Chukker would track them down too.

As he pressed his lips to Loretta's, it was as if he were kissing new life into her. "Go get 'em, sweetheart," he said.

But even as Loretta accepted what Chukker told her, she knew that Palm Beach wouldn't. "They'll say it's only power and pull."

"It makes the job easier, darling. They just wish they had it. Remember when I told you about Mrs. Dodge? 'Pearls in the daytime?' they asked. And she answered: 'I used to feel that way, too. But that was before I had them.' "

Around the table, the three of them took turns proposing toasts—to each other, to Mrs. Dodge, to Cardinal Downey, to Wilson, and, yes, even to Chukker's old pal Richard Nixon.

" 'Palm Beach Plague Poisons Fighters of Bigotry,' " Donina shouted, waving the July 4 issue of the *Herald*

*Tribune*. Wilson's piece was on the front page. It had taken a while, but at last the papers were beginning to pick up his "Plague" series.

> A bogus minister was bribed by Palm Beach society figures to destroy the reputation of Loretta Worship Dunbar, the leader of a movement to erase bigotry in this exclusive resort community. The report that the "minister" was paid to "expose" Mrs. Dunbar as a "harlot" is expected to rock Palm Beach to its core. . . .

As the summer's shadows lengthened, Nixon's term grew shorter. Watergate wasn't shaking the President's world, it was toppling it. Wilson had little time for anything but. Loretta, burning with ideas, would have a barrage waiting for him so that when the new Palm Beach season started, they'd be ready to fire. Loretta swore she would never go back, but she could launch her missiles from afar.

Chukker had made plans to travel in Europe, but when Donina pointed out how happy Loretta was in Capri, he let himself be persuaded to stay.

Autumn followed soon after Nixon's resignation and President Gerald Ford's unexpected pardon. Even though Chukker was Nixon's old friend, he found the entire affair disgraceful.

Donina laughed. "Why not just look at it this way? Ford is a golfer. Ike was a golfer. Ike was the war. We met in the war. So Ford for our future is good."

When they finally heard what happened to Big Luke, it was what Chukker had predicted, yet with one twist that even he in his wildest dreams wouldn't have dared wish. In a last, desperate attempt to make people believe he was sane, Big Luke, as he was being led off to the state psychiatric hospital, told reporters that he'd been given the five hundred dollars by two men named John and Walter.

The linotype could not have been dry before John and Walter issued their own statements. Of course they had no idea who he was when they'd handed him the envelope. They hadn't even recognized him the night of the ball, he looked so different. Since their shop was located in West Palm Beach near the Port Authority terminal, they had merely done Mary Dodd the favor of handing someone named Luke Worship an envelope.

Every time Chukker read the story, his heart raced and the veins in his temples bulged to the beat. He wondered how many other innocents had been her victims. But whatever Chukker would have done to Mary Dodd, it could not have come close to the skewering she received from her legion of conspirators. Finally, each blackmailed buddy had the opportunity to do unto her what she had done her whole life long. In a matter of days her Palm Beach "pals" had turned Mary Dodd into society driftwood, and she had departed on "an extended vacation." Many thought she might kill herself. Those who'd dreamed of doing it for her didn't care anymore.

But many Palm Beachers still believed what Big Luke had said. Even if he wasn't a real minister, those big, bold, black-and-white posters were real, each one heralding the peaches-and-cream innocence of Mrs. Harrison W. Dunbar.

For the Dunbars and Donina the ache remained constant. It wasn't that Loretta would never be welcomed back; in a town where roots grow instantly in money, Loretta, as Chukker Dunbar's wife, was already Old World. But that wasn't what Loretta wanted. She wanted something more.

\* \* \*

All of Rosefields, especially the Efficient One, also ached for Loretta. Knowing how well and happy she made H.W., Miss Collier had always wanted to do something special for her. But there hadn't been any way but words, and words were not Miss Collier's strength. Still, no computer was programmed better than she was, so when the woman on the telephone spoke her name, immediately something clicked.

Although the caller heard that Mrs. Dunbar was not at home, hearing that this *was* her home set off a crying and talking jag that blurted out a lifetime. It all started, she said, when she saw the newspaper with Big Luke's picture.

". . . Should've been put away long ago. I realized that after my Loretta left. Always a liar and a cheat. Lied and cheated through the Navy. Lied and cheated my folks. Till I saw what Cardinal Downey said I didn't even know he wasn't really a minister. And what with Loretta gone, well, I got to thinking. He made my Paul go to war, killed our boy sure as taking a gun to his head. And about my baby Loretta being pregnant? That's the big whopper. Closest thing ever got near to her sweetness was his ugly . . ." She paused, breathing deeply and wiping her tears. "When finally I left, he even told me how he'd torn all her letters and used all the money, and that he hoped no good would come to her or to me. So when I read 'Middleburg, Virginia,' I had to call to find my baby. I've wanted so long to tell her how sorry I am for how wrong I was. She's a good, fine girl. Never changed since that day at the orphanage. Sweet as that little sweater with the roses. She always loved roses. I used to grow them in the yard. We'd sit in the kitchen, Loretta and me. I'd read her my poems—not mine, but ones I pasted in the book. Whenever they were in season, the roses would be on the table. You know how I named Loretta? . . ."

The Efficient One understood perfectly everything Lillian Worship was saying. But there wasn't time to keep listening; she had to place her own call.

Sergio came to the pool to tell Mr. Dunbar that he had another phone call. Reluctantly, Chukker rose yet again from the cushioned chaise. Between the sheiks and the Greeks, the embassies and the State Department, it seemed that he was shuttling more diplomacy than Kissinger. Even his deep tan couldn't hide the exhaustion.

However, as Chukker started to talk, Donina heard a brightness in his voice that she had missed all summer. It made her happy, although the words "TWA" and "Rome" and "limousine" did not. She knew Chukker and Loretta had to leave, but she'd hoped it wouldn't be now.

"I'm so pleased Loretta's not here," Chukker said as he hung up. Every morning Loretta went to the harbor and brought back the fresh catches they would grill for lunch. Chukker sat on the end of Donina's chair and, like an excited little boy, told her everything. "Loretta's mama—foster mother—you know, the one she loved so much—isn't dead. And I've arranged for her to fly here. She'll arrive tomorrow."

His joy was worth the earth to Donina. She knew what Mama's being alive meant: not only for Loretta's happiness but also to hasten the purge of any lingering taint from Loretta.

Donina and Chukker were like two giddy children as they planned where the surprise reunion should be. They named all the special places they knew, even somewhere they'd never been. Finally, Donina was right. "Tears flow the best at home."

Loretta sensed something conspiratorial in the air the

minute she came in. Donina and Chukker were wreathed in smiles that couldn't be suppressed. Even Sergio seemed different. "I'm sorry, I cannot take you in the morning to the craft show," he said. How odd, Loretta thought, since it was his idea for her to see the jewelry his uncle was bringing all the way from Sardinia. Couldn't whoever he had to pick up at the airport take a taxi?

Airily, Donina changed the subject. "Remember, Loretta, when you planned the lunch and it was superb?"

"I remember I planned it."

"No modesty. Do it again. Do it tomorrow. Surprise me with something you liked when you were a little girl, like we talked about."

Loretta looked at Donina as if she were slightly mad. But then again, she was—that was one of the reasons Loretta loved her.

Chukker threw up his hands. "What can I say, darling? Donina's regressing. But who would mind that?"

"How many tomorrow?" Sergio asked.

"Just the family." Donina looked naughtily at Chukker.

Loretta looked at them both, smiling herself; their gaiety was infectious.

"Perfecto," Chukker said.

"Which means how many, signora?" With the Contessa, "family" could mean anywhere from three to three dozen.

"*Quattro*," Donina answered.

All day long, Loretta thought about the game they had to be playing. She didn't mind being kept in the dark, because she knew that she would soon be let in on it, and in the meantime everyone was in such good humor.

As the sun left the sky and stars started dripping into the lagoon, Chukker wondered if he would be able to get to sleep at all or if the impending surprise would afford him the best night he'd had in months. When eventually he awoke after a sound night's sleep, his body was bursting with energy.

Loretta, however, woke several times during the night, thinking about her conversation with Donina, about the creeping smells of her childhood in the kitchen, about the stews with everything thrown in.

In the morning, when the pungent scent of leeks and garlic, peppers and coriander and bunches of basil wafted from the kitchen to the terrace, Donina hugged Loretta and breathed deeply.

"Even a cook in the kitchen," Chukker said heartily, his arm around Loretta.

"Should we tell her?" Donina teased.

Chukker pretended to consider it. "What do you think?"

"No."

"Good."

"No good is exactly what you both are," Loretta said, laughing.

Without looking at each other, Chukker and Donina felt a simultaneous panic upon hearing the car drive up in the courtyard. Chukker was so nervous he didn't know where to put himself. By the time he'd decided to stand next to Loretta, Loretta was already rocking in the arms of their surprise. Donina and Chukker were also disabled, as crying and laughter took over the room.

Mama's new old-looking dress, her new secondhand purse, and the wasteful amount of crayon on her hair made her look just like someone you'd call Mama, even though it was obvious that, as she would say, she was "all fixed-up." Yet nothing mattered except her joy at being with Loretta.

Loretta and Mama hugged a long time, stared at each other, then hugged more. In between there were lots of "I can't believe it"s and "thank God"s.

"You're so beautiful, Loretta! I can't believe how beautiful—prettier than a movie star!" Mama kept pushing her hair from her face, and the crayon kept smearing her forehead.

Loretta put her arm through Mama's and walked her to the terrace. She didn't even notice that Donina and Chukker had disappeared.

"Loretta! Where are we? Heaven?"

"Yes," Loretta answered, happier than she remembered ever being. Her mama was here. Gone were the nightmares of Mama's stricken face, her hate-filled eyes, her harrowing screams. All that came to mind were happy memories.

When Mama and Loretta finally stood silently watching the marina, Loretta was able to absorb the moment, to know that it wasn't going away. She wasn't even afraid anymore to touch Mama for fear that she'd disappear.

All at once the story of how Mama got there poured from her lips. The newspaper, the telephone call, everything about Big Luke. "I told that Miss Collier all about you, what a good girl you were—*are*—about *us*, our poems and our roses . . . and then it seems before I hung up I was on a plane, over the ocean, and in Rome. I was only in Rome at the airport. I wanted to light a candle, see the Pope, thank him—even though we're not Catholic. You know what I mean—you always did. . . . Oh, I can't believe it. Look at you! So beautiful! You really are prettier than any star—in the movies, on television—anywhere. . . . Is he good to you? He's much older, but he must be good if he brought me here. He looks good. I like his eyes. They're good eyes. Not like those crazed . . ."

"He's good, Mama. He's wonderful. I love him very much."

There was more silence, and then Mama jabbered on.

"You know, Loretta, no one's got anybody to complain to

about the management of life. Just never give up hope. You know, Loretta, *I* never gave up hope. I almost gave up living, but I never gave up hope of finding you, especially after he told me about those torn-up letters. That's when I could—"

"Hush, Mama," Loretta said, again reversing roles.

"Is this your house?" Mama asked suddenly, almost fearfully.

"No, Mama. It's Donina's."

"But he's rich—I read about him when I saw your wedding picture. He's rich? Right?"

Loretta smiled and shook her head.

"That's not why you married him . . . ? Loretta? You didn't marry him for money, did you? Remember when I'd tell Luke not to place all that importance on money? To look where it finds itself? I don't mean now with him. But *you* don't need money, Loretta. You didn't marry him for that, did you?"

"Never, Mama. Never." She knew Mama knew it already but just wanted to hear her say it.

Loretta began to fill Mama in on the recent years, and Mama told her about working in a flower shop, interrupting herself only to marvel at the flowers and name the ones she knew. As spectacular as everything was, Mama seemed more appreciative than overwhelmed. Her daze was from seeing Loretta, not from the riches around her.

It was not hard to grow attached to Lillian Worship. Her goodness, her life with Luke, her life altogether made Chukker and Donina feel sorrier for her than Mama had ever once felt for herself. Mama was grateful for all her blessings— the most blessed being Loretta.

While Mama stayed in Capri, Wilson's "Plague" series, filled with quotes from Lillian Worship confirming that Big Luke's words had been lies, appeared in the *Tribune*. Mama was thrilled because her statements pronounced on Big Luke the final sentence he deserved. Even Mouth, sensing that Loretta was no longer merely a threat but a power, extolled the virtues of Wilson's piece.

When at last Mama returned to her tiny apartment in Tampa, no one remarked on how her intended several days' stay had turned into several wondrous weeks while four people, each connected by chance's slimmest thread, became closer than if conceived from the same cloth.

# 21

Labor Day had long since come and gone when Loretta and Chukker arrived in New York. Since Chukker had been surfeited with work and longed for autumn at Rosefields, they stayed only a week in the city.

Loretta couldn't wait for Mama to come to Rosefields. She was sure she would like it much more than Palm Beach, although Loretta wanted Mama to visit there, too, now that Donina had persuaded Loretta that she must go back. She'd run away once, and she couldn't run again. She had to go back to fight to win. She and Wilson had started something, and if she quit now, the wrongs would be proved right.

Chukker agreed, of course, that Palm Beach needed shaking up, but he didn't want Loretta to be the prime mover. She'd been hurt enough. And he was selfish, too—he wanted Loretta to himself.

Blazes of orange and red were already igniting the trees and burnishing the mountains as Baines drove the green wagon with the painted rose through the boxwood hedges. The entire staff of Rosefields stood outside to welcome Mr. Chukker and Miss Loretta back home. Tea was waiting on the cart, a fire was crackling, and in the middle of the big library desk stood a picture of Loretta and Chukker in a Dunbar-crested frame.

As autumn flooded the countryside with still more gilded brilliance, Chukker and Loretta read, walked, visited with neighbors, but mostly just luxuriated in their happiness with each other.

One afternoon as Chukker was leafing through *The Chronicle of the Horse*, he came upon some legal-size yellow pages filled with Loretta's writing. At first they appeared to be nothing but lists of famous names. But when he noticed Loretta's marginal reminders to tell Wilson certain things, he realized their significance.

Wilson, check if it was Eddie Cantor or Roosevelt who founded March of Dimes . . .
IMPORTANT!

When was Goldberg's vaccine first proved effective? Fifties? Possible 20 year party for the gala of '75.
BE GREAT!

The first time Loretta felt dizzy was the morning she accompanied the Crestbournes to a museum opening in Richmond. Chukker was in New York with Embiricos, Niarchos, and some new Arab shooter, Adnan Khashoggi. Loretta thought that the nausea had been brought on by the crowds—so many faces she couldn't place. She didn't know how long she'd knelt in front of the basin—long enough for Mrs. Crestbourne to come looking for her.

Dr. Crestbourne gave his wife a wink and a meaningful look when she told him what had happened.

"Little darlin'," Dr. Crestbourne said to Loretta, his arm around her shoulder. "I think I might venture the diagnosis

as 'heirin.' Heir-in? H-E-I-R-I-N? So you both drive carefully back to Middleburg—understand?" He didn't have to
spell it.

When Loretta's shock faded, she knew, somehow, even
without a test, that he was right. She couldn't wait to tell
Chukker this most wonderful news in all the world. Had he
been staying longer in New York, she'd have flown up. But
since he planned to come home the following day, she'd tell
him at the airport. "You'll know me," she giggled into the
phone. "I'll be the one with wings on."

Loretta set out from Middleburg early the next morning.
During the night there'd been a message that Chukker would
not be flying commercially to Washington but instead would
fly privately to the Aldi airstrip near Upperville, only minutes from home. The plane would land at eight. All the way
from Richmond she could scarcely contain her excitement.

She had told the Efficient One and the Efficient One had
told the staff, and now all of Rosefields was buzzing with
happiness. Noreen and Angela were thrilled, and Zinnia
couldn't stop saying, "Lord a-mercy." Donina could hardly
speak through her tears, knowing the years this would add
to Chukker's life. And Mama, certain the baby would be a
girl, kept saying, "Make sure it ends in an *e*, not a
*y*—B-e-t-t-e."

Everyone Loretta told she implored to keep the news
secret, remembering from her maternity training how much
longer pregnancy seems when everyone asks "when" from
the beginning.

Loretta couldn't get hold of Wilson. And for some reason
his secretary sounded surprised that she was calling.

"It's coming in now," the control tower announced as
soon as the blip turned up on the radar screen. Loretta ran
to the gate. Shading her eyes, she scanned the sharp fall
sky.

She rushed onto the field even before the steps were lowered. A somber Wilson descended, kissed her cheek, and put an arm around her shoulders.

Right then she saw the coffin.

The stroke had been swift, sudden, and merciful. Jab, the butler, who'd been alone with Chukker in the apartment, said he'd been in fine spirits. Since he'd had a long day and wanted to get an early start, he'd changed his plans for dinner. He wouldn't be going out. Like everyone who worked for Chukker any length of time, Jab both admired and loved him. Chukker had even given him his nickname—for the "Jackson Adams Buchanan" on his birth certificate, each of whom Jab swore was a blood relative. Even if it wasn't true, Chukker thought, Jab was a damn sight classier than the boys Chukker'd grown up with who had the same names.

"Mr. Dunbar was standin' at the window, lookin' at the park, sayin' what he wanted for dinner. All of a sudden he clasps at himself and hits the floor. When I went to get him up, he just shook his head. He didn't look scared. All he said, clear as a bell, was 'Tell Miss Loretta to go get 'em. Go get 'em, sweetheart.' I said, 'Sure, 'nough,' and he never said nothin' more."

The same minister who'd married Loretta and Chukker performed the simple service. Only Loretta, Wilson, and the staff of Rosefields attended. Wilson went alone in the helicopter with his father's ashes. As it circled overhead, Loretta watched Chukker and the land he loved become one.

# 22

"How dare she come back!"

"She belongs here."

"Fucking him to death's the same as murder."

"He loved her more than life."

"Obviously."

"What about what Big Luke said?"

"The man's nuts. He's a liar."

"The pictures aren't."

"What about her mama?"

"More white trash."

"She's made a lot of friends."

"Spics and kikes and losers."

"Wilson?"

"She's probably let him in, too—the whore!"

"That's what we said in the first place."

The longer Loretta lingered at Rosefields after Chukker's death, the more unbearable the time seemed. Although Mama had come to stay for a while after the funeral, her grief for Loretta was constant, and as Dr. Crestbourne warned: "Loretta darlin', I know how good your mama means, but grief is not what we want now. It's well meanin', but not doin' anythin' to make you well. The same with her feelin' sorry. It's not the feelin' you need round you. And Rosefields shouldn't be round you either—not if you want all those memories to stay pretty and yourself to stay pretty along with them."

Although everyone at Rosefields was exceedingly kind and helpful, Loretta knew that Dr. Crestbourne was right. She needed to preserve the memory of the place where she and Chukker had fallen in love.

When finally she did decide to leave, many believed that the demands of mistressing such a big house had been tying her down. But Loretta knew it was Chukker's constant presence that ultimately made life at Rosefields unbearable. Not a day passed when she didn't see him in the gardens, in the stables, in the house. And the echo of Donina's words about running away kept merging with what Chukker had said about the Lorettas of the world changing the status quo. Now more than ever she wanted to effect changes. She knew, too, that Chukker would be just as desperate to make the world in which their child would live a better place. Sometimes, Loretta thought, you have to leave so that you can go back.

At first, Palm Beach didn't seem any easier than Rosefields. Whereas Loretta thought of Rosefields as theirs, Palm Beach was Chukker's, a world she had barely squeezed into. She might have been able to manage the Blue Ridge Mountains, but life in Palm Beach made her feel dislocated. The one person she needed to coax her, just as she had once coaxed him, from small steps to giant strides, was gone. Everything was different. Even the protective hedges looked alien and ungovernable, and the graceful vines of bougainvillea seemed to wriggle and slither rather than cling.

As Loretta stood silently on the terrace of their beach cottage overlooking the ocean, the intensity of the late October heat couldn't lessen the chill as she watched the sun's afterglow ignite the horizon. Thinking about the horror of losing both Paul and Chukker, she felt her faith recede with the relentless surf. Still, how lucky she was to have had both of them in her life. And hadn't so many people she loved suffered losses in their lives? Mama? Donina? Noreen? Julietta?

What pained Loretta most was knowing that Chukker would never see his child and that the child would never have Chukker for a father. She was grateful she'd sworn those she'd told about the baby to secrecy. Gossip from the world's most practiced mythmakers was something she couldn't handle.

But what she suddenly thought she *must* handle—what all at once became almost a mission—was the renovation of the big house.

Pressing the tiny Saint Christopher medal between her fingers, Loretta prayed for Paul and for Chukker as the sky darkened. But it was to Saint Jude, patron saint of the impossible, that she prayed for herself and her unborn baby.

As the weeks passed, Loretta tried to recover some semblance of what had been her Palm Beach life. How right Chukker had been when he predicted that redoing the house would become her dream as much as his!

The excitement started soon after Noreen had said, "Remove that whole third floor. Take all those servants' rooms off. It's not that big a deal." That same day the architect drew up rough plans. Since Mizner had elevated the ground before the original construction, the ocean view would remain unspoiled.

Too often, though, Loretta found her days stretching into

bouts of exhaustion as she learned about oil deals, shopping malls, foundations, and trusts. As she was beginning to understand the scope of Chukker's fortune, she realized also how cleverly he'd chosen his colleagues. Without the patience of Chukker's Musketeers, she knew she'd never have grasped so quickly the intricacies of Dunbar Enterprises, with its countless checks and balances. The more Dunbar made, the more the people running the company made. Now she understood what Chukker had meant by "The money they make makes their morality." It wasn't an aversion to money that had ever made Wilson and Loretta uninterested in the vast Dunbar machinery. It was just that their priorities, especially now, were elsewhere.

Although Thanksgiving had passed, the hospital's walls were still lined with crayon drawings from the children's ward of feathered turkeys and buckle-shoed pilgrims. Loretta and Julietta entered the hallway as they left the boardroom, where the vote had been unanimous for Loretta to chair the next hospital gala—except for Loretta. She would have to give it a lot of thought, because it would require so much time.

As usual, Julietta ran alongside Loretta just to keep up, jabbing Loretta's arm to make her points truly felt. To Loretta, all the Carristas—all the Cubans, in fact—were like gardenias on bushes and oranges on trees, happiest when they were touching.

"Your 'Plague' story, eet's everywhere—even in Havana," she said, her hands moving as fast as her mouth. "Of course, Castro uses eet to say whosoever comes to America will live here worse than jail."

"He won't say it long," Loretta answered, her determination fiercer than ever.

Julietta nodded. She had no more breath to waste talking. She could never understand why Loretta walked so fast. In Cuba, after all, Julietta wasn't considered short.

"You know, Julietta," Loretta said, "Palm Beach may be a tiny pebble to some, but pebbles start small. When the avalanche hits they'll all know what happened."

Little wonder Wilson's latest "Palm Beach Plague" piece assumed national disdain for the morals of Palm Beach. It exposed the shocking incident of Leonard Bernstein's being refused entrance at the gate of a "guest rule" club after conducting a charity concert whose audience was mostly composed of that same club's fine, charitable members.

Three hundred newspapers across the country printed Wilson's series, but in Palm Beach it was carried in only one of five: Jack Newirth's *Pictorial*. "Even if they all ran it, it would fall on blind eyes," Noreen Newirth said. "They believe what they want, even when what they don't want is staring them in the face. Not too different from the queen who yelled 'Let them eat cake,' who sewed her diamond earrings into her hem the day before being guillotined since she knew it wouldn't happen." Incredibly, Noreen told Loretta, those same earrings were now owned by Marjorie Merriweather Post, who wore them the very night of the Bernstein debacle.

What all Palm Beach did read, however, was what all five newspapers carried on the front page: the terms of Harrison Dunbar's will. Somehow it had gotten leaked to the press that he'd written it before they'd married. No one could understand why he would have left so much to her even when he didn't have to. Obviously, she had diddled him into some sexual insanity to make him marry her.

Loretta and Wilson could now own Palm Beach if they wanted to, instead of wrecking it for everyone else.

Finally, Loretta agreed to chair the hospital gala. The

date would coincide with the twentieth anniversary of the polio vaccine, and she prayed that Dr. William Goldberg would accept the invitation as honored guest. He'd certainly be a far cry from the defrocked royals they usually got.

For as long as Palm Beach had had money, it had been as addicted to titles as the titles were to being bought. Many a princely member of many an impoverished crown had earned his living serving as best man or great old chum to someone he'd never met. Medals and sashes strapped on, tiaras intact, royalty reigned in Palm Beach long after they'd been deposed in their mother countries. In fact, after the abdication of Edward VIII, Palm Beach was so delighted to offer the disgraced Windsors asylum that a worshipful crowd waited hours to curtsy, bow, and faint when the exiled couple deigned to give a royal wave from the balcony of the infamous "guest rule" club. Not so splendid, however, was the incident several years later when the duchess was refused credit at Palm Beach's Saks Fifth Avenue because of what had already become a legendary trail of unpaid bills. No matter, she would continue to reign supreme in a city where many of the worst members of the best families lived in similar exile.

Palm Beach was truly astonished when Loretta decided to chair the hospital gala. Unlike so many other charities, whose headquarters were elsewhere, the hospital was all too unattractively here, which meant that chairing required real work. Those who always distrusted their own motives couldn't understand how, given the terms of Chukker's will, this could be the way Loretta wanted to live.

"Why," Angela queried as she and Loretta worked on the gala, "are you so gung-ho on Jews? They seem perfectly happy. Why would they be in Palm Beach if they weren't?"

Loretta's first reaction was disbelief, but then she realized that, like Chukker, Angela had never had to edit her life on account of prejudice. Perhaps a tightly packed pain had to burst inside you or someone close to you before you felt the urgency to act.

"But they *are* here. Explain how in God's name a porn queen murderess can be allowed in and a Nobel Prize-winner like Goldberg isn't? The issue isn't Jews, Angela, it's the quality of life!"

Angela nodded. She'd go along with Loretta because she was her friend. She'd just never before thought of ruffling waters that hadn't washed directly over her.

Determined to keep busy, Loretta displayed amazing energy. Her mind, honed by Chukker's gray men, enabled her to throw herself into hospital finances, see where prices could be cut and wastefulness curtailed. The hospital seemed thrilled with the possibility of William Goldberg, although a chorus of disapproval spread through town. Loretta wouldn't listen. She refused to believe her efforts might be hobbled by people whose bodies without Dr. Goldberg might have been as mangled as their minds.

She also threw herself, with Michael and David's help, into overhauling the big house. It was a great job for them, made the more pleasurable not only by Loretta's caring but by her having learned to enjoy being rich. For her, hanging a Renoir had nothing to do with framing money.

When Loretta first wandered through the musty rooms, with furniture still covered in sheets, she hadn't realized how much bygone beauty could be salvaged. Yet with careful polishing, such as she'd seen at Rosefields, the pearwood library walls had come alive, and by pushing the books back slightly, as she'd seen done at the Chatfield-Taylors', pictures and objects could be set on the shelves, lending new warmth to it all.

Since Loretta couldn't remember everything she'd bought in England, the arrival of the huge wooden crates turned into a mini-Christmas. What on first glance looked like a warehouse of furniture was so quickly swallowed up that Loretta couldn't help thinking what Chukker had kept repeating: "Your only regret will be what you *don't* buy." Her favorite was the Regency bird cage, whose two-foot steeple had been separately packed in thousands of pasta-shaped pieces of styrofoam. It found its perfect home on the "rug-up" needlepoint of parrots that ran the full length of the ornately tiled gallery. Not even in the Brighton Pavilion could it have nested any more brilliantly.

As gardens of new cabbage roses bloomed on old sofas, and lawns returned to their intended green, a feeling of lightness began to emerge. Gradually the aged Mizner mansion took on the youth of its new mistress, while still retaining its past elegance.

The nursery became the focus of particular attention. It was Loretta's special project. But Michael and David found the artist who painted its walls with the Little Prince and its ceiling with yellow stars and a sunset.

Mama loved the way everybody in Palm Beach made a fuss over her. Yet Mama would always be Mama. When, just a day or two after Mama had arrived, Loretta tried to wipe the extra bit of crayon from her brow and unpin the nylon bouquet from her dress, Mama pushed Loretta's hand away.

"Being poor doesn't mean I don't know," Mama said quietly, so her voice wouldn't crack.

"Mama, you're not poor. I told you. I'll keep telling you. You can have anything."

"I have everything," Mama said, winding her arms around Loretta's waist. "Right here." Then Mama went to the mirror to spruce up the violets flattened by the hug. At least, Loretta thought, she didn't water them.

The ten days Mama stayed in Palm Beach seemed too short to all concerned. But Wilson was due to arrive, and Mama had to get back to her garden and her endless chores.

What amazed Loretta about Mama's visit was how in so little time she had managed to fall into a routine. Her day started early in the morning, when she'd go with Loretta through the tunnel to the big house that Mama never thought too big, too grand, or too anything except just right for her Loretta. Mama liked all the shiny wood pieces, the long mahogany table behind the living-room sofa with all the pictures on it, the oak tea tables on either side of Loretta's bed, the red-lacquered Chinese bookcase with all those leather books. No, the pieces weren't rounded like Hollywood, but they looked good. They were fine like Loretta. What Mama liked best, though, were the old, pink mirrors in Loretta's dressing room that had been installed with the foundation. "Flesh glass," she announced triumphantly, looking in them and expecting to see something prettier than she'd ever seen before. "In the twenties all the big stars had them. You know how they use pink gauze on the lenses? It's exactly the same." Even Michael and David had never seen flesh glass, but they couldn't help thinking how a fortune could be made in Palm Beach alone if it ever came back.

"I can't believe it," Mama said ecstatically, rushing to the dolphin faucets, dolphin towel bars and toilet flush. "Gloria Swanson had these exactly," she said, caressing each one.

By the end of her stay, there was almost nothing in the house that Mama hadn't touched, sat on, or admired. Her suggestion about the outside roses matching the chintz was accepted at once, and as each day more beauty unfolded, Mama kept saying, "It's paradise before my own eyes." And as she kept calling it that, the others did too.

When she wasn't at Paradise or at the hospital with

Loretta, Mama was likely to be found having lunch with the girls. Although she thought the club was "certainly pretty," in her opinion, it didn't "have a patch on Sam Simeon." On the other hand, the beach house built for Marion Davies in Santa Monica didn't compare to "your beach club here." After lunch Mama would walk along Worth Avenue, where she'd even become friends with some of the shopkeepers. And when the huge Christmas tree was put up in the midst of the avenue's glittering elegance, it was Mama who dragged Loretta to see it lit.

The only thing that disappointed Mama was finding out, the day before she had to leave, that Douglas Fairbanks, Jr., lived in Palm Beach. She couldn't believe that Loretta hadn't mentioned it. But in the little time that remained, Mama at least managed to arrange a drive past the driveway.

"Please don't go," Loretta pleaded, watching Mama smooth and fold her clothes before putting them in the suitcase. "Please."

"I have to, Loretta sweetheart. I have to go home."

"This is home. Rosefields is home. Home is where we are together."

Mama didn't look up, just kept smoothing and folding.

"I'll be back. To Rosefields, too. Besides, Wilson's coming. You have to finish your 'Plague' pieces and do those business things. It's good for you, Loretta. He'll put your mind to work and mine at ease."

Wilson wasn't the only reason Mama was going home to Tampa. She was leaving, too, for much the same reason that Loretta had left Rosefields: so that she could come back.

"Why don't we go to the porch?" Mama said, sensing Loretta's anxiety. "I'll finish packing later." She looked down at her daughter's bare limbs. "Don't you think you better wear something besides those skimpy tennis things?"

"They're already the next size," Loretta said, patting her stomach.

"That's some of what I want to talk about."

Mama held Loretta's hand as they sat in the soft sea air. "Hard to believe it's almost Christmas," Mama said. "But I'm a lot happier leaving than coming. When I came I didn't know what I'd find. I know what I'm leaving, though. I'm leaving a woman, Loretta."

"Mama, I'm not a wom—"

"Hear me out, Loretta. When I come back, I'm going to find even more of one. You did a lot of growing fast, but you had to." Squeezing her daughter's hands, Mama looked across the ocean's darkness toward the distant green of the Gulf Stream. "You did the growing, 'cause it was in you to do it. It was there that first day at the sisters'. Genes, Loretta—genes. There's never a promise without talent, honey. Used to be in the movies, when looks alone could do it. But no more, Loretta. No more."

As a gull swooped toward the sea, Loretta wondered if it, too, were working to feed strength to its family. "But you're all I have, Mama." Desperately, she wrapped her arms around her mama.

"Families keep together by love, Loretta. Right now you've got to keep at what you're doing for B-e-t-t-e as well as for you. Everything you've started—that pebble—is for you and her." Mama took Loretta's face between her hands and smiled as serenely as if her life were one blessed memory.

Loretta wiped her eyes and recited the lines Mama had taught her, lines that made the smile in Mama's face appear even more beautiful:

> "If I can stop one heart from breaking,
> I shall not live in vain;
> If I can ease one life . . ."

\* \* \*

Loretta's first thought upon seeing Wilson was that the last time she'd seen him he'd been scattering Chukker's ashes over Rosefields. Although they'd talked on the telephone, their conversations were invariably about the 'Plague' series or about Dunbar Enterprises.

"I was positive Palm Beach would have mined the roads from the airport," Wilson said, not knowing where to begin. He was tired, but there was an energy in his voice, and he looked fresh despite the trip.

"My God," Loretta said, happy she could break the ice neutrally, "you shaved your beard!"

"Since the Palm Beach *News* labeled me 'the creative destroyer,' I decided to see what such a fine fellow looked like."

As Wilson walked across the room to the bar, Loretta was amused at how much he looked as if he belonged to everything he hated. She was relieved that he seemed relaxed. He seemed surprised she was so happy to see him, since everything on the phone had been so strained.

She had intentionally glossed over the subject of redoing the house, since she knew that Wilson's old memories weren't entirely pleasant. But now, even with the roof off, she felt like showing it to him. She turned out to be right.

Wilson was full of praise. He loved the crisp colors that would soon cover the walls and the bright fabrics that were pinned to the drab sofas and chairs. He had long believed that he could never like the house again, but now he saw that this would never again be the same house.

"You should put real birds in." Wilson said as Loretta pulled the cloth off the cage.

"I never thought of it."

"It's incredible . . . it's wonderful. It's too bad . . ."

"Yes," Loretta said. "But maybe he can see it anyway."

"Maybe."

All at once Loretta had a premonition that they should go no further. Not upstairs . . . not to any of the bedrooms . . . not to the nursery.

As they walked back to Dunesday, she scraped a few damp wisps from her forehead and grew warm thinking about the baby.

Whenever Wilson spent time away from Loretta, negative feelings about her had a way of building up until it was difficult to imagine even being civil to her. Somehow the idea of her—not Loretta herself—was disquieting. Curiously, though, his distrust faded once they were together. Curious, too, was that this fact bothered Wilson rather than soothed him.

"You know," Loretta said excitedly, sitting forward in her chair, "even Castro printed your last piece."

"Maybe that's why I shaved," Wilson said, smiling as he pulled his tie through his collar.

"Wait'll you hear this, though," Loretta said, her eyes sparkling at his. "Jonas Salk has accepted our invitation for the hospital gala. And the best part is that the night before I'm going to take him and his wife for dinner at the club. I want that more than anything."

"Clubs just shelter fellowship, my dear Loretta." Wilson hadn't felt so relaxed in this place since that time he'd brought Bernard home. Now that he was here and his doubts about Loretta were diminishing, something deep inside still nagged away.

As he watched her add mint to her iced tea, Wilson searched for flaws. He couldn't quarrel with the simple blue dress, or her hair pulled back tight and unadorned. It wasn't her fault she still looked great. The sandals? The thin gold band? Maybe it was all too simple. Suddenly Wilson had an urge to get it all out, to turn to Loretta and fucking well ask her. What's your racket, anyway? What do you want? Who the hell are you?

Instead, he listened while Loretta told him about Mama, about how she hated her leaving, how glad she was that he was here. The following day he heard her on the phone with Noreen and Angela, with the hospital staff, with the decorators and workmen at the other house. He watched her charm Francisco, the crazy gardener who was beside himself about Mama's cutting the oleanders and hibiscus. She certainly didn't seem impressed by names or trends or those people who spent entire seasons in front of mirrors. But why should that surprise him so? Why did the nagging persist?

After Loretta and Wilson had talked at length about the business, the trusts, his articles, she decided to tell him about the baby. Having had just enough wine at dinner to give her courage, and certain that Wilson would be happy not only for his father but for her, she ordered champagne for the occasion.

"It's a good chaser for brandy," Wilson said, observing an odd kittenish quality about Loretta. Even her gestures seemed coy. It was the way she put her hand into her pockets, then fumbled with that medal at her neck: she seemed so full of herself, especially with that silly half-smile on her lips.

Loretta sat on her heels in front of Wilson's chair. Uncomfortable, he got up to pour himself another brandy. Without thinking, he found himself going back to the same chair to face the same grinning Loretta.

"I have something to tell you," she said, taking a sip of champagne, her eyes fixed on his.

"Shoot," Wilson said, agreeably calm.

Loretta steadied herself by putting her arm on Wilson's

knee. Her voice was filled with confidence. "I'm going to have a baby. Your father never knew, because I was going to tell him that day at the airport—the day you—"

With a wave of his arm Wilson smashed Loretta's glass against the wall. Jerking himself up, he stormed to the bar, never glancing at the sprawled body that had fallen backwards.

When Loretta realized that she was unhurt, her mind raced to sort out what had happened, but the verbal incontinence around her made thinking impossible.

"Gold-digging bitch! Fucking fake philanthropy! I knew it. I felt it in my gut." His hands trembled as he poured another brandy. "A man's gut doesn't lie, no matter how many lies get to it. In the end the gut wins. But this is some fucking victory. I told him about you—God, I told him!"

Her eyes still fixed on his, Loretta crawled back like a startled animal spotted by a wild beast.

Defiantly, Wilson leaned against the bar. "I told my old man everything. But maybe he didn't see it because he was an old man. By God, Loretta, you're clever, right down to the fucking kid, the sob-sister finale. Let's see those tears, Ah-merica, for our angel of mercy, Florida's Florence Nightingale! But don't think I'm buying that song. Nobody changes." Wilson winced as he emptied his drink.

Moving backwards, feeling her way, Loretta found the nearest chair, all the while staring at Wilson.

"You don't have a clue what you're staring at, do you? The truth!" Wilson yelled. "The truth's staring you smack in the face and you don't have a clue. Why would you?" Wilson raised the brandy bottle to his mouth.

The more he talked, the more he didn't know where his thoughts were going as the writer moved uneasily among his words. "You know it always comes out," he went on. "Whether it's a burglary or a baby."

Loretta couldn't believe what he was saying. He was like

a crazed gambler challenging fate to destroy himself and everything around him, and she couldn't let him get away with it. "Listen to me, Wilson, if you can. If you can't, then get out. You can hear that, can't you? If you can't listen, leave."

Hypnotized by the never-veering eyes and the toughness in Loretta's voice, Wilson fell silent.

"All my life, Wilson, I've lived with lies. The way some get candy, I got fed lies. But I knew they were lies. That was *my* gut. And when I lied, I knew it too. I did it to survive or to help someone else live. And I'd do it again. Maybe *you're* the fake, Wilson. Maybe you're the liar, lying to yourself. Maybe your 'Plague' series has nothing to do with anyone except you—your selfish, vengeful self. Your father was the finest person I ever knew. He was proud of you. He only hoped *you* were proud of him."

Loretta's breath came hard; but, unlike Wilson, she had no doubt where every word was going. "For some reason you want what you say to be true. You've wanted those lies to turn out to be real long before you heard about the baby. I'm no angel of mercy, Wilson, but I'm also not the kiss of death you'd like to believe I am."

Wilson was stunned sober and instantly soaked in panic as the front door slammed and the car engine revved. He knew that he was lying to himself when he attributed his panic to his concern for the safety of Loretta's baby.

Anger more than sadness welled up in Loretta as she drove her Mercedes alongside the moon-drenched ocean. The lights in the houses she passed made her even angrier, because they reminded her that she was running again. When she turned left onto the nighttime emptiness of Worth Avenue, the floodlit palms, the giant Christmas tree, even the tinseled windows made the street seem more like a set from "The Twilight Zone" than the most glamorous avenue of the world's most famous capital of wealth.

Where to now—Noreen's? Julietta's? Angela's? Suddenly, just the thought that she could call on all these people, these friends, calmed her. She decided to head in the direction of the Newirths', since it was closest.

The same precision that marked Noreen's life could be seen in her home. Things were bright and cheery, but the rooms' unused perfection gave one the impulse to replump the pillows after sitting. Even Noreen, who certainly hadn't been expecting visitors and whose husband was away, looked as cool as the white canvas chairs.

Seeing Loretta in her thin shift and sandals, Noreen filled with the same protective feeling that Mama had felt before she left. She wrapped her arm like a wing around Loretta as they sat in front of the spotless glass doors that led to the pool. No matter who or what Loretta became, Noreen thought, the wounds suffered as a child would always give her the strength of weakness, the innate force to make people want to reach out to help.

Noreen was not half as surprised at Wilson's outburst as she was at Loretta's reaction. Her resistance, her defense, her meeting it head-on, was hardly the running away that Loretta had interpreted it to be.

"Staying there and keeping silent, believing that he was right, or hysterically trying to convince him that he was wrong—those things would have been running away."

"But what do I do now? It was so crazy. He didn't even look when I fell. Do you think he wanted . . . ?"

"He didn't want you to miscarry," Noreen said, knowing somehow Loretta knew that too.

Without either of them mentioning it, they both felt strangely forgiving toward Wilson as they kissed goodbye.

The note taped to Loretta's door was more scrawl than

script, and the clumsy apology ended with what had remained unspoken when Loretta left for Noreen's. "Easy
sentiments come hard to me." Wilson wrote. What meant
even more was that not until Loretta drove up did the light
go out in Wilson's room.

# 23

Christmas Eve at the Carristas' was the first invitation Loretta had accepted since Chukker's death. Being there with Wilson as her escort seemed even more benign than going alone. Wilson was not only glad to be giving Loretta support but eager to see the Carrista scene.

There wasn't a leaf or a twig of Casa Esperanza that hadn't been turned into part of a twinkling wonderland. In the outside gardens topiary reindeer were hitched to poinsettia-fashioned sleighs by ribboned reins of light, while in the interior courtyard a fifty-foot Canadian spruce stood high as the stars. For days, display experts had balanced ladders and scaffolds hanging delicate baroque figures, huge shimmering balls, and tiers of white candles that rose to the cross of pure gold at the top. All around the giant base, hundreds of red and green foil packages with fat rhinestone bows held the Carristas' traditional gifts: silver frames engraved with "Feliz Navidad" and the date. As the guests took their leave, they were handed the photographs of them taken on their way in. Although the Carristas made sure they covered every important religious holiday, it always appeared as if Bacchus more than Jesus were being celebrated.

Señor and Señora Santa mingled to spread their cherubic jollity, while waiters dressed as elves distributed food and drink. All who were invited turned out for the occasion. Once again, nothing succeeded like excess.

The eyes that always fixed on Loretta ogled her tonight as well, but this time they watched Wilson as well. Although Loretta felt the stares, she was certain they were brought on by the loose Mexican caftan that fell free from her expanding bosom. Self-conscious, she tried to hold herself in. Her hair, barely touching her shoulders, was caught at the sides by tortoiseshell combs, and the makeup she'd applied, though sparse, was sufficiently sophisticated to cover any lingering little-girl look. Her pearls, her sapphire ring, even her charm bracelet were sure tonight to take on the significance of heirlooms.

None of the stares was lost on Wilson. He watched as people who didn't recognize him immediately were informed within seconds. Bemused, he enjoyed himself nonetheless. Actually, he liked the changing scene, the colorful spectacle, the Carristas' irreverent observance of religious holidays. Wilson especially liked watching the old bigots in whose mouths butter would harden unctuously vying for invitations from those they once didn't admit existed.

What surprised him most were Loretta's friends—the fact that they really were friends. He didn't even mind Angela, whom he had always thought he'd dislike forever.

"He's got balls, all right," Lennox Knox said to his Crayola cronies just after telling Wilson how great he thought he and his series were. "All you have to do is take a good look. I'd like to punch the two-faced bastard smack in the nose."

"Why don't you?" Angela Seagrist challenged, slinking her red sequins so close that he backed away, frightened she might actually hit him.

"Fort's just thinking of Chukker," a colorless Crayola defended. "Can't help people wondering why the boy's sniffing around. It's no secret he's never had any use for us, and we've never exactly placed an ad for left-wingers." Running his finger around his collar, this protector of the old guard suddenly grew hot realizing he'd expressed an opinion.

"Dancing on the grave, I call it," slurred a chinless fool.

Fort slapped his thigh hard. Then, in an idiot frenzy, he shook his fist and head—a marvel of coordination, Angela thought, considering his abilities. "His wife with his own son, and Chukker hardly dead."

"And a bullshit Christmas to you all." Angela would have spit, but she didn't want to waste the Dom still lingering on her tongue.

With just minutes remaining before midnight, a giant gong sounded through all of Casa Esperanza, summoning the guests into the grand salon. There, high in the minstrels' gallery, tailcoated violinists took their seats. During the moments of silence while they readied their bows, many around the room made the sign of the cross. When at last midnight struck, the haunting strains of "Silent Night" echoed through the halls in a way that seemed at once miracle and magic.

Wilson returned to Washington early on New Year's Day. The night before he left, he and Loretta spent alone.

Their talk, even when it wasn't about business or baby, seemed centered on Chukker: how proud he'd be of the "Plague" series; how he'd love the idea of William Goldberg being honored. He'd think "How deserving!" long before it would occur to him how it'd get *them*. But when it did occur to him, "He'd tell them all to take a flying fuck." Wilson said these last words well into the early morning.

"You'll see, Loretta. The evil ones like Mary do themselves in just when they're the most clever. What I worry about is the 'I am a camera' ones, with their shutters open, passive, recording, not thinking. They're as bad as the Crayolas. They seem dead, but they're not, because they're still there to be counted."

The Palm Beach papers announced William Goldberg's acceptance of the hospital's invitation alongside a story about Loretta's plan to re-create the great Bradley's Casino for the night of the gala. What wasn't mentioned was the matter of Loretta's pregala club dinner for Dr. and Mrs. Goldberg.

The girl must not know. Someone must tell her. The board? The president? Admissions? There should be no confrontation. A letter. Perfect—a letter.

The club stationery, with its casual crest of palm trees and polo mallets, contrasted sharply with its message.

Dear Mrs. Dunbar:

It has come to the club's attention that a dinner reservation has been made in your name for the evening of February 11th. Upon receipt of your guest list, it seems that several people in your party would be unacceptable as guests since they would be unacceptable as members. In order to avoid any embarrassment, we feel it would be in everyone's best interest for you to make other plans.

I hope we have let you know sufficiently in advance so this causes you no inconvenience.

Most sincerely,
Paul Garvey,
Manager

The very next day, the club's letter, Loretta's list, and Wilson's blockbuster article pitting Palm Beach against the foundations of America were headlined around the world.

Wilson identified by name the chest-thumping members whose Puritan and Pilgrim ancestry of drunkards and traitors enabled them to practice the persecution their forefathers had fled.

In all the years that the club remained cloistered behind the small "Private" plaque, nothing had ever happened that couldn't be handled by a word to the ignorant. Once, a mere laugh from an adjoining table, offending Paris Singer's underbred wife, was sufficient cause to have the laugh and its source banished forever. But country-club novocaine was then in its infancy, and its strength deficient in subtlety.

A hastily assembled board meeting barely managed a quorum, with so many members suddenly called away to perform urgent duties they'd avoided for years. Yet as speedily as the board assembled, it adjourned. Some heretics thought the pressure too strong. Certain defectors actually believed that Dr. Goldberg had a right to invade their turf. No majority vote could be cast, and an emergency meeting, this time with a full complement, was to come after the weekend.

From all over the world outraged mail began arriving at the club. Only once before, when Mrs. Frederick Winston Churchill Guest dared enter its doors with Estée Lauder, had there been even a trickle of controversy.

The club rallied with a brave "no statement" as members met secretly. The bitter blows eventually came from the members themselves, as the shocked old guard realized it had misjudged the insurgents. Undetected, a new young had not only joined the club but joined forces as well. Hadn't some even married spics? Didn't one even mention some crazy statistic about Palm Beach being half Jewish? Didn't they even say that when the money ran out, Jews ran in to renovate the rundown, develop the derelict, and save shops and banks and restaurants from going bankrupt?

When a petition opposing the "guest rule" was submitted, the club's board was devastated. It wasn't so much the number of signatures as the names themselves: many of the club's third and fourth generation; many of the club's old rich. If they resigned, there would be no club.

While all of Palm Beach clamored for tickets to the gala, Loretta and her crew were working overtime to revamp the Flagler Museum, the Gilded Age palace that once had belonged to Angela's great-grandfather. Within these very marble halls Nellie Melba had sung, Woodrow Wilson and Warren Harding had spent the night, and Henry Morrison Flagler had died only a year after the structure's completion, leaving his young bride the second richest woman in America.

Each day the museum grew to look more and more like Bradley's legendary Casino. Even the colors of the colonel's famous racing silks were faithfully reproduced in the green-and-white-striped awning before the entrance to the fabled octagonal gambling den. All that was missing were the machine-gun-toting guards who looked down on the spinning roulette wheels through one-way mirrors behind the criss-crossed trellis of the ornate Victorian ceiling.

On the walls, paintings of Bradley's four Kentucky Derby winners—each of whose names started with the letter B—were interspersed with portraits of Whitneys and Wideners, Dodges and Donahues, all regular patrons. Loretta's favorites were the five portraits of C.W. Barron, the founder of *Barron's* weekly, resplendent in his five different sizes of dinner clothes brought and worn each season as testament to his lack of willpower. The largest portrait was of Bradley himself, in his trademark high, choking collar, looking over the outlawed fun he'd gotten Florida's law-abiding governor to ignore.

What Loretta hoped the hospital would achieve was the success Bradley himself had boasted of: "More money is left on my tables than in any casino in the world." Loretta hoped that the guests would buy endless green and white chips, especially since their winnings could "buy" any of the lavish donations, from a Dior layette to the 1928 Dusenberg owned by Henry Morrison Flagler's partner, John D. Rockefeller. Loretta eyed the layette as the curious eyed Loretta. Tongues had grown loose along with her clothes, but Loretta remained silent.

Loretta had even pressed Donina into service when she learned that Bradley's menu had been the finest in the country. In fact, it was said that when a member once complained to the colonel that his dinner prices were ten percent higher than anywhere else in the world, Bradley replied, "Our meals are also ninety percent better!"

"You must have the freshest of the season. Truffles from Cahors! Fraises du bois from Malaga! Figs from Brazil! Crawfish from Turkey! That, Loretta, is behaving rich!"

Donina's voice filled Loretta's bedroom and her laugh almost made Loretta cry. "Please," Loretta urged, "please come. You won't believe it."

"I would not believe it? I would not believe you? I know it will be a grand success, but never do I want to see another gala. What I do want to see, and what I shall cross the seas to see when the time comes, is my baby."

"Come early, then. In March. For Easter. Come for the magnolias."

"I shall come for you. Flowers I have here. Easter too. I am coming for you, for the baby, for Mama. How is she?"

"Wonderful. Wonderful." Without being aware of what she was doing, Loretta was circling her stomach with the flat of her hand. Suddenly she felt something move.

"How is Wilson? His pieces are a miracle. A miracle. Even people who do not know care."

Loretta told Donina about Wilson, about their fight, the note, the Carrista party.

"He's good, Loretta. Make sure he comes and goes with you when you enter the club."

Loretta laughed.

"You heard Donina."

"I've asked him."

"And?"

"He wouldn't miss it."

"Now remember the truffles," Donina said. "The least-needed thing can be the most important. Truffles from Cahors will be what makes Loretta Dunbar behave rich."

Just as Loretta was going to tell her about her stomach, Donina was gone.

As usual, Mr. Garvey stood at the front door checking the arrivals.

As Wilson drove up in Chukker's old Mercedes, uniformed valets opened the doors for Loretta and her guests, Dr. and Mrs. Goldberg.

The smile on Loretta's lips was unwavering as her glassy eyes froze on Mr. Garvey's pen and his guest list. As she walked toward him, her arm through that of William Goldberg, a monstrous montage of Big Luke, Randy Byrd, Vietnam, even the bloody cross on the altar washed over Loretta's mind. Feeling herself shake, she consciously shook more in an attempt to free herself. At once her thoughts turned to Chukker. Suddenly, the other altar appeared, the one with the lavender roses. Squeezing the arm linked in hers, her smile broadened and her eyes shone.

"Good evening, Mr. Garvey. These are my guests, Dr. and Mrs. Goldberg."

Mr. Garvey's semibow and swirl of arm, though not quite Oriental, were exceptionally cordial as Loretta Dunbar and her party entered the club.

All of Palm Beach was there, and when Loretta and her party walked in the gaping guests seemed to form a parting sea before them. When finally she was seated, a spontaneous applause broke forth from the incredulous crowd. For those who remembered the old Bradley's Casino, the transformation of the Breaker's ballroom was overwhelming, and for those not lucky enough to have bet their millions, it was a sight they would never have dreamed.

Whenever Loretta took to the floor, the oglers danced around her, wondering at every turn how this had happened. It seemed to have come like a thunderclap, without warning. And like lightning, wherever Loretta moved the flashbulbs exploded. Her triumphal success surpassed every expectation.

Loretta was already in Rosefields with Mama, Donina, and the magnolias, awaiting the birth of her baby, when the photographs of herself and Wilson appeared on the cover of the *Pictorial*. And by the time Bette Lillian Dunbar arrived, at a fine filly weight of nine pounds two ounces, the magnolias had come and gone. But as Baines drove the new mother and daughter home from the hospital, rainbows of azaleas stretched across the countryside, while inside Rosefields a profusion of lavender roses waited in every room. How Loretta wished Chukker could see the beauty and feel the happiness.

Mama's single regret was that she ever suggested the name Bette. "Doesn't do her justice," she said again, bending over the crib, moving Loretta's no-eyes teddy to get a better look. "Lana would've been better. Should have been Lana. Lillian, Loretta, Lana. That initial's important for the next generation, for tradition."

Long before Bette was born, Loretta had decided to ask both Mama and Donina to be godmothers, realizing that each would assume what she wished. One of Loretta's favorite sights was watching Donina walk and cradle the baby. Always she would remove her skyscraper platforms, although Loretta thought it wouldn't be long before Donina and Bette would be the same height.

Loretta's biggest surprise, however, was Miss Collier. It almost became a joke that in order to find Miss Collier you had to find Bette. With a seemingly endless vocabulary of coos, the Efficient One managed more gurgles and smiles than anyone.

Since Donina's Capri season was about to start and Mama was already late for green-up time, Loretta decided to have an early christening. Happily, Wilson, who was to be the godfather, was still nearby in Washington.

"Thank the good Lord," Zinnia said, "I arrived early enough to do some fixin'." The family christening gown, worn by each of the Crestbourne boys, actually needed lace added if it was to be worn by baby Bette. "You goin' to be a Globetrotter," Zinnia whispered, as she measured and remeasured the hem.

As Loretta again stood in the small chapel of Upperville's Trinity Episcopal Church, her thoughts were everywhere but here. Memory kept bumping into memory, especially when, out of the corner of her eye, she noticed Zinnia fanning herself with the same funeral-parlor fan she'd used that day on the bus years ago. Loretta smiled. It was a piece of continuity that helped to make everything real.

The unexpected splash of water elicited only the tiniest cry, but nothing could drown out the church bell as baby Bette encountered her first flash of photographers.

In the months that followed, Loretta became an almost daily commuter between Rosefields and Palm Beach. Tirelessly, she attended to every detail of the renovation. Through it all, she kept in mind what Mr. Reffold had told her: "Loretta, my dear, you have that rare instinct toward quality. Use it. Without it, there is nothing. With it, there is sometimes paradise."

The full-length portrait of Chukker with America's last forty-goal team of Iglehart, Hitchcock, Smith, and Phipps still dominated the library, while Renoir's bonneted girls and Monet's gardens at Giverny would always lavish the living room. The refurbished surroundings, however, made even the masters seem grander. Slowly but surely a harmony of old and new flowed through the original Mizner brilliance, and once again one was left with the feeling that gentry who cared were living here again.

The clipping, pruning, and planting of the outside proved almost as much of a challenge as the interior. Still, work was nonstop, and with each turn of a shovel everyone's excitement grew. Loretta, the boys, and their crew worked as one toward their united dream.

Since tight security had been enforced during the entire renovation, speculation from Newport to Paris was rampant: People positively *knew* Loretta was allowing wild birds to fly free through the gallery; that she had sold Chukker's favorite polo portrait of himself at auction; and that two nannies were

already in residence. Noreen, the Carristas, Angela, Donina—
everyone who cared—persuaded Loretta that what she must
do, what Chukker would be proudest of, was to throw the
doors open when the house was finished and the season was
starting.

# EPILOGUE

The party had been called from six to eight on Saturday. Even for Palm Beach the gossip was spectacular. From old whorehouse to new money, everyone knew about the decoration. After all, bullying the club was one thing, but buying class was another.

As the traffic streamed along South Ocean Boulevard, it seemed that everyone was turning into the Dunbar driveway. In no time Paradise was swarming with the best and the worst of the not-so-peaceable kingdom. Even Colonel Bradley wouldn't have booked a no-show bet.

One by one the guests greeted Loretta, incredulous at a poise that still contained an innocence. As caviar and champagne mingled with the beady eyes, head-shaking disbelief prevailed.

It was far into the evening when Loretta finally said goodbye to the last hangers-on. Once again, she had seen them all. And once again every last one had seen her.

Who was Loretta?

"She's smart, she is."
"She's got good taste."

"She bought it."

"She'll get him to marry her."

"He'll be lucky."

"The baby's probably his."

"I wouldn't say that."

"I didn't."

"The club's letting the Newirths in."

"Pigs."

"I wouldn't say that."

"I didn't."

"I can see why Chukker married her."

"She's a helluva woman."

"The best."

"The very best."

"Great for this town."

"The best."

"The very best."

"That's what we said in the first place."

Judith Green is a graduate of Vassar and a former copywriter. She lives with her two children in New York City and, sometimes, Palm Beach.

# BANTAM BOOKS
# GRAND SLAM SWEEPSTAKES
Win a new Chevrolet Nova . . .
It's easy . . . It's fun . . . Here's how to enter:

## OFFICIAL ENTRY FORM

Three Bantam book titles on sale this month are hidden
in this word puzzle. Identify the books by circling each of
these titles in the puzzle. Titles may appear within the
puzzle horizontally, vertically, or diagonally . . .

This month's Bantam Books titles are:

**INDIAN COUNTRY**

**SOMETIMES PARADISE**

**BE HAPPY YOU ARE LOVED**

In each of the books listed above there is another entry
blank and puzzle . . . another chance to win!

Be on the lookout for these Bantam paperback books:
FIRST BORN, CALL ME ANNA, SAMURAI STRATEGY.
In each of them, you'll find a new puzzle, entry blank
and GRAND SLAM Sweepstakes rules . . . and yet another
chance to win another brand-new Chevrolet automobile!

MAIL TO:　　　　GRAND SLAM SWEEPSTAKES
Post Office Box 18
New York, New York 10046

Please Print

NAME _____

ADDRESS _____

CITY _____ STATE _____ ZIP _____

# OFFICIAL RULES

NO PURCHASE NECESSARY.

To enter identify this month's Bantam Book titles by placing a circle around each word forming each title. There are three titles shown above to be found in this month's puzzle. Mail your entry to: Grand Slam Sweepstakes, P.O. Box 18, New York, N.Y. 10046

This is a monthly sweepstakes starting February 1, 1988 and ending January 31, 1989. During this sweepstakes period, one automobile winner will be selected each month from all entries that have correctly solved the puzzle. To participate in a particular month's drawing, your entry must be received by the last day of that month. The Grand Slam prize drawing will be held on February 14, 1989 from all entries received during all twelve months of the sweepstakes.

To obtain a free entry blank/puzzle/rules, send a self-addressed stamped envelope to: Winning Titles, P.O. Box 650, Sayreville, N.J. 08872. Residents of Vermont and Washington need not include return postage.

PRIZES: Each month for twelve months a Chevrolet automobile will be awarded with an approximate retail value of $12,000 each.

The Grand Slam Prize Winner will receive 2 Chevrolet automobiles plus $10,000 cash (ARV $34,000).

Winners will be selected under the supervision of Marden-Kane Inc., an independent judging organization. By entering this sweepstakes each entrant accepts and agrees to be bound by these rules and the decisions of the judges which shall be final and binding. Winners may be required to sign an affidavit of eligibility and release which must be returned within 14 days of receipt. All prizes will be awarded. No substitution or transfer of prizes permitted. Winners will be notified by mail. Odds of winning depend on the total number of eligible entries received.

Sweepstakes open to residents of the U.S. and Canada except employees of Bantam Books, its affiliates, subsidiaries, advertising agencies and Marden-Kane, Inc. Void in the Province of Quebec and wherever else prohibited or restricted by law. Not responsible for lost or misdirected mail or printing errors. Taxes and licensing fees are the sole responsibility of the winners. All cars are standard equipped. Canadian winners will be required to answer a skill testing question.

For a list of winners, send a self-addressed, stamped envelope to: Bantam Winners, P.O. Box 711, Sayreville, N.J. 08872.